The Lies I've Told

A By the Bay novel

J.L. BERG

Copyright © 2018 by J.L. Berg
All rights reserved.

Visit my website at www.jlberg.com

Cover Designer: Juliana Cabrera, Jersey Girl Designs
www.jerseygirl-design.com

Editors: Jovana Shirley, Unforeseen Editing
www.unforeseenediting.com

Formatting: Champagne Book Design
www.champagnebookdesign.com

No part of this book may be reproduced or transmitted in any form or by any means, electronic or mechanical, including photocopying, recording, or by any information storage and retrieval system without the written permission of the author, except for the use of brief quotations in a book review.

This book is a work of fiction. Names, characters, places, and incidents either are products of the author's imagination or are used fictitiously. Any resemblance to actual persons, living or dead, events, or locales is entirely coincidental.

ISBN: 978-1720349471

For my brother,
Even though as kids, you were mean, pushy and sometimes just downright bossy, there was no one I looked up to more than my superhero of a big brother.
I love you Jason.

PROLOGUE

Somewhere, in the dead of night, in a small, sleepy town, surrounded by the sea, two things happened almost simultaneously.

Two things that would seal the fate of two unassuming strangers.

A crime was committed, and a woman went into labor.

As the stone carving of the town's beloved memorial was crushed in anger, the perpetrator reducing it to nothing but rubble and the woman cried out for her husband in the middle of the night, two strangers, though worlds apart, had no idea their lives were about to change.

For better… for worse…forever.

And wasn't that the way with this crazy little thing we called love?

CHAPTER ONE

Aiden

IT WAS A SOLID TURNOUT.

The best of my career—or so everyone kept telling me.

Every piece in the collection had been sold, some for far more than the asking price. It was the biggest gallery showing I'd ever had. After years of scraping by, doing the whole starving-artist routine, begging for my work to be shown in a place like this, I'd finally done it—made a name for myself as an artist. Aiden Fisher, master sculptor. Finally, people were clamoring to get *my* pieces into their homes. Well, the overly inflated, self-indulgent wealthy people were. The regular man-about-town type still had no idea who I was, but in certain circles, I'd become a legend.

A legend who currently had nothing left in his wine glass…

Looking down at the crowd from my private perch on the balcony, I watched as people binged on the free booze and appetizers, pointing and chatting about my work. My eyes naturally gravitated to the heavy-stone pieces I'd put so much of myself into, and I couldn't help but let out a heavy sigh. It really was quite a sight. How many hours of blood, sweat and tears had gone into everything here today? How much of my soul had I sacrificed? Part of me hated to see some of them go.

My hand fell to my pants pocket and my heart clenched, remembering what lay inside. Reminding me that, only a handful of hours ago, I was just as happy and carefree as they were. But in the blink of an eye, everything had changed.

Funny choice of words, asshat…

No, let those pieces find new homes, I decided, as I stood there watching everyone gawk at them. They weren't mine anymore. Seeing each piece now, after the day I'd had, it only tainted everything.

All that hard work meant nothing now. All those memories…

Nothing.

As I leaned against the balcony, my hand threaded through my jet-black hair as I contemplated my next move. My glass of red had been empty for quite some time, and tonight was not a time to be sober.

Out of the corner of my eye, I recognized something. Turning, I caught James entering the gallery.

He was the last person I wanted to see right now.

He shook hands with the director of the gallery, who gave my rat bastard of a brother a welcoming pat on the back as James took a look around. He'd changed since I saw him that afternoon, opting for a slim black suit that looked like something out of *GQ* rather than the white lab coat I remembered from his office.

My eyes narrowed, trying to find a glint of something in his stature.

Remorse.

Guilt.

Sorrow.

But he appeared to be nothing but happy grins and handshakes as he made his way through the room. *Fucking tosser.*

Looking down at my empty drink, my hand gripping the glass a bit tighter than before, I took my growing frustration as a sign that I needed another drink.

With one last look at the scene below, I headed for the stairs.

No, tonight really wasn't the time to be sober, especially with my brother around.

Scratch that, ex-brother.

As I made my way down to the gallery, several people patted me on the back and tried to make small talk. A few women tried to stop me, fawning over how hot my English accent was, like I was the first bloke from Britian to come to this country. I mostly ignored them, focusing on the stairs instead as the dim light made it difficult to see. I held on to the banister, ignoring the female chatter, knowing I was probably coming off as rude. Or perhaps a bit drunk.

Maybe a little of both.

But I didn't mind.

Let them believe whatever they wanted.

I was an artist after all. Weren't we supposed to be temperamental and unpredictable? Now that I was considered a legend in my field, this was just me settling into the role.

Or vacating it, a tiny voice echoed in my head.

The last step onto solid ground felt like a monumental feat, and I mentally patted myself on the back for not stumbling down the stairs like a damn fool. Not that that wouldn't have put a cherry on this epically fucked up day.

Or confirm everyone's suspicions that I'd become a hopeless drunk in my rise to stardom.

Heading straight for the bar, I opted for something a bit stronger, forgoing the wine for straight-up whiskey.

"I just heard the good news," a familiar voice said behind me.

Downing the entire glass, I felt the liquor burn all the way to my gut. Turning, I found myself face-to-face with the one man I'd hoped to avoid for the evening.

Hell, maybe even forever.

"The good news?" I said, nearly spitting out the words, my accent growing thick with anger.

James recognized the subtle change and did his best to keep the conversation light. I'd been in this country for well over a decade, watering down the British accent I'd brought with me. But times like these—when my fists were clenched tightly at my sides and I couldn't do much but breathe through the rage? That accent grew thick.

A warning to leave me the fuck alone.

But James didn't back away from a challenge, especially when it involved me. He was a bastard like that.

"You're sold out! That's fantastic, Aiden," he said, his own accent very much accentuated. Honestly, I thought he sat at home during the weekends and took lessons on how to sound like a pretentious asshole. "The gallery director says he already has people asking when you can get new pieces in."

I didn't justify his words with a reply. Instead, I turned back towards the bartender and demanded another drink.

"I'm not the enemy here," he urged, stepping up to the bar so his words could be heard only by me. "If you'll just come back to the office and talk with me—"

"I don't want to fucking talk about it, James."

He turned to me, his brown eyes round with concern.

No, not concern. Pity.

Fucking pity.

He of all people should know I didn't need his pity.

"This isn't something you can run from, Aiden."

I swallowed hard, the test results he'd so conveniently printed out for me earlier in the day burning a hole in my pocket. Staring straight ahead, I waited as the bartender slid another shot of whiskey my way. Wasting no time, I emptied the glass and turned toward my big brother.

Scratch that, former big brother.

"Watch me," I said, and then I walked out of my own gallery opening and never looked back.

I wandered around the streets of New York City, the bright lights serving as a path for my solitude, but after several hours, I felt no more a sense of peace or solace than I had when I left the gallery.

How many movies had I seen where the hero or heroine simply wandered around a big metropolis and within a few magical movie minutes—backed by a popular soundtrack of course—all their problems were solved?

By the time I made it back to my apartment, I was feeling incredibly let down by the movie industry and life in general. After making my way through the door, I threw my keys down on the kitchen counter and immediately went for the necktie around my throat. The saleswoman at the upscale store had said the dark green satin brought out my eyes. At the time, even though I had known she was flirting with me,

I had taken it as a compliment and bought everything she had thrown at me regardless of the price.

Looking down as the tie hit the floor, I couldn't help but feel anger as I tried to focus on it in the darkened room, but I couldn't. My eyes blurred and strained as that anger boiled up to the surface.

Anger toward James and his constant positivity. Anger toward life and how it never failed to keep throwing shit at me. Anger toward...well, everything.

Yes, that about summed it up.

My phone vibrated in my pocket as I kicked off my shoes. Pulling it out, I saw James's name flashing across the screen.

Ignore.

Undoing several buttons of my shirt, I headed into the small kitchen, hoping to find a silent companion for the rest of the night—one that didn't deliver bad news or give me sad, pitiful eyes. I found just the thing I needed in an expensive bottle of scotch I'd been saving for a special occasion.

Sold-out gallery showing sounded pretty special to me.

Especially if it might be my last.

My stomach clenched as I popped open the bottle. Forgoing a glass, I brought it straight to my lips. Taking a long, hard pull, I tried to drown out my pain with a single gulp.

Coming up for air, I nearly choked on it, the very real feeling of my emotions still so present. Still so real.

So, I drank again.

And again.

Until the tears fell from my eyes and the sobs tore from my lips, and I fell into oblivion.

I awoke to the blinding glare of the sun streaming in through the windows and a buzzing sound against my forehead.

"What the…" I mumbled, waving a sleepy hand in front of my face before I realized the buzzing sound was in fact my phone. Lifting my head proved to be a monumental task, last night's alcohol making me feel like I was being split in two.

"Bloody hell," I cursed to no one in particular as I grabbed my now-silent phone with one hand and my throbbing head with the other.

Deciding I might never get up again if I lay back down, I forced myself up and toward the sink, trying to focus on my phone as I walked. There were several messages and texts from James—all of which I ignored or deleted—a final total from the gallery director, Harry, as well as a request to set up another showing. I chose to pass on replying to that and several others like it and moved on to a rather curious email from a Dean Sutherland.

Why did that name sound familiar to me?

In the fifteen years since I'd left England in pursuit of my artistic aspirations, I'd worked with a lot of clients. In the beginning, I'd done just about anything for a sale even if meant practically giving away a piece. Now, my artwork was world-renowned.

But one thing never changed.

I always remembered names.

But Mr. Sutherland wasn't a patron. No, he was something else.

I couldn't stop thinking about it as I made my way into the kitchen. After I downed several Advil and started an entire pot of coffee made entirely for myself, I decided to finally open up the email and give my poor memory a refresher.

Dr. Mr. Fisher,

My name is Dean Sutherland, and I am writing on behalf of the town of Ocracoke, North Carolina. You were kind enough to lend your artistic abilities to our small town not too long ago when we were in need of a memorial for the thirteen locals and tourists who had lost their lives in a ferryboat tragedy.

The reason I am writing you today is because, unfortunately, our town finds itself in need of your talents once again. Just last night, the monument you'd created was vandalized and destroyed.

Being a close-knit community, we are devastated—not only by the crime, but also because many of our families and survivors, myself included, no longer have a place to grieve, remember, and reflect.

This is why I've taken it upon myself to ensure that this beacon of hope is returned to us—as soon as possible.

The town and I are asking if you could please find it in your heart to replace what was lost—with compensation, of course. I know the art was one of a kind, but I'm hoping you can possibly re-create a sliver of the beauty that once stood on our shores, if only so our town can move on once again.

Thank you,
Dean

His contact information was included, and after reading through the email again, I found myself looking up his name, still stumped on where I'd heard it—because I remembered the man who'd hired me for the job—a old fellow with a gruff, Southern accent with the last name Joyner.

So who was Dean?

Google proved useful as usual, and after a few clicks, I found myself face-to-face with a real-life hero.

Although he hadn't been when I knew him before.

Dean Sutherland was one of the names I'd researched when trying to find my inspiration for the piece I created for the town of Ocracoke. He was a survivor of the ferry boat explosion, losing an arm in the process. But he'd gone on, as I discovered now in my cursory search online, to do a decent number of good deeds—including saving a man from a boating accident and founding several water camps for disabled kids.

"This doesn't have to be the end." James's voice rang in my head as I tried not to compare my current situation with that of Dean Sutherland's.

I remembered the piece I'd made for the small town that had recently been destroyed. I'd poured my heart and soul into that statue, giving it life and movement, grief and resolution and a fluid sense of calm.

It was one of my greatest achievements, and when it had vacated my studio to be shipped off to its final destination, I'd mourned the emptiness it left behind. I'd always hoped I'd be able to see it once more.

But it was gone.

I swallowed hard at that realization.

Everything in this life was so fleeting. It all just came and went.

Dust in the wind.

Grabbing a mug from one of the cupboards, I poured a fresh cup of coffee, not bothering with cream or sugar, quite certain my sour stomach couldn't take it anyway. Heading for the living room once more, I slumped down onto the sofa, placing my phone on the coffee table in front of me.

After a long, hot sip from my cup, I found myself staring at the black screen of my phone, thinking about the email from Dean Sutherland.

"As if I could just whip up another one. Asshole," I muttered, taking another drink of coffee. "And, even if I wanted to, I couldn't. I need to stay focused. I'm a ticking time bomb."

I didn't know why, but the thought made me laugh. It was a chuckle at first; low and rumbly in the back of my throat until it grew into a full-fledged, all-out ruckus. Tears rolled down my cheeks as I laughed at my own fucked up predicament.

"Boom!" I hollered as I clutched my side and doubled over in amusement.

Until I caught sight of that stupid sheet of paper underneath the coffee table.

Where had that come from? I'd thought I'd shoved it deep inside my pocket. Reaching down, I grabbed it, unfolding it as I wiped away the moisture from my face.

I was all laughed out now.

Reality was back, slapping me in the face as I looked down at the positive test results in big, bold script. Like I'd needed it all written down after looking at that stupid grid. I'd known what he was going to tell me by the grave look on his face before he even opened his mouth.

And when he did…

It was like a fucking death sentence.

Or at least, it might as well have been.

I crumpled up the paper and threw it across the room, hating everything and everyone in that moment.

James, for choosing to be a doctor, especially mine.

Dean Sutherland and the fucking town of Ocracoke, for reminding me that everything ended.

And me. Most of all, me. For aspiring to be more than the piece-of-shit orphan I'd started out as.

All of a sudden, everything felt too small.

This room.

This goddamn city.

I needed air.

I needed space.

Picking up my phone once more, I made a split decision.

"Hi, Dean. This is Aiden Fisher. You sent me an email about the monument I sculpted for your town."

"I did. I didn't expect such a prompt reply. Or a telephone call," he replied.

"Well, let's just say, you caught me at a good time. I recently finished up a gallery showing and I'm in between projects. I'd love to come down and work on-site if possible. I think it would be just the inspiration I need."

"On-site? Are you kidding?" The shock in his voice was palpable.

"Yes. Do you think that could be arranged? I'd need lodging with ample space to work."

"Absolutely. When would you like to arrive? I can recommend rentals, or if you prefer, there is a charming inn—"

"No rentals, I hate cooking. And as for my arrival, how does today sound?"

We worked out the rest of the details, and soon I was headed for the airport.

Good-bye, New York.

Good-bye, James. Take your shitty test results, and shove 'em.

It was time for a change of scenery.

CHAPTER TWO

Millie

I TOOK ONE LAST LOOK IN THE BATHROOM MIRROR AND tried not to smile.

It didn't work.

I couldn't help it. This was it.

All my hard work was finally coming to fruition. All those long nights, all the travel, every hour of dedication and putting everyone else's opinions and ideas first.

It was all about to pay off.

But, first, I needed to look the part.

My hair was perfectly curled in that undone *why, yes, I did wake up like this* sort of way when, in reality, no one woke up this way. We all just paid a fortune for high-priced blowouts to make it look like we did.

My makeup was flawless, but it always was. I'd spent far too much time on YouTube learning how to make it so.

As for the sleek, fashion-forward dress I was wearing? Well, considering I worked for the company who designed it, let's just say I'd gotten more than a few double takes on the way up to the office today. And I doubted any of them had anything to do with my stellar good looks or my overpriced blowout.

I did work in one of the top fashion houses in Miami after all.

Here, it was all about the clothes.

"Millie, your shoes are fantastic!" one of my coworkers announced, stepping out of a stall to wash her hands. She eyed my spiked Louboutin leather booties, just off the runway from one of my last trips to Italy.

Okay, sometimes, it was about the shoes too.

"Thank you," I replied, deciding, after another glance in the mirror, a little touch-up on my lipstick wouldn't hurt.

After all, today was a big day.

"Are you nervous?" she asked. "Excited? God, I would be a basketful of emotions."

Pulling out my go-to nude I loved to rock at work, I shook my head, wishing I'd done a better job at paying attention when this newbie made the rounds last week introducing herself.

I wanted to say her name was…Sally? Sarah?

"It's Sadie, by the way," she said, her blue eyes meeting mine in the mirror. There was no shame but not a bit of animosity either.

"I'm so sorry," I said. "I'm usually better with names. It's been a crazy week."

She smiled, a genuine type of smile. One I hadn't seen in a long time. "I get it. You're about to be promoted to one of the highest positions in the company. That couldn't have been easy."

I let out a breath, thinking back to all the long nights without sleep, the endless travel, and the lack of a social life. "It hasn't been; that's for sure. But it's not a guarantee. The position, I mean. It's all rumors at this point."

I was totally lying through my teeth.

That promotion was mine. I'd heard it directly from my boss's lips late last night.

"Well, you're an inspiration, Millie. Truly. I wish you nothing but the best today at the company meeting."

"Thank you," I said, watching her exit.

I returned to my primping, dabbing on a little lipstick before letting out a breath.

"This is it," I said. "This is when everything finally begins."

Wasn't there a saying about famous last words?

When I entered the conference room, it was bustling with energy. Most often reserved for board members and key leaders of the company, today, the usually large space was bursting at the seams.

That was because today was the annual company meeting.

Today, we would recognize achievements across the board. From the support staff all the way up to the top.

And today, that would include me.

I tried to play it off as casual as I made my way in, but the moment I saw my boss and CEO, I broke out into an ear-splitting grin. Lorenzo Russo, sharply dressed in a suit that no doubt had been perfectly tailored to his body, gave me a brief nod before continuing his conversation with a board member. But, as I turned away, I couldn't help but notice the small smirk that had formed at the corner of his mouth.

"Mills!" someone called.

THE LIES I'VE TOLD

I turned to find Kyle Tennant, one of my original friends when I'd started here.

"Over here." He gestured, giving me a full view of the ensemble he'd picked for today.

"Jesus." I laughed, taking the seat he'd saved for me next to him. "Going for shock value?"

He looked down at the plum-colored sequined top and shrugged. "I have to do something to get noticed around here. Not all of us are traveling the world, you know."

Although Kyle and I had started here at the same time, both of us wide-eyed newbies like Sadie from the restroom, I'd surpassed him in rank within the first year. While I met with board members and made decisions about fall and spring lines, he was still grabbing coffee and running errands.

I rolled my eyes, giving him a nudge. "As glamorous as it sounds, it's not all it's cracked up to be sometimes."

He gave me a hard stare. "Tell that to me the next time I'm at your house, crying in the middle of your closet. Have you been in there recently?"

My lips pressed together, trying to cover my growing smile. "Okay, yeah, that part is pretty great."

He just shook his head before glancing down at my shoes. "Speaking of, where'd you get those beauties?"

With my crossed legs, I shook one foot in his direction. "Why? Jealous?"

"I'm jealous of your whole life, honey. But I'd take those the shoes for starters."

I laughed as more people began to find their seats. I leaned in closer to him, catching the familiar fragrance of Chanel No. 5—Kyle's favorite perfume. "How about this? When I get this promotion today, I'll do you one better than a pair of shoes. What if I make you my assistant?"

He gave me a dejected stare. "Assistant? Are you fucking kidding me? I am nobody's assistant!"

I placed a hand on his shoulder, still amused by the amount of sequins on it. Did he ever stop and wonder if that was maybe why he didn't get promoted? Maybe they were scared to put him on design work when he showed up in such ridiculous clothes.

"Hear me out, okay?"

He let out a huff of air and sat back in the chair, clearly not amused. "Fine."

"You want to get out of this office, right? And, with this promotion they're giving me, I will be traveling even more. I'll need help. It's a win-win. Plus, you'll have my ear and I have theirs. Do you see where I'm going?"

His interest perked up. "Okay, I'm listening. So, I'll get to go with you to all these ridiculous places you visit?"

"Yes." I smiled.

"And help you with design."

"You can give me your opinions. I can't promise more than that."

Because that's all you'll ever be able to give. No one is going to take you seriously in this company, a small voice in my head said.

I ignored it, like I'd been doing for years.

He briefly considered it before he spoke, "When you see what I have to offer, you'll be begging for more. Will I have to get you coffee and cut up your food?"

"Cut up my food?"

"Willa, Lorenzo's assistant, says he regularly makes her order him dinner and then cut up his food before he'll eat it."

I tried to imagine my sexy man of a boss doing this. "Um, no. I'm pretty sure I can cut my own food, but I might ask for coffee from time to time."

"I guess I can do coffee, as long as I can get my own at the same time."

I heard someone clear their throat next to us, and my attention went to the front.

"So, are we good?" Kyle asked.

I gave him a thumbs-up as Lorenzo took the stage. Well, there was no stage, but if there were, he would totally have owned it.

"Hey, uh, Millie…I think you have a bit of drool right there," Kyle joked, pointing to my mouth.

I shot him a look before shaking my head and returning to Lorenzo.

"Thank you all so much for taking the time out of your busy day to come together as a team to honor and celebrate this wonderful company. Our annual meeting is always a special occasion because it truly humbles me to see the hard work that goes into making this company great and to recognize much you achieve on a daily basis, both in and out of the office. So, without further ado, let's get this party started!"

Everyone laughed at his attempt at humor. It really wasn't that funny, but with the addition of Lorenzo's Italian accent…well, it helped.

Plus he was our boss, so of course we laughed.

"Here we go," Kyle whispered beside me. "Wake me up when they get to you."

"You're terrible."

"No, I get easily bored and this is fucking long."

He wasn't wrong. We weren't a large company, but we

were by no means small. This was just our corporate office. We had satellite offices in several other countries, and even though none of those people were here, Lorenzo felt the need to honor them anyway.

So, it could get a little long.

We celebrated promotions and retirements and even births and marriages. In Lorenzo's eyes, those were equally important, although none of the top staff members even knew what it was like to be married, let alone have kids since we were all married to our jobs, but we celebrated everyone else with a smile and a round of applause.

Finally, he got to promotions in the corporate office. I hit Kyle in the ribs, causing him to sit up straight and pay attention. Just as Lorenzo was about to open his mouth, several beeps and buzzes filled the room, like everyone's phone had gotten a notification at the same time.

Wanting Lorenzo to continue, I ignored my phone, but several others didn't.

Including Kyle.

He casually pulled his phone under the table, like half of the room, and I watched as his eyes nearly bugged out of his head.

And he turned to me.

Along with everyone else in the room.

"What?" I spat in a hushed tone in his direction.

He didn't say anything. He didn't even make eye contact with me. He just handed over the phone as everyone watched.

"What is going on?" Lorenzo asked, not bothering to conceal the tone of his voice. He was annoyed.

I looked down at the phone, at the email that had been sent out. The title: *Guess Who's Screwing the Boss?!*

Holy shit.

In the body of the email was a video and a single sentence. I didn't have to watch it to know what it was. I could see from the single-preview shot exactly what it was.

Lorenzo and me. In his office. Last night.

I guess we all know how she worked her way to the top.

A single tear fell from my cheek as I read the email. I forgot how to breathe as I looked up at Lorenzo. His annoyance turned to panic. His hand went to his pocket as he, too, found his phone and the email.

The email that ruined everything.

"Who sent this out?" Lorenzo's voice boomed. "Who sent it?"

The room went silent.

I looked down at the sender. It was blank. Whoever had sent it didn't want to be found. I swallowed hard as I handed Kyle his phone back.

"I guess our arrangement isn't going to work out, huh?"

"What?"

"Me being your assistant? Was I going to have to sleep with you, too? Because you know I don't swing that way."

My vision was fuzzy as my only friend began ripping me apart in front of the entire company.

"Kyle, please," I managed to say. "It isn't like that."

"It isn't like what?" he bellowed. "It isn't like I've been working my ass off every damn day for the past seven years while you fucked your way to the top?"

My eyes met Lorenzo as he just stood there, unmoving, unwilling to come to my aid.

"I didn't—"

But what could I say?

I had.

I'd slept with my boss.

I was the cliché, the cautionary tale.

And because of a single email, I'd lost everything.

So, I did the only thing I could.

I ran.

The worst thing about being married to your job?

Outside of my coworkers, business trips abroad, and the clandestine affair I was having with my boss, I had nothing.

Less than nothing.

After fleeing the meeting that was supposed to make all of my dreams come true, I put an end to my career before someone else could.

Taking the high road or what was left of it, I resigned.

Effective immediately.

Lorenzo couldn't even look me in the eye as I tossed the hastily written letter on his desk.

I guessed I knew where that left us.

It didn't take long to clean out my office. There wasn't much in it that was actually mine. A few pairs of shoes I had bought but never took home, a couple of family photos, and a sketchbook I hadn't used or opened for years.

No one said a word to me as I exited the building, but their silence spoke volumes. I knew what they were thinking.

Slut.

Whore.

Gold digger.

I would have thought all that and more if it were someone else.

But it wasn't.

I was the slut. The whore. The gold digger.

I tried to hold my head up high as I entered the elevator for the last time, but it was hard…so damn hard.

Because, in that moment, I kind of agreed with them.

I'd become everything I loathed when I fell for my boss. The hopeless romantic sap of a girl who believed this time was different.

This time, it was real.

I'd really thought I could change him. That, after years of womanizing and philandering, I, Millie McIntyre, could somehow tame the wild Lorenzo Russo with love.

God, what a fool I'd been.

Armed with my pathetic box of mementos, I headed for the parking garage, feeling the Miami heat hit me the second I stepped off the elevator. It used to comfort me, this heat. It reminded me of home—of warm nights out on the patio, roasting marshmallows like a regular family.

We were a regular family—most of the time. If you didn't count the steady stream of guests we had coming and going through the house. My family had come from a long line of innkeepers. My sister and I had been raised in a bustling business rather than a quiet family house. But I wouldn't have wanted it any other way.

Maybe it'd prepared me for the chaos of this life.

Well, maybe not this specific moment in life, but the majority of them.

I'm pretty sure nothing could have prepared me for driving home to an empty apartment with no plans of ever leaving it again.

Walking through the door, I took a cursory glance around. Not a single thing was out of place as I flipped on the lights, admiring the modern styling I'd paid a fortune for.

I couldn't remember the last time I'd spent more than two nights here.

I guess that was about to change.

Heading for the kitchen, I kicked off my shoes, not caring where they landed, as I went straight for the wine fridge.

"Hello, pinot grigio. Where have you been all my life?" I said fondly, pulling out a perfectly chilled bottle. Not even bothering with a glass—because who was I kidding? I was going to drink the whole thing—I uncorked it and headed for the one place I thought would bring me comfort.

My closet.

Half a bottle later, my ass was planted on the floor of my giant walk-in, nestled between a pair of sparkly pink heels and a few sample pieces from the fall line I'd taken home last week. Looking down at them as I took another sip from the wine bottle, I realized that this right here, was my whole life.

This closet. This fucking job. These fucking clothes.

And now, it was gone.

Gone.

"How sad am I?" I said to no one.

But then someone actually answered back. Or at least, that was how I interpreted it when my phone began ringing a few seconds later. Picking it up from the spot where I'd tossed it on the floor, I let out a frustrated sigh.

"Great," I said, seeing my sister's name in big, bold letters staring back at me.

Do I answer or not?

"Hello?" I answered before I had a chance to change my mind.

After all, none of this was her fault. There was no reason to avoid her.

Now, if there were a way to avoid myself?

That I could get on board with, at least for the time being.

"Hey!" she replied, her voice instantly warming my insides.

Molly was older by a few years. Wiser by probably a decade... maybe two.

It didn't matter how far apart we were or how long we went without speaking, she always seemed to cheer me up with just the mere sound of her voice.

"How's it going?" I asked. "Still preggo?"

She laughed at my joke, but I could hear some hesitation in her tone.

"Wait, you are still pregnant, right? You didn't have my niece and not tell me, did you?"

"No," she said.

"There's a *but* in there. I can hear it all the way down here, Molly."

"I'm in labor!" she squealed.

"Oh my gosh!" I screamed, jumping up from my pathetic spot on the floor, as if I could do something all the way in Florida when my sister was going into labor up in North Carolina. "Then, why are you on the phone with me?" I asked. "Shouldn't you be pushing? Or doing heavy breathing or something?"

She laughed.

She freaking laughed.

She was having a baby, casually chuckling through

labor, while I was having a mild panic attack about it in the middle of my walk-in closet.

Maybe I needed to lay off the wine for a while.

Setting it aside, I stepped out of the closet and settled down on my bed, ignoring the way the room slightly spun.

"We're at the hospital and I'm fine," she said. "Remember, I'm married to a doctor. The most neurotic pain-in-the-ass doctor on the face of the planet."

I had a feeling the last part of that was being said at the incredibly neurotic husband. Not me.

"Well, he must be doing something right if you're already at the hospital. How did you manage that? Did he drive you up the coast a month in advance and park you outside to wait?"

She laughed. Again.

"No," she replied. "I was up here for a routine visit. We drive up to Nags Head every week now to see my OB. Jake's made it his mission to see how quickly he can get from Ocracoke to the ferry and then from the ferry to Nags Head. Honestly, I think he's going to miss that part of this whole thing."

I was the one to laugh now. "Well, he'll still be up there visiting patients. I'm sure he can continue his race car fantasies then. But, seriously, how are you? Are you feeling okay?"

"Yes," she answered adamantly. "I'm feeling great so far. They're taking good care of me. But, that's not why I called."

I gulped, wondering if she'd somehow found out about my failed promotion. The one upside to this whole thing was I hadn't told any of my family members, wanting it to be a surprise. So, I thought there wouldn't be any questions.

"It's Mom and Dad."

Panic turned to worry. "What about Mom and Dad?" I asked, wondering what else could possibly be wrong in my topsy-turvy life.

"They're supposed to take over the inn when I go on maternity leave, but I didn't exactly plan on going into labor three weeks early. They're on a golfing trip in Myrtle Beach. I've called them, and they're headed back, but—"

"They'll want to be with you, not at the inn with a bunch of guests."

"Yeah."

I took a quick look around my apartment, the walls already feeling like they were closing in around me. "Say no more, sis. I'll get on the first flight there. Just call me the hostess with the mostess."

"Oh my gosh! Are you sure? There are people I can ask around town, but this is the inn, and I didn't want to leave it to simply anyone."

"I get it. It's a family thing. I'll be there."

"Aren't you busy? I mean, don't you need to fly somewhere or do something really important?"

I bit my lip to keep from snorting. "No, it's fine. I have tons of vacation time saved up, and you know what? It's about time I use it."

"You are my lifesaver, Millie. It will only be a couple of days, promise. Mom and Dad can take over once I'm out of the hospital."

I tried not to think of what I'd do after those couple of days, but I put on a brave face and finished making the arrangements with my sister.

"Oh, and before we hang up, there's one more thing."

"You mean, before you go off to give birth?"

"Right"—she snickered—"that."

"How are you so calm? I would literally be freaking out right now."

"Oh, I am, but I'm good at hiding it. The doctor came in here with this giant hook thing, like one of Mom's crochet hooks, and used it to break my water. Weirdest thing ever."

"Okay, that was more information than I ever needed to know. Thanks for that. Anyway, you were saying?"

"Right." She laughed. "There was some vandalism in town. The statue that was put up at the docks for the ferryboat accident, it was destroyed last night. Dean has arranged for the artist to visit and re-create it."

"That's awesome. I mean, not the vandalism part. But it's quite a generous offer from the artist."

"Yes," she said. "We were amazed. We never expected something like this. He's pretty well known in the art world. So, obviously, I've made arrangements for him to stay at the inn. He should be arriving after you. Can you make sure he gets to town okay? I don't know how he'll be arriving."

I could already hear the worry in my sister's voice. She was overly attached to the inn and how it ran on a day-to-day basis. Before she'd married Jake, it had been her entire life.

Wow, that sounded familiar.

"I'll treat him like royalty, promise."

"Thank you," she said, clearly relieved. "Okay, I've got to go. I can feel a contraction coming on, and I think you should remember me in this moment as being happy and not cursing my husband for being born."

I let out a giggle before saying good-bye.

My sister was having a baby.

She was creating a family.

And I was getting drunk in my closet.

Well, not anymore.

Feeling like I had a new purpose, I jumped to my feet. I still felt a little wobbly, but there was nothing like ambition to cure a tipsy head.

A few days at home? It was exactly what I needed.

There, I could clear my head and get refocused, and when I came back…

Well, let's just say, bitches had better be ready.

CHAPTER THREE

Aiden

"**W**HERE ARE YOU HEADED AGAIN?" THE tipsy woman sitting next to me in first class asked once again.

"Ocracoke," I answered.

"Where?" She giggled, taking another sip of her wine.

I'd been on this plane with her for a grand total of thirty minutes, and I already wanted to kill myself.

Repeatedly.

"Ocracoke," I said slowly. "It's a small island off the coast of North Carolina. That's a state in the southern region of—"

"I know where North Carolina is," she said, her words slurring together.

Normally, I'd go for her type—the well-dressed, expensive, but easy kind of girl who made being single everything it was meant to be. Fun and string-free.

But, today, I wasn't into it. Or her.

She must have gotten the clue when I stopped speaking to her and instead sought out entertainment elsewhere. Slipping on the noise-canceling headphones, that, given my current predicament, were worth every penny I'd spent on them, I plugged them into my laptop and zoned out.

Well, I zoned her out at least.

With music blasting in my ears and an entire hour left on this flight, I pulled up my internet browser, thankful for Wi-Fi and began to surf the web.

At first, it was typical stuff, reviews of my show from the night before to social media, but then I began to feel the itch. Those test results were back in my pocket, and before I knew it, I was typing words into the search bar like a goddamn idiot.

I felt a tap on my shoulder.

It was the drunk girl, looking over at my screen. I let out a sigh and pulled off my headphones.

"My grandma has that," she said, pointing to the page I'd pulled up on Google. "Terrible disease."

I swallowed hard, feeling a trickle of sweat forming at my temple. "Yeah, mine too," I lied before putting on my headphones and immediately shutting down the laptop.

I felt physically ill from her comment, and it took every bit of strength I had to continue sitting there next to her, stiff as a board, while I was slowing falling apart on the inside.

Thanks to a decent layover in Norfolk, I'd managed to knock back several drinks in the airport.

With nothing but time to kill, I didn't want to waste a single second of it thinking. Alcohol had seemed like the only plausible option.

When the pilot and the dinky excuse for a plane finally

arrived to take me the rest of the way to Ocracoke, I was feeling pretty okay. Making my way down to the tarmac, I said my hellos to the older gentleman who looked more like a beach bum than a pilot, but who was I to judge?

I carved stone for a living. It wasn't like I walked around, covered in dust, twenty-four hours a day.

Well, not most days anyway.

After taking my seat, I pulled out my phone and took a quick glance at the latest email Dean Sutherland had sent that afternoon.

Aiden,

All accommodations have been made. You will be staying at By the Bay Inn—the best place on the island. Someone will be at the airport to pick you up when you arrive.

Looking forward to meeting you in person.
Dean

I had some serious doubts as to whether Dean's and my idea of proper accommodations were the same. For some reason, *the best place on the island* drummed up images of a run-down cottage with wood veneer and appliances that dated back to the Nixon administration. But I'd made do with less.

A lot less.

"Are you staying in Ocracoke long?" the pilot hollered over his shoulder as we left the airport.

I looked down as the ground grew farther and farther away.

"Uh, I'm not sure," I answered, feeling less than chatty as my buzz began to wear off.

THE LIES I'VE TOLD

"Ah, well, that's how a lot of us got hooked, you know."

"Hooked?"

"On the island," he explained. "I used to be a Midwestern man myself, until I came down here for a vacation one year. That's all it took. Twelve months later, my wife and I had sold our house and moved down here permanently. Never regretted it for a moment."

I looked out the window, down at the dark blue water.

"Pretty sure I've had all the island life I can handle at this point. This is only temporary."

He chuckled, obviously catching my joke, aiming my displeasure over my country of origin. "Not too fond of jolly old England?"

I swallowed hard as I tried not to let my mind wander back to my childhood. "Let's just say, I won't be going back anytime soon."

He must have caught the hesitant tone in my voice. "Well, I hope Ocracoke works out better for you. Island-wise, I mean. I'll give you some peace and quiet while I work on getting us back on the ground."

"Thank you," I said, taking one last look out the window as the sun began to melt into the horizon.

He gave me a quick wave as he got back to work, flipping dials and doing whatever it was that pilots did, while I sat back and tried to figure out what my next move would be. I promised Dean a new memorial, but the honest truth was, I wasn't even sure I could give it to him.

I guessed time would tell.

At least I was away from my brother and New York.

And all the stress that went with it.

Less than twenty minutes later, the plane landed with a bit of a jump and a jolt. "Strong gusts from a storm offshore," he explained as we taxied into a small parking lot off the runway. "Welcome to Ocracoke," he said as we came to a stop.

I did the typical thing most travelers did when they arrived at a new place. I pressed my head up to the small window, squinted, and took a long, panoramic view of my new surroundings.

There wasn't much to the place. Just a small hut of a building that made up the entirety of the airport and a large parking area for planes and cars.

No fuss. No frills. Only the basics. I had a feeling that was going to be the theme for this little adventure.

I began to gather up my things when a small SUV pulled into the parking lot.

"I have a feeling that's my ride," I said, pointing to the vehicle as the pilot helped me out.

"Ah, yes, I flew her in from Greenville about an hour ago."

"Her?" I said, taking another look out the window.

Unfortunately, the mystery woman kept herself shut inside, preventing me from catching a peek before I headed outside.

"Jesus," I said, the moment the hot air hit me. It was like walking into a sauna. Sweat instantly beaded across my brow, and the air felt thick in my lungs.

"That'll be the humidity." He chuckled. "I'd say you'll get used to it, but I never have. Still sweat like a damn pig and beg for fall every time June rolls around."

"I can see why," I replied, immediately removing my blazer as I stepped onto the pavement. I was no stranger to humidity. I'd been living in New York so long, I considered it my hometown, but this? This made the sweltering summer heat in the city seem like a nice sunny day at the North Pole.

A car door slammed nearby, causing my eyes to jolt forward.

"Be careful with that one," he said under his breath. "I think she's had a bad day."

I let out a sort of muffled snort. "Haven't we all?"

I didn't know what I had been expecting when I saw her step toward us. Maybe a beach bum, like the friendly pilot. Maybe a plain Jane—this was the middle of nowhere after all—but definitely not a sophisticated goddess in heels.

"Fuck me." The words were barely a whisper under my breath, but the pilot caught them all the same and I heard him chuckle beside me.

My eyes narrowed to get a better look, zeroing in on the subtle sway of her hips and the causal confidence she seemed to carry. Everything about her—from the long blonde curls that framed her face to her startling blue eyes—seemed to mesmerize me.

"Jimmy, we've got to stop meeting like this. People will begin to talk," she said to the pilot, stepping up to greet us.

"Aiden Fisher," I said, holding out my hand like a damn fool. In the few seconds since she'd dropped into my world, I'd become completely fixated on her.

A slight curve to her lips sent shivers down my spine, making me wonder what they'd feel like against mine.

Or wrapped around my—

"Okay," she replied, sounding less than enthused. "As you can see, Aiden," she said my name with distaste, "I was having a conversation with my buddy Jimmy. You know Jimmy, right?"

"Uh," I uttered, slightly dumbfounded by her out-of-the-blue animosity toward me. *Couldn't she feel the connection? The heat?* "I don't believe we had the pleasure of exchanging names while I was on board."

A satisfied grin spread across her face. "You mean, you didn't bother to ask for his, did you?"

Jimmy, clearly uncomfortable with our conversation, stepped back. "I'm gonna go lock up. You two have a good night."

And then the man scurried off like a damn weasel, leaving me alone with the crazy-hot chick of my dreams.

"Look, I know you've had a rough day, but I don't think it's exactly fair for you to take it out on me," I said, hoping to clear the air.

Her eyebrows rose as she crossed her arms in front of her. "You know I've had a *rough day*? What the hell is that supposed to mean?"

Whoa.

I shrugged, finding my bearings once again. She might have surprised me with her less than perky mood, but I wasn't about to back down from a challenge.

Especially when it was so damn good-looking.

"Jimmy said something to that effect. In fact, his exact words were, 'Be careful with that one.'"

Her eyes drifted across the lot where our pilot was doing his best to blend into the darkening sky. He slipped into his car and was buzzing away in no time.

Smart man.

"Look, not that it's any of your business, or Jimmy's—God, I hate this town—but I am fine. Totally, completely fine."

I cleared my throat as she began to walk away in the

direction of her vehicle. "Clearly," I said, still enjoying the view.

Even if it was a little crazy.

After we loaded my luggage in the car and set forth for the inn, things got quiet.

And then they got awkward.

Awkwardly quiet.

Finally, after what felt like an eternity of silence, she spoke, "Look"—she let out a long sigh—"I'm sorry. I'm not very good at this hostess thing. Never have been."

"Kind of an awful career to pick then, don't you think?"

Her eyes briefly met mine before focusing back on the road. "What? Oh no. That's my sister you're thinking of. The inn is hers. Well, it belongs to the whole family, I guess, but Molly runs it."

"And you are?" I asked, realizing I still didn't know her name.

"Millie."

"Your parents named you Millie and Molly? That's quite terrible."

"I think they were going for cute. But, yeah, it's pretty terrible."

"So, where is Molly now?"

"In the hospital. In labor. Or at least, she was."

"She's having a baby? Now?"

Nodding, she smiled. "She had one. This afternoon. A beautiful baby girl named Ruby. Or so I've been told."

"You haven't been there? To the hospital?"

"In case you haven't noticed, Ocracoke is a tad remote.

The closest hospital is about two hours away and requires an hour-long ferry ride across the sound."

Things were starting to become a littler clearer in regard to her bad day.

"And you're the one left behind to pick up the British bloke from the airport then?"

She nodded, a slight smile tugging at her lips. "Not really left behind. I flew in from Florida to help, so that is what I'm doing. Helping."

There was a distinct sort of sadness to the way she'd said it. Maybe she was sad she was missing out on such a monumental family moment. Maybe it really was an epically bad day.

Or maybe she simply needed alcohol, like me.

We pulled into a driveway. I took a moment to look around, noticing the pristine landscaping and beautiful entryway.

"How about you offer me a little of that help by showing me the closest bar?"

I heard the car click back into gear as a sly smile spread across her face.

"Now, you're speaking my language."

After a bit of a rocky start, Millie and I seemed to find our rhythm just fine.

I was a little apprehensive when she pulled off onto a sleepy street and said, "This is the most happening place on the island."

After a quick look around, I swore she was joking.

But the second we stepped onto that open-air patio and

I felt the warm breeze against my face, I had to hand it to her; it wasn't half bad.

"Silly Millie McIntyre, back in the 'Coke!" someone hollered from the kitchen as we took our seats.

She turned to see a big, burly guy emerge, holding a few menus as he slung a kitchen towel over his shoulder.

"Billy! So good to see you."

"You, too. Haven't seen you since your sister's wedding, but I figured you'd be around sometime soon. Molly looks like she's about to explode." He made a motion with his hands, making the round shape of a pregnant belly.

"I'm surprised you haven't heard yet, considering the speed at which gossip is spread through this place, but Molly and Jake are now the proud parents of a little baby girl."

"Well, I'll be damned." He cupped his hands over his mouth and hollered. "Drinks on the house, y'all! Our good doctor is a daddy!"

Everyone cheered as Billy took our orders. Millie ordered a Long Island iced tea while I stuck with a whiskey sour.

"I hope you aren't expecting that whiskey to be Scottish because I'm pretty sure Billy only serves Kentucky whiskey, and I'd hate for you to be upset. After all," she said, a slight grin tugging at her bottom lip, "my sister made me promise to treat you like royalty, and I wouldn't want it getting back to her that you were forced to drink Southern whiskey."

"After the week I've had, I wouldn't care if it came from Jamaica as long as it burned on its way down and made me forget."

Her eyes met mine, and time seemed to stand still for a brief moment. "What are you trying to forget, Aiden?"

I opened up my mouth to respond, but Billy stepped in, delivering our drinks before running off to another table.

I picked up the glass and took a large swallow, nearly downing the whole thing in one gulp. "Nothing. Everything. Tell me more about your sister," I said, quickly changing the subject.

She sort of laughed. "Why? Do you want to date her? I think she's a little tied up at the moment."

"No," I replied. "Although, if she looks anything like you, my hat goes off to the good doctor. He must be a lucky man."

Her eyes narrowed in on mine, not falling for my cheap shot at flirtation one bit. "Well, let's see…Molly is fiercely loyal and strong-willed. She believes any problem can be solved with a couple of hours in the kitchen and a few baked goods. And she's kind." She paused for a moment before looking up at me. "Why do you want to know so much about my sister?"

I shrugged, letting my fingers trace circles through the condensation that had formed. "Just a handy trick I've picked up over the years. Works great with clients."

"I'm not your client," she deadpanned.

"No." I laughed. "You're definitely not, but it still works. You see, when you sit down with a stranger and say, 'Tell me a little about yourself,' more than likely, you're going to get a handful of shit."

Her forehead rose in amusement. "Go on."

"People don't often know themselves. Or if they do, they don't like to share it with anyone. Revealing who we really are is vulnerable and scary."

"So, you ask them to tell you about someone else? Why? I don't get it."

"Not just anyone else. Someone close. A sibling is always great because it's such a delicate relationship."

"Okay…"

I'd obviously lost her. "When you were describing Molly, your face lit up with emotion. I saw love and respect but also a twinge of jealousy."

"I'm not jealous!"

I grinned. "See, it's like a window to the soul."

She paused a moment before making a sour face. "All right, so why don't you tell me about your siblings?"

I nearly choked on my drink before composing my features once more. "Can't. Nothing to tell."

"Only child?"

I bit the inside of my lip before responding. *Right now, I am.* "Something like that. Anyway, it's only a theory. Something I use when a client asks for something stupid or impossible."

"Like?"

I flagged Billy for another round of drinks, and he nodded before I continued, "A long while back, I had a couple who wanted me to etch their love for each other into stone."

"Okay. Kind of corny but not really stupid."

"Not stupid, no. But completely impossible, considering he was banging the nanny and she'd checked out of the marriage ages ago."

"And you figured that all out based on your little sibling game?"

"Well, no. The last part was pretty obvious when she came on to me in my office; but the rest, yeah. Although, instead of siblings, I asked them to tell me about their kids."

"Why?"

"I needed to pull the love from somewhere. And seeing

their eyes brighten and melt when they spoke of their sons, it was enough to get the job done. They saw love shining back at them when they saw the finished piece."

"Even if it wasn't for each other? Wow, that's kind of sad."

"It wasn't sad when I deposited that big, fat check they had written me. I'd been living on rice and black coffee for months."

"Mmm, been there. When I landed my first job out of college, I made enough to barely cover my rent. Pretty sure I subsisted on ramen and coffee for the majority of that year."

"And, now, you're running the whole place, am I right?"

She gave me a hesitant smile as she finished off her drink. "Something like that." Looking up at me, those baby-blue eyes met mine, full of determination and wicked intent. "You want to get out of here?"

I couldn't help but smile. "I thought you'd never ask."

CHAPTER FOUR

Millie

MY EYES BOLTED OPEN AS SUNLIGHT FROM THE windows glared down at me.

Where am I?

This was a common question of mine when I woke, having lived the better part of the last three years constantly in transit. But today felt different.

I looked around, somewhat recognizing the room that had once been my parents', growing up. It had changed quite a lot, having gone through some recent major renovations. Since my sister and brother-in-law no longer lived here, having renovated Jake's family home for their own, there was no need for family quarters anymore.

It was sort of sad really.

The end of an era.

I sat up, quietly stretching as if I had all the time in the world.

Because I did, right?

No job. No responsibilities.

Responsibilities…

Shit!

Breakfast for the guests!

I bolted out of bed, frantically searching for my clothes. *Where were my clothes?* I tried to think back to the night before, but it was blurry.

Hazy.

And then the hammering in my head began.

Shit, how much did I drink last night?

"Where are you running off to so early?"

The deep British accent had me stopping in my tracks.

Last night...

I turned on my heels, tugging on the short shirt I had on, wishing it were suddenly a dress. Or a robe.

Or anything longer than a shirt.

Aiden's eyes perused my body with a wide grin on his face as he casually tucked his hands behind his head. I tried not to notice the way the muscles in his arms flexed.

Or the fact that, besides a carefully placed sheet, he was basically lying naked before me.

"Oh my God," I whispered. My fingers raked through my hair as I tried to remember the night before. "We didn't...did we?"

The question had him immediately sitting up in bed, causing that well-placed sheet to shift.

I gulped as all of him—and I did mean *all* of him—came into view.

Oh Jesus, Mary, and Joseph.

I turned around, my cheeks flushing as heat spread through my body. He wasn't just naked. He was naked and very much awake.

"You don't remember?" he asked as I listened to the bed groan as he stood.

"No," I admitted. "Do you?"

THE LIES I'VE TOLD

I heard the telltale sign of jeans being zipped, giving me the courage to turn back around. Sure enough, he was decent.

Well, as decent as a shirtless, hot-as-fuck Brit could be. God, I thought his muscles had muscles.

"Um, no," he answered, but there was a hint of sadness to his eyes as he reached down to grab his shirt off the floor.

I let out a tiny whimper of protest as the black T-shirt slid down his body.

He really was beautiful.

I shook my head, trying to keep focused. "Oh, that's great. Just fucking great. So, what happened here exactly?"

He pointed to the pile of clothes and the mostly empty alcohol bottle on the nightstand, that sadness drying up as he let out a breath and straightened, his features hardening. "I think that's pretty clear."

My arms folded across my chest before I realized that only brought my shirt higher up my waist. Aiden didn't miss the extra peek of flesh either as I watched his grin widen.

"Nope, I don't believe you. I don't do one-night stands. Ever."

"Ever?" he echoed, surprise written all over his stupid face.

"Yes. Ever. Why is that so hard to believe? Do I look like the one-night-stand kind of girl?"

"Well, right now. Sort of."

My hands flew up in frustration. "I can't do this right now. I'm late in setting up breakfast. My head is pounding and—"

And my life just fell apart.

"And what?"

"And nothing. Now, will you help me find my clothes?

I need to go try to save face with the rest of the guests. In the meantime, maybe one of us will remember what exactly happened last night. Like, how the hell we ended up here. I'm not even sure this is your room. Did I even show it to you?"

God, everything was hazy.

He nodded, his face still unreadable as he scanned the room and finally met my gaze. "It is. Your sister—the loyal, overly kind woman that she is—was actually booked solid when I made my hasty trip down here. But these rooms hadn't been opened up for booking yet since they were recently renovated."

"Yes, I believe she was holding off until after her maternity leave to save my parents the added stress of extra guests while they were in charge. But how would you remember that?" I asked as his head turned, focusing on gathering up his things.

"Don't know," he said. "Guess I was sober enough to remember that part."

"This is a nightmare. I've got to go," I said, flustered, turning toward the door.

"Oh, Millie?" he said, making me turn back around.

I could see a hint of amusement in his eyes, but it was masking something.

Something big.

"What?" I said, trying to hold back my anger.

"You might want to put some pants on before greeting the other guests."

I glanced down at my bare legs and the lacy panties that barely covered anything before looking back up at the cold smirk spreading across his face.

God, I hated this man.

Thankfully, Molly had prepared for her departure when it came to food. After rushing into the large family-style kitchen, I began searching for anything and everything that might work as a breakfast for twelve because, although she and I had been taught all the same recipes, growing up, she was the only one to remember them or re-create them without burning anything.

But being the overly responsible person she was, Molly had armed me with enough baked goods—both fresh and frozen—to last through Ruby's first birthday.

Maybe longer.

Now, all I needed was—

"Need some help?"

I twirled around to find the handsome sculptor I'd just run from standing in the doorway to the kitchen.

"No," I said, shaking my head. "No help. Especially from you."

He ignored my words and sauntered in, my eyes unable to look away.

"What do you mean, 'especially from you'? What did I do to deserve such hostility?"

I gulped as a single image from the night before fluttered across my mind.

Him.

Me.

On the bed.

I felt heat pool between my thighs as I turned away. "I told you, I'm not this person. I don't—"

"Fool around with random strangers. Yeah, you made yourself clear on that little matter. But that doesn't change the fact that it happened or that, despite what you might or might not think, you really could use some help. The rest of those guests upstairs are stirring."

I looked at the wide door that led to the foyer, trying to gain a peek at the stairs. Letting out a heavy sigh, I relented. "Okay, fine. Are you capable of making coffee?"

He grinned, moving toward the coffee pot. I took a deep inhale, hating how good he smelled as he brushed past me. "Just call me the coffee master," he said.

"No," I said adamantly.

"That's not what you said last—"

My hands flew up in the air as I tried to keep from screaming at the top of my lungs. "Please, for the love of God, don't finish that sentence."

I watched as he finished scooping out the coffee and added the water.

Then, he turned around and leaned against the counter. "You really don't remember anything?"

"Nothing." I began stacking muffins in a basket.

He mimicked my motions, doing the same with the other pastries.

"But you don't remember anything either, right?" I glanced over at him as his hand froze for a single, solitary moment.

"Nope."

"Any of it?" I pressed.

"Only the little tidbit about the room; that's all."

"So, you don't know if we—"

"We did," he said with a note of finality in his tone.

"How do you know? We could have just made out. Or better yet, talked."

A somewhat forced grin spread across his lips as he

THE LIES I'VE TOLD

grabbed the baskets and ran them over to the table. Then, he turned back around. "There was a condom wrapper on the floor."

"Oh," I said, not sure what to say or do after that.

On one hand, I was glad we had taken precautions. But, on the other…

I looked up and down his body one more time, all those hard lines and toned muscles.

I would have really liked to remember a night with him even if it was wrong.

So wrong.

"I'm sorry if I gave you the wrong idea," I began as I pulled out several other things for breakfast, including eggs. Surely, I could make something with eggs.

He watched as I began cracking them, one by one, before letting out a huff of air and stepping up beside me one more time.

He took several of the eggs and simultaneously cracked them into the bowl. My eyes widened with shock.

"I can do a few things beyond using a chisel and a hammer," he said, a grim line of determination sweeping across his beautiful face. "I'm not a chef by any means, but I am pretty good with eggs. Why don't you go take a few minutes for yourself before the other guests arrive? I've got this."

I pressed my lips together before I spoke, "Why are you being so nice to me? Especially after how I treated you this morning?" I asked.

He placed both hands on the counter, his upper arms flexing as he leaned against it. His face almost seemed lost for a second, like a ship gone astray. But, just as quickly as it had come, the moment vanished, and he was back at the helm, that same emotionless expression on his face. "Let's just say, I know what it's like to have a bad day."

I could see genuine pain in his eyes before I turned toward the door. I thought about asking him what he meant, but I got the feeling it was off-limits and not meant for me, a virtual stranger.

A stranger he'd slept with.

I tried not to think about that on my way back to my room, the one that sat next to his in the old family quarters. Aiden had left the door to his room partially open, and I thanked him for that small kindness, seeing as most of my stuff was apparently in here.

I took a cursory glance around the room. The first thing I noticed was the changes Molly had made. A long time ago, back before careers and responsibilities, this had been a safe haven for Molly and me. We'd run in here when we were scared, huddling under the covers of our parents' large bed when the house would creak and groan in the middle of the night.

But seeing it now, I barely recognized it.

Everything from the paint on the walls to the furnishings had been updated, tying it in with the rest of the inn rather than separating it like before.

A part of me was indeed sad. So many memories had been shared in these two bedrooms that were always ours.

Just the family.

But I was glad to see my sister moving on. Once tied to this place physically and emotionally, she'd found that elusive balance everyone talked about. The perfect mix of career and family life.

Aiden had said I'd spoken of her with jealousy. Looking around at everything she'd accomplished while my own life was falling to pieces, it was hard not to be.

Grabbing my suitcase and other miscellaneous items that had been strewn about during my drunken night of debauchery, I headed out the door to my own room, thinking of only one thing—a long, hot shower.

But the moment I unlocked the door, my phone began to ring. I answered it without bothering to look. I'd already turned in my work phone and shut off all my email accounts, so who could it really be? No doubt, based on the time, it was my sister calling to check on things.

"Hello?" I said, a small grin on my face as I set my things down.

"Millie?" a distinctly male voice replied.

"Lorenzo?" I said, recognizing his accent almost immediately. "What do you want?" I didn't bother covering up my disdain for the man.

When everything had fallen apart yesterday, he'd treated me like everyone else had.

Like a fucking whore.

"I am so sorry, *mi amore*. This was the soonest I could call you."

His little nickname for me, which used to make me blush, suddenly felt wrong. It grated against my ears as I shut the door to my room and took a seat on the bed.

"It's been twenty-four hours since I walked out of your office, Lorenzo. You couldn't carve out a few minutes since then to check on me?"

"I've been dealing with the board. It's been a mess."

I shook my head, unable to believe his bullshit this time. I'd fallen for it one too many times. "It's not like they haven't had to deal with this sort of thing before. You're not exactly discreet."

"Yes," he agreed. "But, usually, it isn't made public to the entire company. Or the press."

My eyes widened as the significance of that email took on a whole new meaning.

"The press?"

Oh God, what would my family think if they found out?

"You should be fine. No one cares who I have affairs with—at least, not anymore. I have had my share of distractions over the years. This is no different."

Distractions.

That was all I was, just another distraction. I should have known.

When would it stop hurting?

"Well, that's great. I mean, you'll come off as a manwhore, once again, gaining you and the brand more exposure and thus making you even wealthier and more pigheaded than you already are."

"*Mi amore*," he purred.

"Don't call me that," I snapped. "I am not your anything. We were a mistake. A dalliance. Nothing more. I don't want anything to do with you, Lorenzo."

"Yes, but you misinterpret my intentions, Millie," he said, dropping the nickname as his tone hardened.

"Oh?"

"I did not call to make amends. To continue what we had would be a huge mistake. I only wanted to make sure you were aware of the press and ask, if they do try to contact you—"

I let out a frustrated huff of air. "You want to make sure I say nice things? That's why you called. To make sure I toe the line."

"Please Millie, don't be difficult."

I swallowed hard as the tears welled up in my eyes. "Oh,

don't worry, Lorenzo. I'll keep my mouth shut."

"Thank—"

I hung up before he could finish.

I didn't want his thanks.

I didn't want his love. Not anymore.

No, I wanted revenge, and I was going to get it if it was the last thing I did.

CHAPTER FIVE

Aiden

IN THE LAST FORTY-EIGHT HOURS, MY LIFE HAD BEEN turned upside down. Plagued with the news from James, I hadn't been able to think about anything else.

Until I'd met her.

Millie McIntyre was a mystery to me. She came off as rude and a bit standoffish yet seemed to possess a deep, abiding love and kindness toward a family she barely saw. Coming here yesterday, I'd had no idea what was awaiting me.

But, after a few short hours, I'd begun to believe it was her.

I'd never been an overly sappy person, especially when it came to the opposite sex and I'd never put any thought into fate, but waking up next to her this morning had felt right.

More than right. It'd felt destined, like the universe had brought us both here to this very place just so we could meet.

But, when I had seen her jump out of bed, not remembering all that had occurred the night before?

THE LIES I'VE TOLD

Everything we'd shared?

Like a giant knife sinking right into the center of my heart.

Now, I didn't know what to believe.

Maybe fate had had nothing to do with this, and it really was what Millie believed it to be—another meaningless one-night stand.

I should know, I'd had plenty.

But nothing about Millie felt temporary or fleeting and I knew she felt the same way, if only she'd remember. I let these thoughts bounce around in my head as I greeted my fellow guests, offering freshly cooked eggs and even some bacon I'd managed to whip up.

She's not going to sleep with you again just because you cooked a plate full of bacon in her absence.

I ignored the voice of doubt ping-ponging around in my head and focused on making sure everyone had what they needed, including me. Helping myself to a plate of food, I made small talk with those around the table. A few were fairly local, driving in from neighboring states, while others had traveled a much greater distance.

Of course, they were all interested in my place of origin.

"New York," I answered after an older gentlemen asked.

"Ah, I would have guessed someplace a bit further," he replied, grabbing another pastry from the plate in the center of the table.

"Not for a long time," I answered.

"And what brought you to New York? Family?"

I shook my head, maybe a little too swiftly. "No," I answered. "Just work. I'm an artist."

"Oh, what kind? Maybe I've heard of you."

This was always fun. Whenever I mentioned what I did

for a living, suddenly, everyone was an art expert.

"Sculpture. I'm a stone carver, mostly granite and marble, but I've done other stuff along the way as well."

"Wow, that's impressive. I have to say, I'm not much of an aficionado when it comes to sculptures, but I do find it interesting. How does one fall into that line of work?"

I swallowed hard. "Dumb luck, I guess."

A memory flashed quickly in my mind.

"Let me teach you, Aiden," a voice echoed in my ears, one I hadn't heard in years.

Even after all this time, I could still remember the exact tone and cadence, as if it'd only been hours since I heard it.

Rather than years.

We continued to make small talk through the remainder of our meal, but I purposely turned the attention off myself and back on him, asking him about his hometown and career. As with most people, he didn't mind talking about himself and did so for quite some time until his wife stole him away to get ready for their sailing lesson.

By the time the kitchen emptied, I felt exhausted.

Emotionally spent.

Rising from the table, I put myself to work, cleaning up. I knew it wasn't necessary—I was, after all, a paying guest—but my hands felt too idle.

"Thank you," a small voice said behind me.

I turned to see Millie enter the kitchen. She was dressed in a casual dress and sandals, and it made for a stark contrast to the woman I'd met the night before. She'd been all business—tailored skirt and mile-high heels. This version of Millie seemed much more laid-back.

Even though the woman wearing it seemed to be anything but.

"Where'd you learn to cook?" she asked.

I gave a noncommittal shrug. "Everyone can cook eggs."

"But not everyone can crack them like that," she countered.

"Cooking show," I answered. "Was trying to impress a girl with my baking skills."

There was a long pause as she stared down at the floor, and I felt like a fool for speaking.

"I didn't mean to be gone for so long," she finally said. "But I can take over now. I'm sure you have things you need to do."

"Things?"

"Yes," she replied, walking toward the table to fetch a few empty plates. "Don't you need to get to work?"

I shook my head in confusion until she clarified, "On the memorial?"

Pressing my lips together, I nodded, finally understanding.

I couldn't believe I'd forgotten about the memorial. The flight here, the email, the test results…it all felt a million miles away after last night with her.

"Yes," I answered. "Of course. I was actually hoping to meet up with Dean Sutherland today."

"Dean?" she asked as she stepped up next to me at the sink.

"Yes. He was the one who contacted me about it. I assume he'll be the best place to start. Do you know him?"

"Of course I know him. This town is about as big as my pinkie finger. Everyone knows Dean."

A twinge of jealousy crept up my spine. "How well do you know him?"

Her eyes met mine. "Are you asking if I've dated him?"

"Have you?"

She let out a frustrated breath, abandoning the dishes to turn toward me. "Not that it's any of your business, but no, I have not dated Dean. He was engaged to my sister though, but that thankfully ended. And, before you scrutinize that sentence, no, I'm not jealous."

I smiled at her obvious flustered state. "I wasn't going to scrutinize. I was merely trying to see if you were involved with anyone right now."

Her eyes avoided mine, causing me to wonder what she was trying to hide, as she answered, "No, I'm not seeing anyone right now." She swallowed hard. "But I'm not looking either. Especially not here."

"Especially not here? What is that supposed to mean?"

She placed her hands flat against the counter as her gaze fell to the floor. "I didn't bust out of this town at the tender age of eighteen just to find myself stuck back here ten years later."

I raised my hands in protest. "No one said anything about you being stuck here. You forget, I'm a temporary guest here as well. After this project is done, I'm out of here."

"Then, why are you so interested in my love life?"

Because I can't go through life having you only once.

Because last night was one of the greatest in my life, and I have to make you remember.

Because I think I might be falling for you.

I met her gaze, her breath hitching as I chose my next words carefully. "Well, I was thinking, since we're both stuck here, we might as well be stuck here together."

Coward. I'm a fucking coward.

Her arms folded across her chest. "I thought we already did that."

"Yes, but did we?" I forced a smile, stepping closer. So close, it made her uncomfortable. I watched her breath rise and fall, and that was when I smiled for real. "If neither of us remembers it, does it really count? I mean, how do I know if we were any good together? Or what if it was so good, it deserves an encore? Or three? Don't you think we owe it to ourselves to at least give it another try? Sober."

She gulped as her gaze drifted down the length of my body. I had to practically hold myself back as I watched the indecision play out on her delicate features.

"No," she finally said.

"No?"

"I can't do this. I can't be another distraction."

"Another?" I asked, not understanding her meaning. "Who have you been distracting?"

"Nothing. No one. It doesn't matter."

I thought we'd told each other everything last night.

But, from the hurt I saw moving across her face, I knew that couldn't be true.

I'd bared my soul. She'd obviously given nothing but a sliver.

Maybe fate was nothing but a joke.

"I think it would be best if we just started over, you as the guest and me as your hostess. Nothing more."

I cleared my throat, an obvious attempt to stifle the stabbing wound in my heart she'd inflicted with her words.

"Of course," I said. "Whatever you want."

She stood straighter as I made my way toward the door, my knees weak from the effort, my reality beginning to crash in around me.

Ticking time bomb.

No way out.

I barely remembered my trip back to my room, thankful I'd left the door open for Millie on my way to the kitchen earlier. My hands were shaking and I wasn't sure I could work a lock if I tried.

I stumbled into the room, finding my way to the unmade bed, remembering the peace I'd felt when I woke up beside her.

All of that was gone now.

Staring into the mirror across from me, I let out a shaky laugh.

God, I was an idiot.

Did I really think I could push all of this aside? That one night with an absolute stranger would suddenly make this all go away?

The years of pain and struggling to survive, and now this? My future had just been reduced to nothing but a bunch of test results.

I was alone.

I'd always been alone.

And, in this lonely world I'd created for myself, I'd find a way to survive this, like I had with every other obstacle that had passed my way.

Because that was what I did.

I survived.

"I need a ride into town," I announced after arriving back into the kitchen just twenty minutes after I left it.

Millie, still looking as hot as ever in that flowery dress

THE LIES I'VE TOLD

that made her legs look a mile long, turned to stare at me, mouth wide open in shock. "Um, what?"

"I need a ride. Into town. Did I stutter? Or was it the accent that made you stumble?"

She'd just finished cleaning the kitchen and preparing what appeared to be a picnic lunch for someone when I boldly announced my demand, causing her to turn abruptly around from the counter to face me.

God, she was gorgeous. Every inch of her skin had been mine last night. Every moan, every—

Stay focused, Aiden.

"I thought we'd agreed this thing between us was going to be strictly—"

"Professional? Yes. It is, which is why, I, the guest, am asking you, the innkeeper, for a ride into town."

She pressed her lips together, causing me to nearly groan. "I'm not sure that's exactly part of my duties."

"What exactly is in the scope of your duties?" I asked, folding my hands across my broad chest.

Her eyes watched as I did, making me horny and frustrated in equal amounts.

"Why don't I give you my sister's car for the day? That way, you can run whatever errands you need to do."

I immediately shook my head. "Nope, sorry. Won't work."

"What? Why?"

She was clearly getting frustrated with me as well, her face growing a shade darker as her stance took on an exasperated appearance.

"I don't have a license," I said.

Her eyes narrowed. "What do you mean, you don't have a license? Everyone has a license."

I shook my head. "Maybe everyone who is born here. But I moved to the States when I was eighteen and to New York City no less. Getting a driver's license wasn't exactly at the top of my list of important things to do. Not when I could take the subway everywhere."

It wasn't an entirely far-fetched lie. Lots of people in the city didn't process driver's licenses. And those who did sometimes let them expire when they were up for renewal because having a car in the city was a hassle.

The truth was, I just didn't trust myself behind the wheel anymore.

Especially in a new town.

Especially with those test results still buried deep in my pocket.

It took her a moment to respond. "Fine," she finally said. "But don't think this means anything. And I can't be gone all day. I have things I need to do, too."

My hands went up in self-defense. "Fine," I answered. "Just a quick trip to meet up with Dean."

"Good."

"And then a trip to the ferry terminal."

Her eyebrows rose. "What?"

"I need to see the remnants of my piece."

She let out an exasperated breath. "Fine."

"And then lunch."

"What?" she practically yelled.

"Well, a guy has to eat."

She muttered obscenities all the way to the car as I followed close behind, trying not to laugh.

This was going to be fun.

THE LIES I'VE TOLD

We headed out of town first. After learning from his brother, Taylor, that Dean was leading a fishing tour until noon, I decided it might be best to spend some time with the ruins of my artwork while we waited for him to return to dry land.

"Taylor said Dean would meet us at that place we had drinks at last night," I said as we sped down the highway out of Ocracoke and toward the docks. "He didn't describe it as such, but I figured it was the same place, based on the location. You can join us if you'd like. I'm sure your mate Billy wouldn't mind another visit."

She gave me a sideways glance before focusing back on the road. "What is that supposed to mean? Oh God, you're trying to figure out if I dated Billy, aren't you? You're relentless."

My eyebrows rose in blatant curiosity. "Well, did you?"

She shook her head.

"I'm merely curious."

"I thought we were being professional," she said, her eyes still set dead ahead.

"I can't be professionally curious?"

She finally looked over at me, a doubtful sort of look that told me she didn't trust me in the least.

Good. She shouldn't.

My intentions were less than honorable.

Millie McIntyre had made herself clear.

Crystal clear in fact.

She'd woken up beside me this morning and basically catapulted her body as far away from mine as physically possible.

She didn't want anything to do with me.

Or at least, the practical side of her didn't. The uptight,

think-it-through, *I shouldn't have sex with a guy I barely know* side of her. But strip that away? Take away all the bullshit and reservations she had been clinging to in her hungover state, and I knew deep down was the woman I'd fallen into bed with.

So, although I'd promised I wouldn't act on my physical feelings toward her…it didn't mean I couldn't make her aware of her own. Misery loved company after all.

"And your professional curiosity extends to questions regarding dating? Is this a normal habit of yours?"

I made a noncommittal sort of shrug. "I'm in the business of emotions. Sometimes, it helps to know where one's heart lies. Or where it's been."

"But I'm not a client," she reminded me. "If anything, it's the other way around."

Another shrug. "Call it a hazard of my job."

She let out an exasperated sigh as I tried not to grin. "Not that it's any of your business, but no, Billy and I never dated. I've always had the feeling that Billy's tastes run a little too similar to my own, if you know what I mean."

We pulled off the road, avoiding the large line of cars waiting to get onto the ferry.

"Good for Billy," I said before asking, "So, who did you date?"

She stepped out of the car, leaving me to follow behind her like a sad little puppy.

I guessed I deserved that.

We passed by several tourists making last-minute runs to the restroom and vending machines before their hour-long adventure across the sound.

"If you must know, I didn't date much in high school. I didn't want any distractions and attachments when I went away to college, like my sister had with Jake. I just wanted to get away."

I looked around at the picturesque setting spread out before us. "Doesn't really seem like a hellish sort of place to grow up."

"It wasn't," she admitted, slowing her gait a little to allow me to catch up. "But I always knew I wanted more. Surely you should understand that, hotshot artist man?"

"Hotshot artist man. Now, that's a title I could get used to." I grinned. "Do you think that would fit on a business card?"

She giggled slightly, making me feel like a king among men. Hearing her laugh again felt like a great victory after being turned down this morning.

I'll make you remember me, Millie McIntyre. Just you wait.

"Well, here we are," she said as I was admiring the way the sun seemed to light up every golden strand on her head.

"What?" I managed to say, looking around before I noticed the police tape. I squinted and stepped a few feet forward, and that was when I saw it. The pitiful remains of my memorial. "Oh, this is just sad."

Ignoring the yellow tape, I stepped over it and felt my heart plummet.

"I'd ask you if you date much, but seeing that look on your face right now pretty much sums it up for me. How could any woman compete?"

I nodded. "An artist's work is often his one true love. And this one?" I said, running my hands along what was left of the granite base. "This one was one of the great ones."

I didn't know how long we were out there, but she stayed silent as I mourned.

As I remembered.

My hands moved over what remained and glided over what was not. I closed my eyes and recalled every chiseled edge, each hard line, and the hours it had taken to make them.

"God, I would have loved to see it here. Finished. Whole. Where it was supposed to be."

"Oh!" Millie said suddenly. "I think I can help you out with that," she said, reaching for her phone. I moved closer to her as she fiddled with the screen for a moment. "I came home not too long ago for my sister's wedding, and when I drove in, I actually pulled off to the side of the road and took a few pictures of it."

"You did?" I said, feeling a bit stunned.

"Yeah," she answered, her eyes avoiding mine as she pulled up the photo.

"Why?"

"Well, I guess you could say I was sort of taken by it."

Her eyes finally met mine, and in them, I saw honesty. Maybe for the first time since I'd met her.

It electrified me.

Moved me.

Scared me.

Not breaking the connection I felt between us, I asked, "You were taken by it?"

She took a deep breath and blinked. Just like that, like a rubber band snapping on the back of my hand, I felt that deep, far-reaching connection break as her eyes tore away from mine.

"Yeah, well, because of Dean, you know? He nearly died out there."

I swallowed, feeling like the worst kind of moron.

"Right, of course. Dean."

"I'm going to go grab a drink from the vending machine. Do you want anything?"

Still no eye contact.

And the photo she was supposed to show me was gone, the phone shoved back her purse.

Along with her emotions.

"No," I answered. "I'm fine."

"Right. Okay."

But I was anything but fine.

I turned back to look at my statue, reduced to nothing more than a pile of rocks on the shore.

Hadn't I learned enough by now?

This was what people did to you.

They used you, destroyed you, and abandoned you.

No doubt Millie was no different.

I needed to stop with the antics. She was never going to remember, and even if she did, so what? Neither of us would be around long enough to see it through.

I needed to get my head back in the game.

I was here for one purpose and one purpose only.

To fix a problem and move the hell on.

CHAPTER SIX

Millie

AIDEN WAS QUIET ON OUR WAY BACK INTO TOWN.

Uncomfortably quiet.

With both hands on the steering wheel, I tried to focus on the road ahead.

I tried to focus on anything but the color of his hazel eyes under the bright summer sun.

Or the way they seemed to speak to me in a way no one else could.

Like he understood me without effort.

Like he knew what I was thinking without words.

Without explanation.

I nearly shook my head at the idea.

It was ludicrous.

I'd just met the guy.

We'd known each other less than twenty-four hours.

Didn't stop you from jumping into bed with him.

I let out a frustrated puff of air, releasing it into the car like a long prayer drifting up to heaven.

"You okay?" Aiden asked.

"What? Oh yeah, I'm fine," I lied. "Just admiring the

blue sky. It's the perfect shade today."

It wasn't much of a lie because, honestly, the sky really was putting on a show today.

I saw his head move forward toward the window as he looked up. "It is."

"Do you work much with color?" I asked, suddenly curious about his profession.

"Not much," he said, still gazing up at the sky. There was a sadness in his eyes, something I hadn't noticed before. Almost as if he were saying good-bye to a good friend for the last time. "I dabbled in pottery for a while when I was learning how to work with clay a long time ago, so I have some experience with colored glazes, and yeah, you do have variations in stone colors, but it's not a vivid color like this."

"You work with clay?"

He nodded, his arms folded around his chest. It made his biceps thicken, and I tried not to notice.

I said I tried.

Thank God I could focus on the road ahead of me; otherwise, I'd probably have drool forming around my mouth from staring at the guns on that man. Who knew stone carvers were so ripped?

"I use it to do a rough workup of most of my pieces. It helps guide me as I'm working. Clay is easy to form. If you make a mistake, you just smooth your hands over it and work it in a different direction. Stone, however, isn't nearly as forgiving."

"Kind of like a sketch."

"What?" His eyes turned toward me once again.

"In design, we work up a sketch first. And then, before we cut the fabric, we'll pin. And pin some more. Because, like clay, fabric is not so forgiving after it's been cut."

"I forgot you were in the fashion industry."

My eyes rose as I briefly turned to him, the Ocracoke sign passing by us as we entered town. "I don't remember telling you I was in fashion."

His forehead furrowed briefly. "I, uh, don't quite remember either, but I do remember you told me. Just chalk it up to another mystery from our evening together."

"The evening we shall never speak of," I reminded him.

"Right," he agreed, clearing his throat before I pulled off the road into a small gravel parking area surrounded by several ancient oak trees.

"We're here! Just in time for your meeting with Dean," I announced a little too loud for the small space we were in. Sharing pretty much any space with Aiden felt too small. I wasn't sure what it was—maybe it was his personality or perhaps it was the raw sense of curiosity I had for the man, but he just seemed to swell up and envelop any space we were in.

Until I felt like I was gasping for air.

Aiden looked out the window, immediately recognizing the restaurant I'd taken him to the night before. It obviously looked different during the day, the water from the bay glistening from the bright noonday sun as kayakers swam up to the dock to order lunch.

"Right then," he said, sounding very English all of a sudden. "Are you sure you don't care to join us? I'm quite certain Dean wouldn't mind the company."

I shook my head back and forth. "No, you go ahead. I have stuff I need to catch up on back at the inn. I don't want my sister to think I'm falling asleep on the job."

I sounded like an absolute idiot.

No, I sounded like a phony.

Because that was exactly what I was.

An absolute fraud.

But I couldn't help it. I needed to get away from him.

Something about Aiden completely threw me off-balance. He was too perceptive. Too intuitive. And, if I weren't careful, I'd end up right back in his bed.

And, this time, I didn't think I'd ever leave.

I should have floored the engine the minute Aiden stepped foot out of the car.

But I didn't.

I made the mistake of thinking like a Floridian instead of remembering where I was.

I was in Ocracoke, a tiny blip on the map where everyone knew each other and you couldn't go two feet without running into half of the town.

I thought I'd be safe, grabbing a to-go order before heading back to the inn.

God, what an idiot I was.

I barely made it to the bar before I heard Dean shouting my name.

"Silly Millie McIntyre! Don't think you can sneak in here without saying hello!"

I pressed my lips together, cursing myself for not being content with a can of soup or leftovers from breakfast this morning.

No, I cursed Billy for making the world's best French fries.

I slapped on a smile and turned to greet him. "Dean!" I said, feeling genuine happiness at seeing the man who'd almost become my brother-in-law. Although no one believed for a second that Molly and Dean would have actually made it down the aisle. Not while Jake still lived and breathed.

"How are you?" I asked, wrapping my arms around him as he wrapped his one around mine.

I'd never seen him without his prosthetic on; he'd always been so sensitive about it in the past. But, recently, he seemed to be okay with his disability, choosing to go with or without it, depending on his mood.

And it suited him.

This was a lighter, happier Dean than I'd ever seen.

"I'm good." He smiled, taking a seat at the table he'd grabbed for him and Aiden.

No doubt they'd already done their introductions as I snuck up to the bar. I tried to ignore the dark-haired man sitting next to him, but it was difficult.

So very difficult.

I cleared my throat and tried to concentrate on Dean, still refusing to sit down. I wasn't staying.

I definitely am not staying.

"You look good. Could this be because of a certain lady in your life?"

His grin widened. "Two actually," he replied.

Aiden kind of let out a choked laugh before realizing Dean was being completely serious.

"Cora, my fiancée, has a young daughter. Her name is Lizzie. Those two, well, they're my world," he said with such conviction and ferocity.

My conversation with Lorenzo came back in that moment, and I felt suddenly bereft.

Nothing but a distraction...

What would it be like to be someone's entire world. To mean so much to another person? To have someone in your life that meant so much in return?

"You okay?" Aiden asked, jumping to his feet, his eyes full of concern.

"Yeah, fine."

"Why don't you sit down?"

I shook my head as his hand found mine. "I'm okay. I have stuff to do. I really should be going."

Neither of the men was all that convinced.

"Can it wait for a little bit?" Dean asked. "The last time I saw you was at your sister's wedding, and we didn't exactly have much time to catch up."

A small smirk tugged at the corner of my mouth. "If I recall, you were pretty busy during the reception."

He shook his head, a low rumble of a laugh bubbling up from his chest. "Had a black eye and sore ribs for a week after to prove it. Come on, please? I'll even pay your tab."

I let out a sigh. "Okay fine, but I'm ordering the most expensive thing on the menu."

I saw Aiden scan his menu before looking up at me. "You know the most expensive thing on the menu is fried calamari, right?"

I glanced down at my own menu before confirming what he'd just said. Scrunching my nose in disgust, I announced, "Okay then, the second most expensive thing on the menu. I hate seafood."

"Fried clams?"

"Jesus," I cursed. "Just order me a burger."

Dean laughed. "You know, I have a little girl at home who once hated seafood as much as you."

"Oh yeah? Let me guess; you cured her of it?"

"What kind of fisherman would I be otherwise?"

I shrugged. "The kind who knows kids hate seafood?"

"You're not a kid, Millie," Aiden reminded me, his gaze dark and deliberate.

"Well, I can still eat like one."

"Oh come on, Millie, You travel all over the world for that fancy job of yours, right? Surely, you don't order French fries and burgers when you're in Paris?"

I gave Dean an exasperated look, trying to ignore the fact that I was not a world traveler anymore. "Of course not."

"Well, that's a relief—"

"In France, they're called *pommes frites*."

Aiden broke out into laughter while Dean shook his head and said, "You're exasperating. And that's saying a lot. I live with a six-year-old genius."

"Well, I'm sorry. I'm an adult, therefore I can eat, or not eat whatever I want."

Billy arrived, and although Dean rolled his eyes at my plain cheeseburger and French fries, he kept his word and added everything to his tab, including Aiden's fish and chips.

"Do they remind you of home?" Dean asked.

"What now?" Aiden asked, seemingly caught off guard as he had been staring off at the bay.

"The fish and chips—do they remind you of England?"

"Oh no, not really."

The way he'd said it with his arms folded across his chest and his eyes still fixated on the subtle waves rolling into harbor told me it was a topic he wasn't keen on elaborating on.

But Dean pressed onward nonetheless. "Do you miss it?

Your home?"

"No, not in the least."

It was a surprising answer. Didn't everyone miss their home, even just a little? I knew I did.

"Where in England are you from?" Dean asked.

I turned toward him, my eyes widening to an unnatural size.

His shoulders rose as he mouthed back to me, *What?*

Clearly, he wasn't getting it.

Maybe it was the accent, but of all people, the emotionally scared Dean should see when a person was retreating from a subject, and that was Aiden. It was as if there were a bright white flashing sign above his head that said, *This Topic is Off-Limits*, and Dean was blind to it.

"Nowhere significant," Aiden replied.

Suddenly, I caught a wisp of auburn hair. I turned to see Cora as she made her way onto the deck, and I breathed a sigh of relief.

"Oh, look! Cora's here!" I announced rather loudly, dragging Dean's attention toward his fiancée.

I saw Aiden let out a breath of air. I couldn't help but wonder what had happened to make him never want to return to England.

That meant never seeing his family again.

Does he have any family?

I shook my head at the thought.

Everyone has family, right?

"Hi, everyone!" Cora said, taking the seat next to me.

"Aiden, this is my fiancée, Cora. Cora, this is the sculptor I was telling you about, Aiden Fisher."

They shook hands as Aiden greeted her.

"So lovely to meet you," he said in a very proper way,

taking her hand, which caused her to blush.

"Oh my gosh," she nearly squealed. "You sound just like the Doctor."

"The what?" I blurted out, looking from Aiden to Cora and finally to Dean, who seemed to be fairly amused with his fiancée's behavior.

"The Doctor," Dean said before they all answered in unison, "*Doctor Who*."

I still had no idea what they were talking about.

"It's a British sci-fi show Cora and her whole family are kind of obsessed with."

She nodded, still staring at Aiden like he was some sort of god. "It's kind of our thing. Star Wars, Harry Potter—pretty much anything geeky. Oh my gosh, you kind of sound like Harry Potter. Oh! And maybe that hot guy from *Game of Thrones*."

Aiden chuckled. "So, basically anyone British that you've seen on the telly then?"

Cora turned to Dean. "He said telly!"

I swore, she swooned.

"Babe, don't you need to order some food before you head back to the clinic?"

Her eyes widened before she grabbed her menu. "I'm so sorry. I'm back to normal now. And I really do apologize for crashing your lunch, but we managed to empty out the clinic, so I thought I'd run out for a quick bite."

Aiden's eyebrows rose in confusion.

Dean translated, "Cora's the nurse at the town clinic."

He nodded his head before saying, "*The* nurse, as in the only one?"

She sort of laughed, a crimson blush spreading across her pale skin as she fought her inner fangirl. "Yes, it's just

THE LIES I'VE TOLD

me. Well, me and Dr. Jake. There are a few volunteer EMTs who help with emergencies, but for everything else—coughs, colds, and flus along with the everyday accidents—that's all us."

"Wow."

I turned to him, my lips pressed together. "Wow?"

"I guess I didn't really fathom how small this place was. I mean, you sort of see it as you drive in, but I don't think you can really put it all together until you hear something like that."

Dean's eyes met mine. "Should I tell him the size of my graduating class?"

I laughed. "No. Mine was smaller."

"It was not!" Dean protested.

"Was to," I replied. "Carter Dodd dropped out halfway through his junior year, which brought us down to four."

"Four?" Aiden said, his voice sounding incredulous. "As in four people?"

Dean nodded. "How many were in yours?"

Aiden's mood suddenly shifted, and I could almost feel it in the air. "Uh, I don't recall. Definitely not four."

"So, don't you two have business to discuss? A statue to resurrect?" I interjected, calling for an immediate change of subject.

I might not want to sleep with the guy again, but I could at least offer him some common courtesy.

Okay, that wasn't true.

I definitely wanted to sleep with him, but I wasn't going to.

Out of the corner of my eye, I caught him glancing at me. The tiny flecks of green in those hazel brown eyes reminded me of sand.

From far away, it looked brown.

Just basic, boring brown.

But palm a bit of sand in your hand, spread it out, and really look at each individual grain, and you'd find a virtual rainbow of color. There were flecks of red from crushed up shells, blue and green from sea glass and a dozen other colors all scattered in between.

That was what I saw in Aiden's eyes and it dazzled me.

Nope, definitely not sleeping with him again, I reminded myself.

I shook off his deep stare and tried to focus on Cora. "So, how have you been?" I said, sort of out of the blue. "You need food. We should order you some food."

She didn't seem caught off guard by my rambling, but, as Dean had said earlier, she was the mother to a tiny genius, so she was probably used to this by now. I flagged Billy, who took Cora's order of fish and chips, while Dean and Aiden began talking business.

"I left in in a hurry. I need to have some things shipped here," Aiden explained. "Supplies."

"That shouldn't be a problem. We are fairly modern in that respect, although it might take a bit longer than what you're used to in New York. You can even have your stone material delivered, if you'd like."

Aiden shook his head as I listened in on their conversation, having already given up on my attempt to ignore them. "No, that's one thing I won't be ordering."

"Oh?" Dean and I said in unison.

"Stone is a fickle medium to work with, and I am particular. I'll have to hand-choose the piece I work with."

Dean shrugged, unfazed by the decision.

I, on the other hand, had some serious reservations.

"What do you mean, you'll have to choose the piece by hand?"

His eyes met mine. "It means I'll have to go to the quarry and select it."

"And will you be driving there yourself? Can't we just go to a store and pick it out?"

Why was I even bothering to ask? Had I ever heard of a giant rock store?

"Uh, no, it's not like I'm putting in a countertop here. And I was hoping you'd take me."

I let out a breath, trying to keep my cool. "And where is this quarry?"

"Mount Airy."

My eyes nearly bugged out of my head as I calculated the driving distance. "That's nearly eight hours away."

He nodded, turning his head toward the bay again. "You're right. It's too much to ask. I'll ask the pilot who flew me to take me."

My gaze traveled to the water, wondering what he was so fixated on. "He won't take you. He's strictly tours and airport travel only. It's fine; I'll take you. But we'll have to wait until the day after tomorrow when my sister returns from the hospital, so my parents can take over the inn for me."

He nodded, not turning away from the sparkling blue waves. "Good."

"Okay, sounds like a plan," Dean said, taking over as I sat back in my chair.

I'd hoped to get back to Florida the day after next.

A quick day with the family and my new baby niece, and then back to reality.

Back to getting my life together.

Back to figuring out who had stolen it all away from me,

because I was going to make them pay.

Right after I finished clawing my way back up to the top.

But, for now, all of that was on pause because this beautiful conundrum of a man needed a favor.

Again.

I guessed revenge could wait another day.

"You want to get out of here?" Aiden asked, a look of challenge spreading across his handsome face.

I couldn't help but smile. "I thought you'd never ask."

He quickly paid our tab, which wasn't much, considering we hadn't been there long. I had no idea what his intentions were when we left the restaurant, but with the drink I'd nearly inhaled buzzing through my veins, I was up for anything.

As long as it didn't involve work, Lorenzo, or the email that had ruined me.

"I don't suppose there is anywhere in this tiny little town to purchase alcohol, is there?" Aiden asked as we hopped in my sister's car and pulled onto the desolate road.

"At this time of night? That would be a no. But I might be able to scrounge something up back at the inn."

"Sounds promising," he said before a long, silent pause.

I looked over to see him peering out the window. He appeared thoughtful, his eyes taking in every detail as we drove the short distance home.

"What is it that you do, Millie McIntyre?" he asked, turning his attention back toward me.

I swallowed hard, hating that my one wish for the evening—to not have to think about work—didn't even last the car ride back to the inn.

"Um, I'm in fashion."

I stopped the car in its normal place beside the house and shifted it into park before the engine shut off.

"And what does that mean exactly? Fashion? Do you design clothes? Sell them?" He paused for a moment, his eyes lingering on the subtle curves of my body. "Model them?"

My hand fought at my side to find the door handle.

Was it hot in here?

God, I felt like I was on fire.

"Um, sales mostly. I want to design though. I mean, that was—is my goal…eventually."

"Impressive," he said. "Although you'd make an excellent model."

I let out a tiny laugh, half-humor, half-nervousness. "Clearly, you don't know a thing about the fashion industry. I'm about as far from what they deem a perfect model as you can get. I'm too curvy, far too short, and—" I looked down at my chest, feeling my cheeks heat instantly.

God, I was acting like a fool. What was with me tonight? I was never this nervous around men.

That damn email…

"Well, let's just say, I'm all wrong for that particular profession."

His eyes, those beautiful hazel eyes that seemed to include every color under the sun, stared deeply into mine. "Well, I guess that explains why I've never been into models. I prefer curves."

Hot. So hot in here.

"Drinks?"

"What?" he replied as the connection between us snapped.

"You wanted drinks? Do you want to head inside?"

"Oh, right. Yes, of course."

My hand finally found the handle, and as I pushed the door open and the summer air rushed in, I couldn't help but take a deep breath and look to the heavens.

Dear God, what was I doing?

I awoke to the sound of my phone and the ear-piercing alarm I'd set the night before.

Blinking several times, I looked around, my mind still a haze after my dream about Aiden.

I was still in the weird bedroom that looked like my childhood bedroom but wasn't.

Same screwed up life.

Different day.

At least, today, I'd woken up on time.

And alone.

Way to go, Millie.

I gave myself a mental pat on the back as I proceeded to the bathroom my sister had tastefully renovated, admiring the subtle coastal vibe she'd given it with the white subway tile throughout and cool blue accents. It wasn't cliché like a lot of beachy accommodations with shells plastered literally everywhere, but it gave a serene vibe that screamed relaxation.

Unfortunately, I didn't have time for any of that and needed to get a move on. Hopping into the shower, I spent a few minutes getting clean, and within thirty minutes or so, I was presentable in a fresh pair of linen shorts and a floral top.

Sweeping my hair back into a side braid and putting

on some light makeup, I felt confident and better prepared about going into breakfast than I had the day before.

I stepped into the hallway, doing my best not to press my ear against Aiden's door—that would definitely not be professional—and headed for the kitchen.

As soon as I entered, I nearly tripped over my own feet.

"Hey, sweetheart!"

Sitting at the table, drinking coffee, were my parents.

But that wasn't what had me nearly choking on my own saliva. At the stove, cooking them breakfast, was Aiden.

Freaking Aiden Fisher.

My guest.

My honored guest. The one I was supposed to treat like royalty.

"Um, hi, Mom. Dad," I said before running over to give them hugs and kisses. "How are you? How's the baby? And Molly?"

Why are you here?

Why is he here?

We finished our mini-reunion, and they returned to their coffee at the table.

"We're good," my mom said. "The baby is fantastic, but you'll see that for yourself. Jake, Molly, and little Ruby are being discharged this morning. We decided to leave early and avoid the traffic. Plus, I figured I could get some things set up for them at the house."

Okay, I guessed that made sense.

"And you needed breakfast?" I asked, glancing over to Aiden, who threw one of his devil-may-care, panty-melting grins at me. Except I thought he missed because my mom seemed to melt into a puddle behind me and broke into spontaneous laughter.

No, not laughter. A giggle.

My mom fucking giggled, like a little schoolgirl.

"We popped in to see if you needed anything and found Aiden here, making himself a cup of coffee. And wouldn't you know it? He offered to make us breakfast. Isn't that kind of him?"

I looked from my mom to my father, who seemed a little less thrilled with the idea. He looked up at me, his forehead wrinkled in obvious disbelief.

He couldn't believe my mom was acting like this either.

Good. Glad I wasn't the only one.

I gave him a small smile, and he returned it.

"Well, why don't I take over since Aiden is our guest, and you can tell me all about my new little niece? How does that sound?"

Aiden, who had remained quiet through this whole family reunion as he flipped bacon and scrambled eggs, continued to ignore what was going on. As if he didn't know what he was doing to my mom. He probably lived for flirting. God knew he'd done his fair share with me.

My thoughts briefly drifted back to my dream, the memories of that car. To the words he'd said.

He'd probably flirted his way right into my bed.

Or his.

Whatever.

"Oh, I don't—" my mother protested, clearly enjoying the view of Aiden cooking.

"That sounds lovely," my father interjected.

"Good." I smiled, turning back toward Aiden. "Thank you so much for accommodating my parents after their long trip home. It's really polite, but the *professional* thing for me to do is to cook for you, and I wouldn't want you to think I'm not *professional*."

The emphasis wasn't lost on him, and as our eyes locked, I saw disappointment in his.

"Right. Of course," he said. "I overstepped."

I'd expected some sort of snarky response. A rebuttal. Even a flirtatious remark.

But not disappointment.

Who was he to be disappointed with me?

I watched as he cleaned his hands on a dish towel and set it down next to the stove.

He gave me one last look before heading for the hallway. "If you'll excuse me, I think I'm going to get a run in before breakfast."

My eyes didn't waver until he disappeared around the corner, leaving me wondering how I'd hurt him.

And why it affected me so.

"The least you could have done is shown up in sweats, Millie. Or put your hair in a messy bun. Come on," Molly said as she pulled open her front door. "I just had a baby, level the playing field a little! You look ridiculously hot. Is that contouring?" She pointed to my makeup and shook her head.

I bit my top lip to keep from laughing but couldn't help it when she pulled me into a giant hug, causing my attention to drift downward to her slippers.

"Oh my God, what are those?" Stepping away, I saw the grin on her face as she modeled whatever was on her feet.

"Like them? Mom got them for me, so I'm guessing they're mom slippers. I don't know, and I don't care because whatever orthopedic, memory foam crap is in these ugly things is honestly the second best thing that's ever happened to me."

"Heard that," Jake hollered from the living room, causing us both to laugh.

"Want to meet your niece?"

My eyebrows rose in excitement. "More than I want to stab a knife through those horrible slippers of yours."

"Don't you dare! Come on in."

I chose not to make a comment about the huge pink robe she had wrapped around her. I mean, she had just had a kid two days ago. She did deserve some slack. But I made a mental note to send her something of the silk variety for her birthday; otherwise, poor Ruby might end up being an only child.

The living room had drastically changed since the last time I'd seen it. Scattered around the room was evidence that a baby now lived here. No, not lived. Ruled. A baby definitely ruled this place, and she'd only been here a handful of hours.

A portable changing table had been set up in the corner, next to the sofa, along with a place for the baby to nap. There were boxes of diapers stacked in the hallway and unopened gifts from people who'd stopped by while they were away.

"Wow, it's like baby central in here."

"This is the bare minimum. Wait until she's older and we have a swing, a high chair and toys," Jake said, rising from his spot on the sofa to give me a hug. Well, a side hug at best because in one arm, he held Ruby.

I bent down and felt my eyes well up with tears.

"You guys," I said, surprised at the emotion in my voice.

"I know," Molly said, standing next to me.

I wiped a tear from my cheek. "Look what you made."

"Do you want to hold her?" Jake asked.

I looked down at her, so new to the world with her pink skin and soft folds. "Are you sure? My experience with newborns is limited. Well, not limited. It's nothing. As in none. I've never held one. Actually, I've never even seen a newborn this young before. Am I rambling? What if I drop her?"

My sister's head tilted to the side, a curious gaze in her eyes, before she answered, "You won't drop her, Millie. Here, let us teach you."

Jake showed me how to cradle her head and support her body, and before I knew it, I was holding that tiny bundle of joy.

My niece.

Mine.

I'd never felt such pride for something so small.

So real.

"I think I'll go finish unpacking our stuff," Jake said softly, placing a tender hand on his wife's shoulder before vacating the room.

"Let's sit down," she suggested. "I don't know about you, but I could use the rest."

We did, and I could tell Molly was exhausted by the way she exhaled the second her body melted into the couch cushions. Her usual never-ending well of energy had been seriously depleted over the last few days.

I looked back down at the sleeping baby in my arms. "She's perfect Molly, truly."

I heard the smile in her voice as she replied, "Yes, she is."

When I turned to my sister in that moment, it was like seeing her for the first time. Something in her had changed.

She'd become a mother.

And, even though I'd made fun of her slippers and rolled my eyes at her silly robe, the light and love that radiated from within her, it was the most beautiful thing I'd ever seen.

"You okay, sis?" Molly asked, a genuine look of concern on her face.

I pried my face away from Ruby. "Yeah, why?"

Her eyebrow rose in disbelief. "Well, for one, I've never heard you ramble like that. Ever. And two, the fact that you were able to drop everything just like that to babysit the inn. Care to explain?"

I pressed my lips together as I avoided her gaze. "I have been known to ramble from time to time," I said, thinking back to lunch with a certain Brit. "And I told you, I had vacation time saved up. Lots of it."

Another lie.

Unfortunately, lies were easier to tell when you were on the phone, and your sister wasn't staring you down.

"Try again," she said, her face deadpanned. "And, if you don't tell me the truth, I'm taking away the baby."

I looked down at Ruby, my face scrunched in agony. "Okay fine, but that's just dirty, using my niece to get me to talk, only minutes after I've met her."

"Still waiting," she said, not even messing around.

"I'm getting there!" I said sternly. Well, as sternly as one could be while whispering to avoid waking a sleeping baby. "I lost my job."

"You what?"

"You heard me. I lost my job," I reiterated as Ruby began

to fuss in my arms, making me instantly panic.

A sleeping baby was one thing. A needy, crying baby was another.

"Give her to me, and start talking," she said, handling Ruby like a damn pro.

If I didn't know better, I would have sworn my sister had done this whole parenting thing before. I watched in awe as she cradled that tiny little newborn in one hand and disconnected her bra with the other. Within seconds, Ruby was latched and feeding like a champ.

"Wow. Is it always that easy?"

"What? Breastfeeding? No," she explained. "Every woman is different. Every baby is different. It's always a mixed bag. Thankfully, everything has worked out pretty well so far, and the hospital had an amazing staff to support me. But enough of that. Stop stalling. Your job?"

"Right. Well, the gist is, I had a job, and now, I don't."

"Millie," she nearly growled.

"Fine," I growled back. "I was up for a major promotion, and then someone sent an email around to the entire company that had some pretty incriminating information about me. And…well, instead of being fired, I resigned."

Her eyes widened. "What kind of incriminating evidence?"

I tried to look away, but her tractor-beam gaze caught me first. "That I slept with my boss," I said, sort of slurring it all together.

"You slept with your boss?"

Of course she'd understand my mumbled speech.

"Yes, okay? I am a horrible person. I'm the office slut who let her emotions get the best of her and slept with her boss."

A moment passed before she spoke again, "Do you love him?"

I took a deep breath. "I thought I did."

"But you don't anymore?"

I found myself looking down at the hardwood floor as I wrung my hands together. The only sound in the room was the sweet, comforting noise of my newborn niece nursing.

"No," I answered finally. "Not anymore. Honestly, I'm not even sure I know what love feels like."

"So, what will you do now?" she asked, placing a gentle hand on top of Ruby's head as she looked at me with warmth and compassion.

I should have known my sister would be there for me.

"Well, work my way back up, obviously. I have my own contacts, my own resources. I can do it. But, first, I want to find out who sent that email."

"Why?" she asked.

"What do you mean, why?"

"What difference does it make?"

"Molly, that person ruined my life. That email literally ruined my life."

She turned her head and looked at me without saying anything, and then she gazed down at Ruby and smiled. "You lost your job, Millie. Not your life. Learn the difference."

Before I had the chance to offer a rebuttal, the doorbell rang, and the dutiful Jake came running to answer it. From the living room, Molly and I could see Cora enter with a large bouquet of flowers and a gift basket full of baby items.

"Dean sends his love, but he had a fishing tour this afternoon. Weekends are a busy time for them," she said, handing over the basket to Jake, who took it along with the flowers and headed for the kitchen.

"Yeah, especially this time of year," Molly said. "Where's your little one?"

"Oh, Lizzie's at a friend's house. I wasn't sure you wanted kids around the baby yet, but she's dying to meet her. She's already told me at least a hundred fun facts about babies since we got the news—and some of them were definitely not PG-13."

That caused us all to laugh as Cora took a seat on the large couch next to us.

"She looks like she's doing well, latching," Cora said, a professional tone to her voice, as the resident nurse in town.

"She is. I think Lizzie might have a run for her money in the smarts department. This one is turning out to be a young Einstein." Molly laughed, making Cora grin.

"Hey, how is Lizzie doing in school?" I asked. "I remember Molly mentioning in one of our conversations at her wedding about there being some issues?"

She nodded. "There was. Being in such a small area, there were some concerns that the school wouldn't be able to keep up with her. But Dean and I are working with them. She takes some classes at a school on the mainland, she's done some work with a tutor, and she'll be skipping a few grades in the fall."

"Wow, that's a lot," I said.

She shrugged. "You do what you have to. She loves it, so that makes it all worth it." She gave a short pause before her eyes locked back on mine. "So, tell me about the hot British guy from yesterday. Did I totally embarrass you when I geeked out over his accent?"

"What? No. Why would you worry about embarrassing me?" I asked, feeling like all the attention in the room had suddenly shifted to me.

"Who's the hot British guy, Millie?" Molly asked before her eyes widened. "You mean, the artist who's staying in the inn?"

Cora nodded her confirmation, but the way her eyes widened told my sister there was more going on to this juicy story.

"Oh, man, I'm gonna need a couple more details," Molly said, shifting a very milk-drunk Ruby from one side to the other.

Once she was back in place, both sets of eyes came right back on me, and I swore they blinked in unison.

Creepy.

"There is nothing to tell," I said, gulping back saliva in my throat perhaps a bit too loudly.

"She's lying," Molly said in sort of a sideways conversation to Cora. "You can always tell she's lying because she refuses to look at you."

Cora glanced over at me. "Isn't that a telltale sign for most people?"

"What?" Molly replied. "I don't know. But, when we were kids and she was trying to lie to Mom and Dad, they'd sit her down in one of those wooden chairs in the kitchen and kneel down, so they were eye-level with her. It would be the funniest thing, watching her head bob around, trying to avoid their gaze. Decades later, nothing's changed."

I rolled my eyes at her. "Oh, like you're any different."

She rolled them right back—a real mature move for a brand-new mother. "That's right because I wouldn't lie in the first place."

Letting out a laugh, I just shook my head in disbelief. "Right, because you didn't spend twelve years lying to yourself that you were over Jake."

She scowled and made a disgusted sound deep in her throat. "That's different," she said.

"Oh, yeah?" I pushed. "Why?"

Her face turned to the side before she finally met my gaze. "Because that happened to me."

Silence fell between the three of us as I processed it, and finally, I couldn't help it. A chuckle tumbled from my lips and then one more.

I met my sister's eyes, and then the dam broke.

And, soon, the room was filled with laughter.

Quiet laughter.

Because we were not about to wake the baby.

We weren't that crazy.

I stayed at my sister's long after Cora had come and gone. I picked up dinner for all of us and cleaned up the kitchen after we ate. It was nice to feel needed now that the inn was in the capable hands of my parents, although I'd offered to help if they needed it.

But who was I kidding? They didn't need it.

It was nice to spend time with my sister without having to rush out the door somewhere.

Because, for the first time in a long time, I didn't have anywhere to be.

"So, you're just driving him all the way across the state?" Molly asked.

Oh, right. That.

Well, I guessed I did technically have someplace to be.

But that was tomorrow.

Tonight was all about me and my sister.

Molly and Jake had finally put Ruby down for a nap. We were enjoying a little quiet time, because, in no time, that kid would be up and crying again, and that would be my cue to leave.

"Pretty much," I said, answering her question as we sat on the couch once again, but this time, it was just her and me.

Jake had gone upstairs to catch a quick nap himself while Ruby slept beside us in the bassinet.

"Is there more to this story you're not telling me? Because that's an awful big thing, and you aren't usually the person to—"

"To what? Do nice things for people?"

"Go out of your way," she said. "Ever since you left for school, it's been all about Millie and her career. I'm not knocking that. Everyone has a passion, and you've made a fantastic life of yours. But, when you're suddenly jumping in the car—my car," she corrected, giving me a pointed look, "and driving a perfect stranger nearly across state lines, you can't blame me for being a little interested. So, fess up."

I let out a sigh, knowing it was a lost cause, trying to keep anything from my big sister, and honestly, deep down, did I want to? I could put on a mask and pretend to be okay for the rest of the world, act like I had it all together in front of my parents and even Aiden, but at the end of the day, I needed her.

I needed this.

"I don't know," I finally said. "It's complicated."

"What could be so complicated? He's only been here two days."

She looked at me, that staring-in-the-soul look that

sisters did, and I watched as her eyes widened. "You didn't?"

"I think I did?" I replied, taking a sip of wine.

"What does that even mean?"

"Well, there was a lot of alcohol involved."

Just as I was about to take another sip of the fruity pinot grigio Jake had poured me at dinner, it was whisked out of my hand.

"Okay, no more of that for you. Clearly, you are not old enough to handle it."

"What?" I said, appalled. She set it on the coffee table, her eyes meeting mine in a clear challenge. "You're mean as a mom."

"You're slutty as an unemployed drifter," she countered.

"See? Point made. Mean."

"Okay, so let's start with the easy stuff," she suggested, leaning her elbow on the back of the couch cushion. "Tell me what he looks like."

I mimicked her movements and rested my forehead against the palm of my hand. "You know Tom Hiddleston?"

Her eyebrows rose. "Like Thor's younger brother, Loki? That Tom Hiddleston?"

I laughed. "Yeah."

"Damn."

"He has this wavy black hair and intense hazel eyes. And did you know sculptors are buff? Like, why did I not know this information sooner?"

An amused expression tugged at my sister's lips. "Anything else?"

"He's an unimaginable flirt," I went on, remembering the flashback of our night together. "That is exactly why I need to stay away from him, Molly. I just had my heart crushed by someone exactly like him." I turned away, inhaling deeply into my lungs.

"Then, why take him on this trip? Why put yourself in that position? You're not the only person on the island who could drive him."

"I know," I acknowledged. "But there's something about him. Something not right."

"What do you mean?"

"It's a bunch of little things, but like yesterday, at lunch, Dean asked him about England, and Molly, the look on his face, it was haunting. He told us he didn't miss it in the least. Isn't that sad? So, when I got back to the inn, I naturally looked him up. His bio on his website says he's from a prominent family in England. It sounds like he had a very nice upbringing. Why would he never want to go back?"

"Maybe he didn't." She shrugged. "Have a nice upbringing, I mean."

I let out a sigh. "Maybe not."

With her head to the side in a look of total apathy, she took my hand in hers and asked, "But, sis, even if you do go on this trip with him tomorrow and he does happen to open up to you, what then?"

I shook my head. "I don't know, but I need to find out."

CHAPTER SEVEN

Aiden

I AWOKE THE MORNING OF MY BIG ROAD TRIP WITH Millie to the sound of my phone vibrating on the nightstand next to the bed.

With bleary eyes and a weary outlook for the hours that followed, I grabbed the phone and tapped the home screen to read the incoming text message. It was from James.

Aiden, please call me. Don't shut me out like you do with everyone else. I can help.

Another one came in almost immediately afterward.

Also, where the fuck are you? You remember what the date is?

I sat back in bed, my head resting on the borrowed pillow that wasn't my own, as I contemplated what to write back.

Or if I should even write back to begin with.

I'd ignored a dozen other calls and texts already. But no, this time, I had to reply, and he knew it.

Because, this time, he'd brought up the date.

Yes, I know what date it is. I'll be back for Ben.

I hit Send and headed for the shower as memories of a past life flooded my mind.

"It's going to be all right," the brown-haired woman with the pink coat said.

She'd told me her name last night when she came to take me away from my foster house, but I didn't remember.

She was nicer than the last one though.

And the one before that.

"This family has two other boys around your age. You'll have brothers."

I gulped loudly. "Brothers?" I managed to say.

She nodded happily in the driver's seat next to me as I slouched down, trying to become invisible.

I'd had a brother once. His name was Rufus, and just like the lady with the pink coat, the person who'd placed us together was so delighted to make a happy little family of orphans.

But then she'd left.

And that was when Rufus had laid down the law.

"Listen, kid," he'd said even though we were less than two years apart, "I don't want anything to do with a brother, and don't think for a second, I'm sharing anything with you."

And he hadn't. He'd eaten all the food and blamed me for everything, and when he saw kids beating on me in the schoolyard, he'd turn his head and pretend he didn't know me. I'd never been so happy to get out of a place.

And, now, the lady in the pink coat wanted me to do it all over again?

If I had the guts, I'd pop open this car door and jump

right out.

"Ah, here we are," she said, looking more optimistic than I'd ever seen anyone look in my life. Maybe it was her first week. Hadn't she seen the place she pulled me out of?

We got out of the car and I followed her, my feet dragging behind me. We stepped up to the front door. As usual, we were greeted by smiles, and I found myself rolling my eyes. Those smiles would turn into frowns soon enough.

They always did.

I was nothing more than a paycheck to these people.

Even the lady in the pink coat.

I tuned out as introductions were given. I didn't care.

I truly didn't.

Soon, the smiling couple and pink-coat lady were escorting me toward the back of the home.

"This will be your room. Boys, do you want to meet Aiden?"

Their request was met with nothing short of a few murmurs, but as I entered, I found myself face-to-face with my so-called brothers.

One of them curiously eyed me, his glasses falling to the bridge of his freckled nose as he stood to greet me. "Hi, I'm James," he said.

And the other was a short, pale boy with red hair and a small smile, who followed suit. "And I'm Ben."

Although I hadn't seen Millie since our lunch the other day with Dean, we'd communicated via text on our departure time.

I'd been sort of surprised to see her name pop up on

my phone the day before, considering our rooms were literally inches apart, but I'd answered her questions and gone about my day.

But, as the evening drew to a close and there was still no Millie, I began to wonder if she was indeed avoiding me.

And if so, why agree to this trip?

Although I guessed I hadn't given her much of an alternative.

And why was that, Aiden?

I shook my head as I closed the door to my suite and made my way to the kitchen.

Stepping into the kitchen, Millie was the first thing I noticed. Dressed in a simple black slip dress, she looked casual and elegant at the same time. Tan sandals adorned her feet, and I couldn't help but smile at the flirty pink polish on her toes, nor could I tear my eyes away before soaking in every last inch of that gorgeous tan skin.

The inn was still quiet as Millie and I took advantage of the late breakfast hours on Sunday morning to grab a quick bite to eat before we got on the early morning ferry.

"Good morning," I greeted her before she noticed me standing in the entryway, checking her out.

She started a little, turning around to face me. "Good morning." She blushed, caught in the middle of shoving a bear claw in her mouth. With frosting on her thumb and pointer finger, I couldn't help but laugh. "Sorry. I swear, I gain, like, a million pounds every time I come home. My sister is a genius."

I nodded in agreement, heading for the coffeepot first. "I must agree. Although I didn't grow up having them, I've grown fond of them since arriving here. They're quite splendid."

She laughed a little under her breath, amused by me somehow. "Splendid," she said. "I'll have to tell her you said that." There was a momentary pause as she finished her last bite before she said in a nonchalant way, "I bet you had amazing pastries, growing up, didn't you?"

The comment caught me off guard, the memories of James and Ben still so fresh in my mind. "What?"

"Sorry," she said, that blush flaming bright red. "I saw your bio on your website. That's creepy, isn't it? But I was curious. And, well, where you grew up, I figured you would have had nice pastries in a house like that."

I could see the panic in her eyes, probably in response to the panic in mine.

"Right, of course. Excellent pastries. You're correct."

She breathed out in relief, as I held mine. "I've always thought English pastries are so fancy compared to ours. Well, anywhere really."

She began to ramble on about France and madeleines while I tried to carry on, politely nodding. I opened the cupboard, grabbed a cup and set it on the counter.

Suddenly, there was a loud crash.

"Oh!" Millie cried as we both looked down at my coffee cup in pieces on the floor.

"I'm sorry," I said, frazzled, looking up at the counter, down at the floor, and back again. The counter seemed to wave, making my eyes blink several times.

"This isn't something you can run from." James's words began to ring in my head.

"I think I'm gonna make sure I have everything I need for the car. Would you mind packing me some food to go?"

I couldn't even look at her. What if she could see it in my eyes, sense it in my demeanor?

"Um, sure," she said. "But are you okay?"

I nodded, already fleeing the kitchen.

"I'm fine," I lied.

I was definitely not fine.

We made it through the long two-and-a-half-hour ferry ride to North Carolina with little to no conversation.

It was brutal, but I didn't know what to say.

How did I talk to a woman I'd confessed my soul to just days earlier and act like none of it had happened? Besides James, she was the only one who knew about my diagnosis.

But she didn't remember.

Honestly, it was probably better this way.

The moment the car engine flared to life, and we were given the signal to disembark the boat, I breathed a heavy sigh of relief. At least I'd have something new to stare at instead of the minivan full of kids currently parked in front of us. Although, the tiny screens in the seats, displaying the movie *Frozen* had helped pass the time, even if it was slightly excruciating.

"Do you need to stop?" Millie asked, her voice such a stark contrast to the deafening silence that had been ringing in my ears for so long that I nearly jumped.

"What? Oh, um, sure. Might be nice to stretch my legs or grab a spot of coffee."

She didn't reply but merely pulled off at the first gas station we came upon. "I'll fill up while you run in," she said.

The gentleman in me wanted to offer to do so for her, but the tone in her voice was clear; she didn't need it. So, I simply nodded and made my way into the convenience store. The door dinged as I entered and I gave a polite nod to the cashier. There were a few others inside, mostly waiting in line to pay for gas or purchase items for the road. I recognized the father from the minivan that had been parked in front of us, dragging one of his kids through the aisle. She was in tears, a wet spot down the front of her pants as tears fell from her eyes.

"There was a restroom on the ferry. I asked you a dozen times if you needed to go!"

She sniffled, her voice small and meek. "I'm sorry, Daddy. I didn't know I had to go until just now."

The dad stopped mid-aisle, between the chips and crackers, as I stood frozen, unable to look away.

"How can you not know, Olivia? You are seven years old. Your four-year-old sister knows how to piss in the bathroom. Why can't you fucking figure it out?"

With every word he spoke, his grip on her tightened, and her eyes grew wide. Panic filled the little girl's features as if she seemed to know what was coming.

It was a scene I recognized all too well.

"Let her go," I said between clenched teeth.

The father looked up, shock written across his idiotic face. "What did you say to me?"

"I said, let her go. You're obviously scaring her, and you've made your point."

He straightened to his full height, the little girl scrambling back behind him as he sized me up. I was about six inches taller than him and had about fifty pounds of lean muscle to his very impressive beer gut.

"This ain't any of your business."

"When you decide to manhandle your child in the middle of a convenience store, you make it my business."

His eyes narrowed in on mine before he seemed to come to some sort of conclusion. "Come on, Olivia, let's go."

He brushed past me, a last attempt at one-upping the chump who tried to keep him from backhanding his kid in a public place. Grabbing the first bag of crackers within arm's reach, I turned toward the counter and found Millie standing in front of me, her gaze warm and steady.

How long had she been standing there?

"The car is filled up," she said, dragging her eyes away from mine. "I came in to grab a few things myself."

"Right," I mumbled. "Of course."

With a clenched fist, I watched her step past me as I headed for the counter, feeling like the world's worst fool.

Setting my crackers on the counter, I quickly grabbed a bottle of water from a nearby cooler and set it down in front of me as well.

"My dad used to knock me around like that. Yours, too?" the cashier said, not bothering to look up at me as he rang up my purchases. He was an older gentleman with more gray on his head than brown. He sported several tattoos, most of them weathered from years gone by.

"Yeah," I said. "Something like that."

He didn't say anything more, just let out a long sigh as he looked up at me and handed over the small plastic bag with my things inside. I saw it then—the same pain I saw when I gazed into a mirror too long or reminisced with James about our childhood after one too many drinks.

It was the same pain that little girl would carry for the rest of her life.

Like a goddamn brand.

"Thanks," I said before I walked away, still shaken

to my very core. I didn't wait around for Millie to finish. Instead, I headed for the car and soaked up the silence inside for those precious few seconds as I tried to push away the past.

Thankfully, by the time Millie returned holding a giant paper bag, I'd regained some of my composure. Seeing her fumble her way into the car with that bag didn't hurt either.

"Did you buy the entire store?" I asked, taking the bag from her arms before she fell into the car.

"Well, not quite. But pretty close," she said as I began to snoop around at what she'd purchased.

"Jesus, there is enough food in here to feed an army. Not very well, mind you, but still."

"I have a bad habit of eating a lot of junk food when I travel," she confessed.

"Don't you travel for a living?" I asked.

Shit, was I supposed to know that?

"Um, yes," she said, giving me a curious glance as she buckled in her seat belt.

"You mentioned it the other day at lunch with Dean."

Her eyes lit up. "Right!"

Good save, I told myself.

In truth, I knew she'd actually just walked away from her job and felt like an absolute failure for doing so, but if she wanted to keep up this ruse, I'd allow it.

After all, she'd forgotten everything about that night.

I might as well, too.

"So, basically, you eat terribly all the time. Is that quite accurate then?" I asked, pulling out a bag of beef jerky as I made a face.

She laughed. "Okay, so I don't have the best eating habits."

I couldn't help it; my eyes roamed the length of her body. "Couldn't tell from looking at you."

That earned me a faint blush and a smile. "I work for this body. This is the result of hours and hours in the gym. I earn my junk food."

"Well, what would you like first?" I asked, waving the beef jerky as she turned the ignition.

"Definitely not the jerky. Maybe something sweeter?"

"All right," I said, diving back into her huge bag of treats. I grabbed three sweeter options and held them up.

She'd already navigated us out of the gas station and onto the highway once again, but she did a cursory glance in my direction.

"Yes," she said.

"Yes?" I asked, splitting my attention between her and the three types of candy I had in my hands. "To which one?"

"All of them."

I shook my head, feeling a smile tug at lips. "You really are a junk food addict."

"Rip open those bags, my friend. Let me show you my ways."

I did as she'd commanded, opening the large bag of peanut M&M's first. "I'm not much of a candy guy," I admitted.

"What? Who doesn't like candy?"

I shrugged. "Me, I guess. I don't know. I didn't have it much as a child so perhaps I didn't develop a liking for it."

"That's just crazy talk. Pop one of those M&M's in your mouth, and hand one over to me."

I did as she'd instructed, giving her a few as I grabbed one for myself.

THE LIES I'VE TOLD

"Now, place it in your mouth, like so," she said as she placed a single M&M on her tongue.

A flashback of that tongue all over my body came racing back to the forefront of my mind, and I involuntarily cleared my throat.

"You're not following instructions," she said.

"Oh, right," I said, popping a brown M&M into my mouth.

"Now, here's where you have to decide what kind of candy person you are. Are you a cruncher or a melter?"

"What?" I laughed. "That's ridiculous."

"No, it's not! Which one you choose can be very insightful to your personality. You ask weird questions about people's loved ones…and I do this. So, Aiden, are you going to crunch it or let it melt?"

She turned her head toward mine for a brief moment, and I caught her smiling at me. I felt my stomach flip-flop from the force of it.

Jesus, she was beautiful.

"Melt," I answered. Feeling the chocolate making a delicious puddle on my tongue.

"Exactly as I thought," she answered before chomping away at hers.

"What? Why am I so predictable?"

She grabbed a few more from the bag I'd placed between us and tossed them into her mouth, and I couldn't help but watch.

"You're an artist, right? Naturally, you've got patience to spare; otherwise, every piece you did would be a huge disaster."

I grinned. "Quite right."

"Whereas I have the patience of a gnat, and bite into

that M&M as fast as I can."

"Okay, I'll give you that," I said, grabbing another couple from the bag. "But you know what this means?"

"What?" she asked.

"We can never share a bag of candy again," I said, straight-faced.

She suddenly looked concerned. "Why?"

"Because you'll eat the whole bag before I even get through two."

She burst out laughing as I handed her several more, loving the sound as it filled the small space around us.

"Do you want to play Twenty Questions?" she asked, making my head nearly spin, the déjà vu hitting me hard in the gut.

"Do you want to play Twenty Questions?" Millie asked as she poured another round of whiskey.

"All right," I said. "Pick an object."

"What? That's not how you play Twenty Questions!" Her voice sort of boomed throughout the small suite we'd shut ourselves in, and her eyes immediately widened as she realized just how loud she'd become. "Oops," she whispered.

"It is, too!" I said. "You pick an object or person, and then in twenty questions or less, the other person tries to guess what it is."

She looked rather unimpressed. "Oh, well, I don't want to play that," she said. "I just wanted to ask you twenty random questions. What's that game called?"

"Uh, a conversation?"

"Yeah! Let's play that!"

I tried not to look over at her, my heart hammering in

my chest.

"Uh, sure. Do you want to go first?" I asked, unsure if sober Millie did in fact know how to play the real game or if she was just as clueless as drunk Millie.

"Okay, sure," she replied. "Is the chocolate in England really as good as everyone says it is?"

I let out an amused sigh. *Yep, just as clueless.*

"Yes, these M&M's taste like horseshit compared to our milk chocolate. And that's coming from a guy who doesn't even like candy that much."

She rolled her eyes, but I could see a smile peeking out the corner of her pouty pink lips. "Asshole," she muttered. "Okay, you're next."

I thought back to the first time we'd played this game, remembering everything we'd shared. One of these days, I'd have to teach her the proper way to play this game, but for now…

"What made you go into fashion?" I asked, already knowing the answer but wanting to see if it'd change without the truth goggles alcohol provided.

"I don't know really. I guess I always loved design and the creative process," she answered with a bit of a shrug.

I stared into her eyes, recalling her completely different answer only days earlier…

"I know it sounds cliché, but growing up here, I didn't have a lot of options for clothes. There was only one store, Beachcombers. I would go there and pick out a dress or a skirt and then take it home and alter it. I even created my own homecoming dress one year, and I don't know, I guess it just stuck. But here I am, ten years later, still doing other people's designs while mine collect dust."

Now, the question was, *Who was she lying to? Me or herself?*

"My turn again!" she announced, bringing me back to the present. "How'd you get into stone carving?"

I let out a long breath before answering, "Pass."

"What? You can't pass!"

"Sure I can. I just did."

"That's not fair," she said. "How are we supposed to get to know each other if we can choose to pass on half the —"

"My brother taught me."

Silence settled between us before I broke it, "Now, it's my turn. When was your last relationship?"

"Pass," she nearly squeaked.

I gave her a hard stare. "No passing. Remember?"

Her forehead furrowed, and she let out a few choice words as I grinned. "Fine. It was recent."

"How recent?"

"No! It's not your turn anymore."

I let out a growl.

"Why'd you approach that man in the gas station?"

Now, she was really digging deep.

"Because he was an asshole," I answered. "How recent?"

"Very."

My fists balled at my sides.

"Did your dad treat you like that? Like the man with little girl?"

"That's two questions," I said. "And which one? I had lots."

"What?" Her eyes widened.

"Nothing. Yes," I answered flatly. "Did he hurt you?"

"Who?"

We were rapid-firing these questions so quickly; I

thought we were both getting confused. But I was willing to give her information in exchange for answers in return.

Especially this.

Because this was something she hadn't even shared with me the night we supposedly bared our souls to one another.

This was sacred.

"No," she replied before amending. "Yes. It's complicated."

"How?" I asked, not even caring in the least that it wasn't my turn.

She seemed to pick up on that little tidbit and didn't bother challenging me.

"He led me to believe…" She let out a deep sigh. "You know what? It doesn't matter. This was a silly game."

I reached out for her hand, causing her breath to hitch. "He led you to believe what?"

A single tear fell from her eyes. "He was my boss. I was stupid. It's over."

I wanted to ask if this was why she'd quit her job, but I didn't.

Instead, I squeezed her hand and let her drive in silence for a while, knowing I'd do anything to make the pain go away.

Even if it meant forgetting everything I felt for her, because, now, it was starting to finally make sense. I was the distraction she couldn't afford.

And she was right.

I'd break her heart just like he had, only it wouldn't be intentional. Because, as much as I wanted to believe in our magical night together, as much as I wanted to believe it meant we were as destined as two souls could be, I was still speeding headfirst into a future she didn't deserve.

And, as much as I didn't want to break her heart, I knew it'd happen just the same.

Because I was a ticking time bomb, and like all explosives, I was bound to cause serious damage.

CHAPTER EIGHT

Millie

TWENTY QUESTIONS TURNED INTO FORTY, WHICH turned into sixty and so on. Thankfully, the questions became less invasive as time went on, both of us exhausted after our lightning round of extremely personal questions.

Although part of me wanted to go back because, now that I had a sliver of information about him, I was craving more.

So much more.

And yet I knew I was treading on dangerous ground. In only a handful of days, I'd be gone, back in Florida, and this would all be over. So, why push this? Why try to get to know a man I'd never see again?

Because you like him, my inner voice pressed.

I let out a deep breath as the endless road passed by the window. We'd been on this particular boring stretch of North Carolina highway for what seemed like an eternity, but thankfully, we were almost to Mount Airy.

"You all right?" Aiden asked, his voice soft, as if he didn't want to startle me.

"Yeah, sorry. Just bored."

"Guess we ran out of questions," he said. I could almost hear the smile in his tone.

"Yeah, but we gave it a good run. I think, if I'd bought more junk food, it would have lasted longer."

"It's really quite terrifying how much sugar you can eat without going into shock."

I shrugged. "It's a gift."

That heavy silence settled between us once again. We'd spoken for hours during the first leg of the trip, and now, it was complete radio silence. Maybe it had been the sugar rush, propelling me forward and giving me the courage I now lacked. Or maybe I finally realized how much I didn't want to go home.

"Here's a question for you," I finally said. "If you're still up for them—more questions, that is."

"Sure," he answered, a sly smile creeping across his face.

"Why granite?" I asked. "I mean, why not marble or limestone? Or do you use those, too? Basically, tell me more about what you do."

He laughed at my ridiculous attempt at a question, and I couldn't help but join him.

"What? It's not like you meet a sculptor every day, you know?"

I could see him nodding out of the corner of my eye. "I know. We're a rare breed."

"So, educate me."

His voice deepened. "I'd love to."

I swallowed hard, knowing his words meant so much more than stonework and chisels. I felt my cheeks redden as I stared straight ahead, trying to stay focused on the road.

"So, granite?"

I could hear the smile in his voice as he spoke, "It's native to North Carolina; that's why I chose it. But, to answer your question, yes, I use other materials. Just last week, I held a gallery showing with several different types of stone."

"Do you prefer one over the other?"

"Granite is definitely more challenging."

"Why?" I asked, thoroughly interested.

"It's a hard stone. Much more difficult to carve than something like limestone."

"Wow, I had no idea."

"And what about you? Is there a certain fabric you love to work with?"

His question caught me off guard. "Oh, well…I mean, I haven't really done much design."

I turned and saw his eyebrows rise.

"Really? Why not?"

"Well, I've dabbled but nothing serious. Just suggestions here and there."

"But you want to? Design, I mean."

I nodded, feeling like I was under a microscope. "Of course, that's what I went to school for. But…"

"But what?"

I shook my head. "It's complicated."

"What's complicated about it?"

I don't have a job.

The promotion I was supposed to get that would allow me to finally design was taken away from me.

I'm currently blacklisted from probably every major designer in the world because I fucked my boss.

"There's a hierarchy. It's corporate crap. Oh, hey!" I said, pointing to the exit up ahead. "We're here."

His eyes followed the motion of my hand. Sure enough,

we'd made it to Mount Airy and in record time, too. The fact that we hadn't stopped for lunch and eaten junk food the entire way here helped.

We didn't say anything to one another as I pulled off the highway and followed the GPS to the address Aiden had given me. He'd set up a private meeting with one of the distributors since we would be arriving after hours. Pulling into the large parking lot, I turned off the engine and made a move for my seat belt.

Aiden's steady hand stopped me as his intense gaze met mine.

"Nothing should stop you from getting what you want, Millie. Nothing."

And then his lips were on mine, like a hot, fiery brand. His fingers cupped the back of my neck as his mouth captured mine for a fraction of a second, and then, just as quickly as it'd begun, it ended.

Leaving me breathless, achy, and wanting more.

By the time I regained my composure, he was gone.

And I was left wondering if his words had been meant for me.

Or for himself

What the hell was that?

Still feeling dizzy from the kiss that could end all kisses, I stumbled out of the car and followed Aiden, who was already greeting a tall, bulky-looking man with a beard.

"Nice to meet you. I'm Thomas and I'll be the one working with you tonight," the bearded fellow said, holding a hand out to Aiden.

Aiden did the same, before turning to introduce me. His eyes lingered on my lips a little too long. "This is my friend Millie. She was kind enough to drive me today."

Thomas, a big bear of a man, came over to greet me, his giant hand engulfing my own as he shook it. "Nice to meet you both. You ready to go look at some rocks?"

Aiden nodded as Thomas led the way. I chose to linger a bit, enjoying Aiden in his element as he spoke with Thomas about the various choices they had for him. Apparently, he'd done business with this company before, having used them for the original memorial that had been destroyed.

I wonder who drove him then?

Did he kiss all his chauffeurs?

Letting out a sigh, I watched as he ran his hands over the large boulders, seeing how the light reflected off it.

He was intense and passionate and insanely thorough.

It was sexy as hell, and it made me wonder just how hot he would look drenched in sweat, shirtless, with a chisel in his hand or a chainsaw even.

"Millie?"

"What?" I said, suddenly looking up to find him looming over me.

"We're done."

"So soon?" I asked. "That was quick."

He shrugged, his eyes meeting mine. "When you know, you know. And this place has excellent granite, so it wasn't hard to find the piece I need. They're going to deliver it later this week."

Even if I tried, I couldn't tear myself from that gorgeous hazel stare. "So, um, dinner?" I finally managed to say.

He blinked, and I made myself look away. "Yes, that would be lovely. Thomas was actually telling me about a barbecue place down the road. I think we passed it on our way here. Do you like barbecue?"

I smiled, my mind still whirling. "What kind of Southern girl would I be if I didn't?"

"Of course. Well then, off we go."

He marched on ahead toward the car while I stood in place, wondering how the hell he'd managed to kiss me one minute and move on the next as if nothing had happened.

I let out a breath and decided that if he could be so nonchalant about the kiss, then so could I. After all, I was the one who'd said we should remain professional, wasn't I?

Yes. Yes, I was.

Catching up, I hopped in the car and revved the engine, making him look over at me with a curious glance.

"Sorry, just hungry," I said as I made quick work of getting us back onto the main road. A quick peek in the direction of the passenger seat had me noticing a sly grin on Aiden's face. "What?" I asked, briefly turning my head to face him.

"Nothing," he answered, pressing his lips together.

"That grin is not nothing! If you have something to say, then say it."

"You're flustered. It's adorable."

"Adorable?" I echoed. With a quick jaunt to the right, I pulled us off the road. Dust billowed around us as I put the car in park. "I'm not adorable! I'm pissed! Why did you kiss me like that and then act like it didn't happen? Am I that forgettable?"

"Forgettable? You think *I* forgot?"

"Well, it certainly seems like it!" I fumed, all the pent-up frustration I'd felt from watching him saunter around with Thomas, laughing and joking like he hadn't just given me the kiss of a lifetime only moments before.

He shook his head, his hands running through his jet-black hair as he let out a deep breath of air. "Jesus Christ, Millie," he whispered. "I remember everything."

"What?"

His eyes met mine, and it was there again, that frightening intensity that seemed to pull me in like a goddamn tractor beam. I felt like I was flying and falling at the same time, and heaven help me if I didn't want it to end.

"I remember every minute of that night. Every bloody second. And, when I look at you, I can't help but want to pull you into my arms and make you relive it all, so you can know the misery I've been living for the past two days, knowing I'll never have it again."

My heart was running rapid in my chest at his confession, and my breath ran ragged. "Make me remember," I said without thinking.

I was done thinking.

I'd thought through every aspect of my affair with Lorenzo, and look where it'd gotten me.

Jobless and miserable.

Nope, no more thinking. My loins were driving the bus now, and they were headed straight for the sexy British guy sitting next to me.

"I need to know that you're serious," he growled, that panty-melting ferocity seeping from his eyes once again.

I tried not to gulp. "I am."

"Good. Then, let's go grab dinner."

"Wait? What?" I found myself saying, my thighs still clenched from the sexual tension ricocheting between us.

"We haven't eaten all day, and for what I have planned, you're going to need more than just a handful of candy."

The look he gave me meant nothing but business as he gestured to the road. I did as he'd instructed, my insides doing double flips as I put the car in drive.

"Plus, there's a hotel next to the restaurant, if I'm not mistaken."

My face spread into a nice wide grin as I bit down on my bottom lip.

Now, he was speaking my language.

Dinner between us was like a long-drawn-out hour of foreplay.

The appetizer consisted of fervent stares, a subtle gaze here and there, and I threw in a playful laugh to top it off.

By the time our waiter came by and we ordered our food, I was so horny; I didn't know if I could actually concentrate on real food when Aiden's large hand was wrapped around mine, his thumb slowly circling the tender skin of my palm down the length of my wrist and back again.

Like he was memorizing every inch.

It seemed like such an innocent thing to anyone watching us, but inwardly, I was on fire. A burning inferno as I quietly watched him trace lines up and down my arm.

"Why are we even here?" I finally asked.

"I told you," he simply stated.

I rolled my eyes. "I know; I heard. But do we really need to sit down and have a meal? Can't we just get takeout?"

A wicked grin spread across his face as he leaned forward. "No."

"You're frustrating. I thought guys were all about instant gratification."

"Melt versus crunch, remember? I don't think this has anything to do with gender."

I had known that M&M conversation would eventually come back to bite me in the ass. "Okay, fine. But don't think I plan on making this easy for you. I'm going to lick barbecue sauce off pretty much everything on my plate. Including my fingers."

He chuckled before pulling my hand to his lips and kissing each digit, one by one. "Or you can eat quickly, and I could lick barbecue sauce off of you when we get to the hotel room."

I nearly choked on my own saliva as the words rolled off his tongue.

He could recite the damn alphabet or read the phone book aloud, and I would fan myself. That accent made every word he said ten times hotter.

"I think maybe we need to set some ground rules," I managed to say.

"Like what?"

"Like, is this a one-time thing?"

His forehead furrowed. He didn't like that idea. Not one bit. "Do you want it to be?"

My lips pressed together as I contemplated the idea of walking away after today. My heart felt heavy, and I didn't know why.

"No," I answered honestly.

"Then, let's not make it a one-time thing."

I let out a long breath. "But where does that leave us? Neither of us is staying in Ocracoke long."

"So, can't we simply enjoy this—whatever it is—for however long we have?"

"And then we part ways? Just like that?"

He nodded, though part of me wondered if it pained him to do so, and I watched his eyes lower, and his lips part.

"Just like that."

Our deep conversation was broken as the waitress brought over our food, and we both thanked her for doing so. Some of the flirtiness from before had long since passed as I looked down at my platter, brimming with barbecue sauce.

"Do me one favor though, will you, love?" Aiden's voice brought my eyes back up and forward.

He was staring straight at me with that dark, brooding gaze once again, and I felt my heart quicken.

"Of course," I replied.

"Guard your heart, Millie," he warned. "I can't offer you more than this, and I don't want to be responsible for breaking it."

I found myself nodding, unable to speak, as I watched him unfold his napkin.

At first, I thought about replying, *What heart?*

Mine had already been trampled by Lorenzo only days earlier, but then I remembered all the times it had fluttered in response to the sound of Aiden's voice, or the touch of his hand.

How wildly it had beaten in my chest when his lips found mine.

No, my heart was still very much alive and beating, waiting to be loved.

Waiting to be destroyed.

I looked up at Aiden one more time, knowing I should end this before it even began. I was playing with fire, and the only one who was bound to get burned was me.

And yet I couldn't turn away.

THE LIES I'VE TOLD

Like a moth dazzled by a flame, I knew I was skating the edge between love and desire. I told myself I could handle it.

I could stifle my budding feelings for Aiden Fisher.

So, I did the only thing I could do. With a brief nod, I agreed to his terms.

For better or for worse.

Aiden was indeed correct about there being a hotel next to the restaurant we'd dined at.

Although calling it a hotel might have been a bit of a stretch.

"Are you sure you want to stay here?" he asked after paying the ridiculously low rate for our room.

He dangled the key in front of me, a look of challenge spreading across his face.

Grabbing it from his hand, I stalked forward toward our designated room. "Are you coming?" I asked over my shoulder as I shoved the key in room number thirty-four.

"Right behind you. Are you sure you don't want me to go in first? Do a quick check for dead bodies? Or police tape?"

I rolled my eyes as I pushed the door open.

To put it bluntly, it was pretty horrifying.

"It's fine," I said, holding my head up high as I made my way in past the peeling wallpaper and the clunky old air conditioner.

"Have you ever stayed in a place like this before?" he asked, stepping past me to take a peek in the bathroom.

"Have you?" I asked, unsure of where to sit exactly. *Was*

the bed even safe? Maybe if I removed the comforter.

"A few times," he answered, returning from where I could only guess the shower was.

"Well, if a rich kid from Yorkshire can rough it, then—"

"London," he said suddenly. "I'm from London."

My brows furrowed in confusion. "But, online, it says—"

"I know what it says online, but I'm from London."

There was a pleading tone to his voice, and I knew not to ask any more questions.

"Well then, boy from London, I believe I was promised a night to remember."

A small smirk tugged at the corner of his lips, making my stomach flutter. "I don't think that's exactly what I said."

"I might be paraphrasing." I grinned.

He took a couple of steps closer, and I used those precious few moments to appreciate the man I had here with me. If I could sculpt the perfect male form from clay, it would be Aiden Fisher. He was what I imagined when I closed my eyes at night.

And he was standing right here, all hard, lean muscle from years of honing his craft. I couldn't wait to run my hands along each ridge and curve of his body and feel the power hovering beneath. With bewitching hazel eyes and shiny black hair made for touching, I knew I was in for one wild night.

"If you keep staring at me like that, this is going to be over quicker than I planned." He was so close, I could feel his breath, hot and warm against my neck as he bent down to whisper in my ear. "Are you sure, love?" he asked softly.

My insides melted. "Yes," I answered, my legs shaky from his voice alone.

I felt his lips brush my collarbone, and I nearly moaned. From the moment he kissed me in the car to the flirty foreplay at dinner until now had all felt like a fucking eternity.

I was so wound up; I thought I might just orgasm right then and there.

"Relax," he whispered.

"Easy for you to say; you're a melter."

He chuckled against my ear, his hand sliding around my waist. "Just wait. By the end of the night, you're going to have a vast appreciation for the art of patience."

A tingle went up my spine as his fingers began slowly pulling up the hemline of my dress, inch by inch. The cool air hit my bare legs as his warm hands spread across my backside.

"Were you this appreciative the other night? Or are you making up for your drunken haste?" I asked, doing a little exploration of my own as my hand found the bare skin under his T-shirt.

Hello, abs. I smiled.

"I wasn't that drunk," he said, and my brow lifted in challenge. "Okay, I was, but at least I wasn't drunk enough to skip over the good stuff."

"And what's the good stuff?" I asked, looking up at him.

He grinned, a full-faced sort of grin that made a small dimple appear in his left cheek.

How had I not noticed that before?

"You'll see," he replied.

Before I had the chance to question him, I was lifted off the ground. I wrapped my legs around his hips as he moved toward the bed.

"If you put me down on that nasty bedspread, I swear, I'll kill you."

He laughed but managed to toss aside the tattered thing before throwing me down beneath him. My dress pooled around my waist, exposing my lace thong and bare stomach. I watched as his nostrils flared and eyes darkened in response.

"See anything you like, Aiden?" I smiled.

"Simply remembering all the things I've done between those legs," he answered, his voice raspy and full of promise.

Oh...my.

His hand reached behind his back, and in one swift movement, he pulled his T-shirt up and over his head.

And I forgot how to breathe.

All those smooth, hard muscles I'd felt under his shirt were now on full display, and I didn't waste any time in checking him out.

"Damn," I muttered.

"You said that the first time, too." He grinned.

"It's still true," I purred. "Now, what were you saying about my legs?"

He watched as I made a show of slowing spreading them apart, his eyes narrowing, brimming with desire. Never looking away, he hastily unfastened his belt, the clank of the buckle hitting the floor in mere seconds, soon followed by his jeans.

He stopped short, leaving his boxer briefs on as he climbed onto the bed.

"Always the melter," I said, grabbing hold of the waistband of his boxers and letting go with a snap.

He grinned, his body aligned above mine as he lifted my dress higher and higher. "Always the cruncher." I felt his hands on the delicate lace of my bra, sliding the fabric aside. Cool air brushed against my nipples as his eyes met mine.

"Although I guess I could see the appeal, digging your teeth into something," he said just before he bent down, licked a wet circle around my areola, and gently bit down.

Every part of me suddenly went ablaze as he pinned me down, sucking, licking, squeezing, and then repeating. My thighs were bound so tightly together, I felt like a grenade, ready to explode.

And he knew it, too.

He knew, one single touch to my clit, and I'd go off so long and hard, the whole state of North Carolina would hear me screaming his name.

"Not yet, love," his breathy voice whispered in my ear.

I nearly whimpered when his mouth left my tender nipple, trailing a path down my stomach to the top of my panties. His fingers curled around each side and tugged.

Watching him slide that thong down my legs?

So fucking hot.

Seeing him stop to unbuckle my sandals, resting each foot on his bare chest as he did so?

Heartwarming.

"Guard your heart, Millie."

I shook my head, getting back into the game.

This was about sex.

Nothing else.

"Take your dress off all the way," he instructed. "And that sexy little bra of yours. I want to see all of you."

I did as he'd asked, feeling incredibly sexy under his intense gaze. The moment my bra hit the floor, his lips were on mine and his hands were everywhere. It was like his tightly wound control suddenly snapped, and he was running purely on instinct.

It was electrifying.

We rolled around on the bed as he pulled me tight against his body.

"Fuck," he growled. "I need to be inside you."

I smiled against him. "What about patience and melting?"

He pushed me onto my back, pressing his arousal deep into my center. "Fuck patience."

"Good plan," I agreed.

Reaching toward the nightstand, he grabbed a condom, one that I hadn't even noticed he'd placed there. "Where did that come from?" I asked.

"Your purse."

"How did you..." I started to ask, confused by how he know about the secret stash of condoms that I kept hidden in my purse before realizing. "Last time?"

He nodded.

"It's really annoying that I don't remember any of it."

He cupped my face with the palm of his hand, bent down and placed a tender kiss on my lips. "Let me refresh your memory."

I reached up and met his tenderness with something deeper, longer, and all-consuming. Just like that, we were back to fire and passion as my hands reached for the waistband of the only barrier left between us.

My eyes widened as his boxer briefs fell to the floor.

Yowza.

He made quick work of the condom, and soon, we were back to heavy petting and rolling around in the sheets.

Naked fun time with Aiden—my new favorite thing.

For a man who'd just declared he was done with patience, he was quite thorough, kissing a path from my breasts down to my thighs and back again. My heart raced as he fingered my clit, making me moan deep in my chest.

"Aiden," I uttered.

"Tell me what you want, love."

"You!" I screamed, not giving a shit who heard me.

"Beg for it, Millie," he demanded, spreading my legs wide as he loomed over me.

"Please!" I felt the tip of his cock at my entrance, making my eyes roll back in my head from the sheer pleasure of it.

"Please, what?"

"Please fuck me!" I cried out.

He didn't waste any time, slamming into me the moment the words left my lips. He was brutal and gentle at the same time, each thrust sending shock waves to my core as his slow, languid kisses melted a piece of my heart.

It was ecstasy, the feeling of our bodies joined together.

Now, I understood why he'd said he'd been so miserable.

Sex with Aiden was like a drug.

And I could very well be on my way to becoming an addict.

"Oh God, Aiden," I moaned, feeling my body tighten and my breath shorten.

"That's it," he said in my ear. "Come for me."

His pace quickened. The room filled with the sounds of our lovemaking as I began to cry out my orgasm.

"Oh, yes! Oh God, yes!"

"Louder, love," he demanded, his thrusts penetrating deep and long.

"Aiden!" I called out his name as I came so hard, I nearly passed out.

His movement pressed on through my orgasm, prolonging it, as he rubbed my clit and then finally came himself.

"Fuck!" he groaned, drawing out each letter as his eyes rolled back in his head.

Both of us were breathlesss, unable to speak. He pulled me into his arms, and I lay next to him in the crappy hotel room, wondering just how I could have forgotten a night with this man.

Because I was never forgetting this.

Not as long as I lived.

CHAPTER NINE

Aiden

I WOKE UP EARLY THE NEXT MORNING, THE SUNLIGHT streaming through the dirty old window of the dodgy motel room, and I rolled over in bed and watched her sleep.

What a mess I'd made of things.

A beautiful, wondrous mess.

I'd like to say being cooped up in that car all day with her had fried my brain cells to the point that I had no bloody clue what I was doing when I kissed her in the middle of that dusty parking lot.

But the truth was, just like last night when I'd removed every bit of her clothing and had my way with her over and over until we both collapsed from exhaustion, I had known exactly what I was doing when I stole that kiss.

I wanted Millie McIntyre.

No, I needed her. And I was done fighting it.

Even if I could only have her for a handful of days, I'd take it.

I'd take and take and take until she walked away.

Because she would.

She had to. I'd make sure of it.

No one deserved to be shackled to a man like me.

Not with the future I had coming.

"Oh my God, I can't move," she said into her pillow, slowly stretching her naked body in a catlike movement beside me.

Unable to resist, my hand glided along her side, following the natural curve of her hip to the deep valley around her waist.

She was perfection personified.

When she rolled toward me, my hand found its way to her belly, and my eyes met hers.

"Good morning." I smiled. "Seems like you're moving just fine. Should I take that as a criticism to my performance?"

She sensed the teasing tone in my voice and grinned. "I'm pretty sure I'm going to be walking bowlegged for the next week. Your pride can remain firmly in tact. No worries."

My grin widened. "So, does that mean you're too sore for an encore?"

Her breath hitched as I began to dip my hand lower, drifting past her belly button to the juncture of her thighs.

When I heard a tiny moan escape her lips, I knew she was more than ready.

Wasting no time I shifted on the bed, placing myself between her legs, like a man knelt before an altar for prayer.

Maybe Millie was the only kind of religion I needed.

"I've dreamed of this," I said, running my hands along her silky thighs as I dotted kisses down each one. Her legs quivered in anticipation. "The first time I did this, I made you come so hard, you had to scream into a pillow to keep from waking the other guests in the inn." I looked up at her one last time. "Don't hold back this time. Wake this whole fucking flea bag motel if you want."

The moment my tongue tasted her sweet flesh, I was in goddamn heaven. I felt her body jolt, and her breath heave.

"Shit!" she screamed.

Smiling, I clamped my hands down around her hips, pinning her to the bed as I fucked her with my mouth.

Hearing her moans and cries of passion made me feel like a bloody king.

"Oh God, Aiden!" she uttered as I flicked her clit over and over with my tongue, plunging three fingers into her core at the same time.

"Yes! Oh, yes!" Her body arched, accentuating her breasts and those tight pink nipples.

It was too much. It was all too much. I knew I couldn't finish without being inside her.

Reaching for the nightstand, I grabbed a condom, ripped the goddamn thing open, and slammed that thing down on my throbbing dick. Grabbing her by the hips, I flipped her onto her knees, and in one swift motion I slammed into her with a guttural grunt.

"Oh shit," I groaned.

It felt so good.

Withdrawing to the tip, I didn't waste any time. I was like a mad man possessed.

Thrust after thrust.

Moan after moan.

I couldn't stop.

Gripping her hips, I fucked her hard. So bloody hard.

Reaching underneath her, I pressed between her thighs, finding her clit once more, sending her over the edge. She did as she had been told and didn't hold back, crying out her release to the heavens and everyone else between.

So primal. So real. And all mine.

It was the sexiest damn thing I'd ever heard.

And my body responded in spades, coming so hard, I saw stars.

And I wondered, in that moment, how I was ever going to let her go.

Stepping out of the shower, I saw Millie checking me out in the mirror as I toweled off my hair.

"Do I risk it?" she asked, still lounging in bed after our mind-blowing morning sex.

I grinned at her through the mirror and glanced in the direction of the questionable shower. "It's not the worst I've been in, but for you? I'd skip it. Plus, I like the idea of you traveling home today with my scent all over you."

That earned me a sheepish grin.

Sitting up in bed, a thin white sheet draped across her, she cocked her head to the side and asked, "How is it that a boy from Yorkshire but actually from London is so familiar with grimy bathrooms and seedy motels?"

Looking down so that she couldn't see my smile collapsing, I tried to find the words to answer her. But how would I tell her I was just a nobody?

An orphan from the wrong side of the tracks?

I should have never said anything last night about London. I should have let her go on believing I was the rich, spoiled brat she and everyone else in the world thought I was.

The persona I'd made them believe, because I was too scared to share the real me with anyone.

But, in that moment, I'd wanted her to know something about me.

Something real. Even if it was as small as where I was from.

Of course, now it was coming back to bite me in the ass.

Just as I was about to open my mouth and spout out yet another lie about going to boarding school in London, growing up, my phone began to buzz on the counter next to me.

Seeing James's name flash across the screen was like a punch to my gut. I'd been so focused on Millie, I'd felt like the rest of the world had melted away.

But it hadn't.

And I had responsibilities outside of this motel room.

I hit Accept and answered, "Hello?"

"I guess I can cancel that search party then," he said, his voice less than cordial.

"I'm fine," I said, noticing Millie in the mirror as she tried to look busy, grabbing her clothes from the floor. I appreciated the semblance of privacy.

"I booked you a flight home. I wasn't sure which airport was the closest to that ridiculous island you're staying on, but I think you'll manage."

"You booked my flight, James? Who are you, my mum? And how do you know where I am?"

He let out an audible sigh. "No, I'm your brother, and you left me with no choice, Aiden. I haven't heard from you in days. I tracked you through your credit card."

Setting the towel down on the counter, I ran my hand through my wet locks. "That's not true, I texted you several times. And stop going through my shit."

"You texted me once. Once, Aiden. I don't enjoy breaking into your apartment and logging into your computer. Last time you disappeared like this, I had to track you down in another country."

I rolled my eyes. I knew I shouldn't have given him that spare key. "I know, and you never left."

"We've both made a decent life here, and I owe a lot of that to you. I would have never had the guts to make the move if you hadn't done it first."

"Well, you're welcome."

"But let's not forget, you have a tendency to make rash decisions when shit hits the fan."

My eyes found Millie once again in the mirror as I let out a long-winded sigh. I leaned against the counter, suddenly feeling heavier than I had before, like I was carrying the weight of the world.

"When do I leave?" I asked.

"Tomorrow," he said. "Just in time for—"

"I know," I said, cutting him off. "I'll be there."

I hung up before he could say any more, feeling the walls drawing closer.

Reality was coming, and I wasn't ready for it.

Not even close.

By the time I finished up with James, Millie was more or less ready to go. Deciding to skip the sketchy shower after all, she'd gotten dressed and packed up what little things she had back in her purse. Her hair was braided to the side, and even though she wore little to no makeup today, she was still gorgeous.

Maybe even more so.

I liked seeing the normally polished, put-together woman a little disheveled, especially knowing I was the reason she was so out of sorts.

"You ready to go?" she asked as I finished tying my last sneaker.

"Yes, you?"

She nodded. I could sense a tension that hadn't been there earlier.

"You heard my phone call?" I said, stepping closer, the warmth from her body like a beacon to mine.

"Yes," she simply said, her eyes focused on the grungy carpet.

Cupping her chin, I tilted her head upward until those baby blue eyes I adored were gazing into mine.

"You're leaving?"

I simply nodded.

I could see the struggle in her eyes as she shifted away from me. "I should probably go, too."

Panic filled my lungs.

"Come with me," I said without thinking. I did a lot of that around her.

"What?" Her eyes were wide with shock.

Mine probably were, too.

"Come with me," I said again. "Have you ever seen New York through the eyes of a real New Yorker? I'll take you to all the best places. You can watch me geek out at museums."

She grinned, excitement already blooming across her beautiful face.

"Are you sure? It sounded like you were needed for something."

I scoffed, "That? It's not a big deal. And, besides, it's at night. You won't even know I'm gone." I tried not to look away as I lied.

It was a big deal.

The day after tomorrow was the anniversary of my little brother's death. No one, outside of James and me, even knew about it.

And I'd just invited a virtual stranger to the party.

She's not a stranger, and you know it.

"I'd love to!" she said, standing up on her tippy-toes to kiss me on the cheek.

"Great!" I said, faking enthusiasm, and I swallowed down a ton of dread.

James was going to kill me.

We'd only just landed in New York an hour ago, and I already felt on edge. I hadn't realized it before, but North Carolina, with its laid-back calm and chill atmosphere, had already begun to grow on me.

I'd always thought of myself as a city person, growing up on the streets of London and then translating myself to a busy life in New York, but less than a week in Ocracoke, and suddenly, the cars were too many, the horns were too loud, and the people were too overwhelming.

"How long have you lived in New York?" Millie asked as we sat back in the cab while it drove us to my downtown apartment.

"Fifteen years. I moved here when I was still a teen to study art."

She turned to me, a knowing smile on her face. "That

would explain it."

My brows furrowed. "Explain what?"

"Your accent."

Curiosity got the better of me, and I pressed further. "What about my accent? I thought you found it rather sexy."

"Oh, I do. But it's not quite as pronounced as I'd expect."

I chuckled. "And you would be the expert on British accents then?"

She puffed her chest and stuck her chin out. "I do watch a lot of *Game of Thrones*."

I let out a laugh. "It's true. I have lost most of the slang of my youth, but I'm all right with that."

"Why don't you miss it?"

"England?" I specified, shrugging. "I've moved on. This is home now."

I knew she was looking for a deeper answer, but this was all I could give at the moment. Being back here, so close to the day we'd lost Ben, I felt raw and wounded.

"What about you?" I asked, changing the subject. "When was the last time you were here?"

She blinked several times, maybe a little caught off guard from my topic change but decided to go with it. "Um, last month," she answered.

"Last month?" I found myself saying, slightly amazed that this remarkable woman had been roaming the same streets as me only weeks ago.

"Yeah. I'm actually here quite often for work. But, if you asked me when was the last time I was here without a phone glued to my ear, the answer would be never."

"You've never really been to New York then."

"Technically, no. I've been to several lovely hotels, a dozen fashion houses, and a couple of really nice restaurants.

But, no, I've never been to New York. Not outside of work."

"Well then, I guess I've got my work cut out for me," I said, lunging forward in my seat to get the attention of our driver.

"Could you stick around?" I asked as he pulled up to the curb of my apartment building. Turning to Millie, I gave her a quick kiss on the lips. "Don't move."

"But where are you going?"

"I'm taking your things inside."

"And I can't go with you? I want to see your place," she argued.

Stepping out of the cab, I leaned my head in through the window, enjoying the adorable pout on her face. "No time," I explained. "If this is your first trip in New York, we've got a lot of ground to cover, and I'm not about to waste it by showing you my poor excuse of an apartment. So, hold tight, and I'll be right back."

To my surprise, she reached up and planted a deep and urgent kiss against my lips. I returned it, cupping the back of her head through the open window as onlookers passed by, whistling and cheering.

"Don't be long." She grinned when I finally pulled away.

I did as I had been told, grabbing her luggage out of the back of the car and making my way into the apartment building with haste. I was in such a chipper mood after that kiss, I swore, I was singing show tunes all the way up the elevator.

That was, until I walked down the hallway and found James standing at my door.

"You were supposed to land this morning. What happened?"

Leave it to James to get right to the point.

I cleared my throat, my smile dying the moment I saw him. "I changed my flight," I said simply as I noticed his eyes lingering on the scruff that had begun to accumulate across my jawline.

"You've got lipstick on your face," he said, not bothering to wait for me to unlock my own door. He pulled out his spare key and did it himself, taking note of the luggage in my hand.

"So, who is she? Flight attendant? Waitress?"

"Jesus, James. Do you really think so little of me?"

"You have the track record. I'm just working off previous experience here."

He pushed through the front door, and I followed him, going for the bedroom to drop off Millie's things.

"She's different," I said.

"Oh?" he said from the living room, sounding genuinely interested. "How so?"

"I don't know. She just is."

"Come on, Aiden. I've heard this before. Every so often, you meet a woman, and you say she's different. And then, two weeks later, she's gone. So, please, do me a favor and—"

"I told her about Ben," I blurted out, instantly ceasing his words.

I left out the part about how she didn't quite remember, but it did the trick. His eyes widened, and he understood.

"Do I get to meet her?" he asked, taking a seat on my sofa, all doubts gone.

He had always been comfortable here, more so than I ever was at his ridiculous Manhattan high-rise. Even though I was at the top of my field, he would always make more.

But James had always been the most ambitious of the

three of us. Ben had been the dreamer, and James was the take-charge, older-brother type. Me? I was the drifter. The one caught in between.

But that had all changed the night Ben died.

His death had given me a purpose.

And I'd been honoring his legacy ever since.

"No," I said. "You won't get to meet her."

He let out a ragged breath. "So, she's not different from the rest."

"She is," I replied, heading for the door. "She's extraordinary. That is why I have to let her go, and you know exactly why."

I knew he wanted to argue with me, but I couldn't listen to it.

I had an entire day planned with Millie, and I was going to enjoy every second, because, soon, that was all I'd have left.

Days, minutes…and finally, seconds.

And then I'd have to let her go.

Forever.

When I'd promised Millie a day to remember, I hadn't been lying. I wanted her to see New York—the real New York, not the tiny sliver she'd been accustomed to all those years of flying in and out for business.

So, first, we did a few touristy things—things I hadn't even done in my fifteen years of living here. We went to the top of the Empire State Building and took cheesy photos together while wind whipped through our hair, and the world looked so small and far away.

I took her to a restaurant with nothing resembling junk food on the menu and forced her to eat vegetables that were not fried or served with melted cheese. To her surprise, she actually enjoyed it, although I thought bribing her with sexual favors helped immensely.

I kept my promise, and we soon found ourselves at the Metropolitan Museum of Art.

"It's huge!" she exclaimed as we walked up the massive staircase.

"Just wait until you step inside."

The place was packed, but it usually was during the summer. Wall-to-wall people filled the place the moment you walked through the heavy wooden doors.

"Stay here, and I'll go grab us tickets."

She nodded, her head already moving in every direction, trying to capture the height of the ceilings, the beautiful stone sculptures, and the enormous floral arrangements. I made quick work of purchasing tickets, and thankfully, Millie didn't stray too far from the spot where I'd left her; otherwise, in this crowd, I might never have found her again.

"Where do you want to go first?" I asked.

She shrugged, her face alight with excitement. "You lead the way. You're the boss today, remember?"

I wagged my eyebrows. "I'll remember that."

She shook her head, a slight blush spreading across her lovely cheeks. Taking her hand, I headed for my favorite section of the museum.

"Oh my gosh!" she said the moment we stepped into the room. "It's so bright."

"It's my favorite in the whole museum."

We took a moment to appreciate it. I didn't know how

many times since moving to New York I'd come to this particular part of the museum for inspiration, for support.

For solace.

Looking up, I felt like we were in an ancient city with its Roman architecture and beautiful stone statues. But the light from the glass ceiling almost gave the feeling you were stepping into a garden.

"It's wondrous."

I tried to sound impressive as we walked. I pointed out my favorites and told her about the history of stonework.

"Do you hope to have your own work in a place like this one day?" she finally asked as we wandered into the modern art gallery.

I swallowed hard, looking at a particular statue completed only a few years earlier, knowing I had only a finite amount of time before I had to give this all up.

"I don't think I'll ever reach this level of greatness," I said.

I'm on borrowed time...

"Well, I'd like to be here when it finally happens, so I can lean over and whisper in your ear, *I told you so*."

"I would love that," I answered honestly, trying to imagine what it would be like to be surrounded by my friends and family. To have Millie by my side as my life's work culminated to this one great achievement.

But it would never be.

Life would fail me once again.

"Do you want to say it this year, or should I?" James asked as we stood on the rooftop under the New York sky.

It was just past midnight, a warm breeze blowing through the buildings, reminding me of summer days long since past.

My back stiffened as I looked down at the still-bustling city below. Clearing my throat, I said, "Not by birth, but by choice. Brothers for life. Brothers forever."

"He really was a sentimental son of a bitch, wasn't he?" James said as we held our double shots of whiskey in remembrance.

"Yeah, he was. But he was the best of us."

James nodded. "He really was."

Our glasses came together with a definitive clink before we each downed the amber liquid, commemorating our fallen brother on the day of his passing.

It was something we'd been doing since we moved here a decade and a half ago. Piss poor and drowning in grief, we'd found ourselves on the rooftop of our apartment building on the first anniversary of his death, unable to do much else but drink away our sorrows.

Ever since then, we'd made it a yearly event. Our place of residence might have changed over the years, but this remained the same.

Ben would always be remembered on this day.

At least by the two of us.

"Have you ever wondered where we'd be in life if Ben hadn't died?" James asked, taking a seat in the rickety folding chair. He poured himself another shot of whiskey as he leaned back and looked up at the sky.

"He'd probably be making statues for local churches—pro bono, of course, while living on crisps and biscuits."

"He did love biscuits." He smiled.

"And we'd be working our asses off at God knows

where to make sure he didn't starve to death."

He nodded. "I'd be working my ass off. You'd probably be chasing tail at the local pub."

I shrugged. "I'd like to think I would have done something better with my life eventually."

He gave me a meaningful stare. "You would have. Ben would have made sure of it. It's why he taught you how to carve in the first place."

I let out a deep breath, remembering the moment I'd found Ben sitting outside, under a tree, humming to himself while he carved a rock with an old knife.

"What are you doing?" I asked, my eyes wide with fright. Usually, in my experience, a knife meant bad news.

"Making a bird," Ben said very plainly.

My head cocked to the side as I sat down next to him. "A bird? Out of stone? How do you do that?"

He smiled. "Very carefully."

I made a disgruntled face. "I'm not daft."

At least, I didn't think I was. But this kid was younger than me, and if he knew how to turn a rock into a bird, surely, I did, too.

"You simply have to carve away at it. Bit by bit. It takes a lot of patience."

I looked down at his progress. So far, it only looked like a misshapen rock, definitely nothing close to a bird.

"How long have you been working on it?"

"A few months."

My eyes nearly bugged out of my head. "A few months? No offense, but I don't think it's working."

He shrugged. "I'll get there eventually. Patience, remember? Let me teach you, Aiden."

Reaching into my pocket, I pulled out my most precious possession. The stone bird my brother had carved.

It had taken him months, and I'd watched him with skeptical eyes, convinced he was half-crazy. But then, slowly, I'd become enamored by the process.

And so, I'd finally taken him up on his offer and learned.

It hadn't been easy.

We hadn't exactly been blessed with the correct tools or equipment, but Ben had been resourceful. He'd created tools out of household items our foster parents had thrown out and used rocks from the garden.

It had been his talent, but it'd soon become my passion.

Placing the tiny stone bird on the ledge in front of us, I held out my glass and saluted it in a silent nod to my brother, the dreamer.

"We need to talk about your diagnosis," James finally said, cutting through the silence like a knife.

"No," I answered, a note of finality in my tone.

He ignored it and pressed on, "Aiden, I told you, this doesn't have to be the end. There are dozens of things we can try. Please don't shut me out. I'm not the bad guy here."

I let out a dark laugh.

"Did you ever think that maybe I went into this field, so I could one day help you? My own brother? That maybe this isn't a cruel twist of fate but actually a good thing?"

"There is nothing about this that is good," I growled.

He leaned forward in his chair, his eyes level with mine. "How would you even know? You checked out the moment I broke the news to you."

"Because you ruined my life!" I roared. "And what's worse is, less than twenty-four hours later, fate handed me the perfect woman! And I can't have her because what kind of life can I offer her now that I…" I couldn't even finish the sentence.

"A few days ago, it was just my career I was losing, which, at that moment, was my whole life, but then I met Millie, and suddenly, this whole other world of possibilities was shown to me. I could get married, have children."

"You could still have all that," he said.

Ignoring him, I went on, "It was like a knife to the gut. I wasn't only losing my livelihood as an artist. I was losing an entire future."

"Have you even told her?" he asked, his voice barely a whisper.

"No."

"Why? Don't you think she deserves to know? To have the choice?"

I let out a deep sigh as I leaned back in my seat, the empty shot glass still in my hand. "She'll stay," I said. "She's good and sweet and kind. She'll stay, James, and then what? Maybe it will be great for a while. Really great. But, eventually, I'll just become that mistake she made, and I can't be the reason she ruined her life. She's ambitious, James. She has dreams—some she hasn't even realized herself. I can't stand in the way of that."

"Then, why do this at all? Why bring her here? Why prolong the agony?"

Running my hand through my hair, I avoided his gaze and finally settled on the little stone bird. "Because I'm the selfish one, remember?"

I heard him sigh. "No, I don't remember that at all." He paused for a moment before continuing, "Ben taught you to carve because he loved you."

"And look who's famous for it," I snidely replied.

"He would be proud, Aiden."

"Yeah, well, he's not here," I said, rising from my chair in search of the only thing that could bring me solace when my mind was filled with chaos.

Millie.

CHAPTER TEN

Millie

"What if we don't remember?" I asked, our bodies still slick from sweat as we lay side by side on the bed, wrapped in silk sheets.

"I don't think that's possible," he said, his hand gently cupping my face.

"But what if we don't? What if I wake up tomorrow, and this"—I reached forward, placing a tender kiss on his lips—"is gone? Just another drunken night forgotten."

He pulled back, his eyes downcast. "Then, maybe it'd be for the best."

"What? Why would you say that?"

"Because I'm nothing but damaged goods, love. And you deserve more than that." His gaze found mine once more, and I was struck by the pain I found. "So much more."

I awoke in Aiden's bed, the smell of him so fresh on the sheets, it was as if he were here with me. Pulling the pillow close to my face, I inhaled his woodsy scent as I listened to the sounds of the city below.

Over the years, I'd been offered a handful of jobs here, and a few of them had been tempting; after all, New York was an epicenter for fashion. Much more so than Miami where Lorenzo had based his thriving business. But my parents had instilled a sense of loyalty in me that forced me to stay and work for my success rather than jump the line.

That, and the thought of braving a New York winter really scared the crap out of me.

But part of me wondered now, if I'd taken a position here, would I have met Aiden? Maybe at a bar after a long day at work, or perhaps at a fancy art gallery?

Or would we have been destined to be close but never near?

I turned my head, gazing out the window onto the tall buildings that surrounded us. I sounded like a lunatic.

Fate and future?

None of it mattered. Not when he lived here, and I was going home in a few days.

"Guard your heart, Millie," he'd said.

I'd do well to heed his words.

As I settled back against the pillow that smelled far too good, my ears perked up at the sound of the front door unlocking. As I was in an unfamiliar place, in an unfamiliar city, my heartbeat rose in my chest but soon settled at the sight of Aiden in the doorway.

He was quick; deliberate even, as his shoes hit the floor with a thud, followed by his jeans and belt. He swiftly removed his shirt and dropped it as well before sliding into bed alongside me.

His skin was prickled from the sudden blast of the

air-conditioning unit, and he smelled of whiskey, but it was his eyes that set off the most alarms. Even in the dim light, I could see the deep pain radiating from within.

"Aiden," I breathed, "what's wrong?"

His forehead rested against mine as his chest rose with effort. I could feel him shaking. Tears prickled my eyes as he pulled me closer.

"Nothing, love," he whispered.

But then he kissed me, and I knew it was a lie. Because there was anguish and fear in the way his lips moved against mine. Passion and pain all wrapped in one.

We made love slowly, and I knew, with every thrust, a part of my heart went with it.

But, in that moment, I would give anything to ease his sorrow.

Anything to soothe the ache in his soul.

Even if it meant losing mine in the process.

Waking up the next morning, I felt raw.

Like all my emotions had been gobbled up, and I was running on autopilot. Stretching under the covers, I found myself alone in Aiden's bed. When I sat up, as the sunlight poured in, there was nothing of his around. The clothes he'd dropped on the floor last night before he crawled in bed next to me, all gone.

Not one to lounge about, I decided to get up and going. Although Aiden had given me a tour of his cozy apartment last night, seeing it in the daytime was quite different. Rising from the bed, I took my time in walking to the bathroom as I checked out the artwork on the walls and, of course, the sculptures.

He'd mentioned several were his, but he had seemed almost shy about naming which ones. The only piece of Aiden's I'd ever seen in person was the memorial he'd done for Ocracoke, and although I'd told him I had pulled off the side of the road to take a photo of it, what I hadn't said was that I'd spent more than an hour there, staring at that sculpture.

I'd been completely enamored by it.

Moved even.

And, yes, at the time, I'd told myself it was because of Dean and Jake; because it was my hometown and how closely it'd affected my life. But, now, as my hand ran over a small stone piece on Aiden's dresser that bore the same fluid lines and drew that same deep meaning within me, I knew it had to be more.

I was so in over my head.

"Guard your heart, Millie."

I let out a pained laugh as I stared down at the beautiful sculpture.

Too late, I thought.

Too damn late.

"That was one of my first pieces." Aiden's voice cut through the silence.

I quickly brushed away a tear that had found its way onto my cheek and plastered on a fake smile before I turned around.

God, he was beautiful.

I didn't think I'd ever grow tired of looking at him. From those hypnotic hazel eyes to the way his hair always seemed to be messy and tame at the same time, right down to the graphic T-shirts he loved to wear like a uniform.

Setting down a brown bag and a couple of coffees on the kitchen counter, just outside of the bedroom, he walked towards me, his hands finding my waist like a compass. I leaned into the warmth of his chest, and his chin rested on my collarbone.

"I was supposed to sell it to this wealthy couple in Manhattan. A symbol of their never-ending love on the their anniversary," he began to explain as his thumbs rubbed slow circles on my bare skin. "But the wife died suddenly, and when I went to deliver it, the poor husband couldn't bear to look at it."

"That's horrible. You would think he'd want to keep it as a reminder of their love," I said, noticing the way the sculpture seemed to capture a couple passionately embracing. It was abstract, no faces or distinct features, as was the style of most of Aiden's work, yet somehow, he'd managed to create such emotion and movement.

"Everyone handles grief in their own way. Some hold on, grasping at whatever they can, trying to keep a sliver of hope alive."

"And everyone else?"

"They run," he said simply as the warmth of his body left mine. "I got bagels, the best in the city. Want one? Oh, and coffee, too."

The sudden change in his demeanor felt like a slap in the face, and I was bewildered by the backlash of it.

"Um, no. Not right now. I think I'm going to hop in the shower," I said, my voice betraying the wave of emotions swelling in my heart.

Our eyes met, and I tried to swallow the giant lump that had formed in my throat. I could see the indecision in his gaze. But I made the decision for him and turned toward

THE LIES I'VE TOLD

the bathroom door, ending the conversation before it began.

"Guard your heart Millie," he'd said to me.

I hadn't listened the first time, and I lost so much already.

If I was going to survive Aiden Fisher, I needed to hold on to what shattered remnants I had left; otherwise, I'd end up like that memorial on the side of the road.

Just dust in the wind.

"I'm light and breezy. Cool and casual," I mumbled to myself under my breath as I gave one final glance in the mirror.

I'd just finished my makeup after a quick shower where I'd given myself one hell of a pep talk. This was not going to end with my heart broken in a million pieces.

I was not going to fall in love with this man.

I let out a cold laugh. I was not going to fall *further* in love with this man.

We'd agreed to a brief interlude.

Nothing more, nothing less.

I was a grown woman. I could sleep with a man and not grow attached. Hell, I used to do it all the time in college.

Having a one-night stand with your lab partner, Bobby Van Burren, because his girlfriend had dumped him and you felt bad for him doesn't count as all the time.

Shut up, brain.

I was single. This was what single people did.

Causal dating. Meaningless sex. It was healthy.

Like going to the gym.

And, if there was one thing my junk-food-craving body needed, it was definitely health.

Grabbing the doorknob, I twisted it, feeling the weight of the door push against me like lead weights.

Looking up at Aiden, the moment I caught his gaze, I felt every word of my pep talk crumble to the ground around me like ash.

Light, breezy, and what?

Oh, right. I swallowed hard as his hazel brown eyes met mine. *Casual.*

"I have that bagel here, if you're still—"

"Let's go shopping," I said, interrupting him mid-sentence.

"Okay," he answered, his brow raised as his emotions seemed to be a mix between amused and perplexed.

Believe me, buddy, so am I.

"Anything in particular?" he asked, handing me the bagel he'd been saving for me.

I took it without complaint, my stomach growling in response as I broke off a piece and tossed it in my mouth.

It really was the best damn bagel I'd ever tasted.

He smiled, watching my reaction, but my mind was already on other things as I eyed the T-shirt he was sporting.

"How attached are you to those shirts of yours?"

He looked down at the fitted gray tee. It had a band logo, one I recognized from our childhood. It was retro and on trend, and it definitely did nice things to his body that I couldn't help but notice.

"You want to give me a makeover?"

"I mean, I don't want to go all *Queer Eye* on you and wax your eyebrows and cut your hair. But, yeah, I wouldn't mind picking out a few things for you."

A slight smirk pulled at the corner of his mouth as I ate another piece of my bagel. "I wouldn't mind seeing you in your element," he said.

And I wouldn't mind the distraction, I thought.

"Just tell me where you want to go," he said, rising from his spot on the bed to give me a quick kiss on the cheek.

I couldn't help but grin, feeling like I'd accomplished some great feat.

See? I told myself. *I can do casual.*

With bagel in hand, I went on a hunt for my phone, intent on looking up stores. I had a few in mind, but having no real clue where I was in relation to anything in New York, I wanted to look at a map and get my bearings.

I did a quick perusal of the bedroom with no luck, but I remembered I'd left it in the living room after Aiden explained the lack of outlets.

"Beautiful high ceilings, ornate architectural details, and, like, three outlets in the entire apartment. That's the trade-off of living in a historical building," he'd said with a shrug after pointing me to one of the few places I could charge my phone, which was near the coffee table.

After quickly packing everything back up in my small carry-on and stuffing the rest of my bagel in my mouth, I headed into the main room and plopped down on the sofa, reaching for my phone but was stopped short.

There, on the small table in front of me, was a small stone bird.

Underneath it was a handwritten note.

I leaned forward, my heart quickening.

Don't read it, Millie.

Don't—

The moment my eyes made contact with the messy writing, it was gone. I exhaled, not realizing I'd been holding my breath, as I looked up and found Aiden, his face a mixture of emotions as he shoved the beautiful stone bird in his pocket and placed the note on a shelf behind him.

"Sorry," he said. "Just a list of supplies for a client I have coming up."

I nodded, still a little bewildered as he took my hand, suggesting we go for a nice walk before grabbing a cab.

His words felt like they were ringing in my ears as I went through the motions, my focus still fixated on that note and the little stone bird.

There was one thing I couldn't get out of my mind.

The fact that he'd lied.

Because, although I hadn't read the letter, I'd managed to see a few key words before he whisked it away from my sight.

Love.

Ben.

And probably the most important one of all.

Millie.

So, unless his new client happened to share my name, this casual business just became infinitely harder.

What was the expression people used?

Oh, right.

Fuck my life.

Yeah, that about summed it up.

"I know you're not a child anymore, but a simple text goes a long way," my mother said as the three of us sat down over a pitcher of iced tea on the patio at the inn.

I'd barely been home an hour before she tracked me down, banging on the door to my suite like a crazy person.

After I'd explained to her where I'd been, she'd calmed down a bit and then politely invited me to afternoon tea with my sister.

But I knew better.

The tea was just a sugarcoated ruse, so she'd have an excuse to interrogate me about my trip. She and my sister weren't all that different.

Come over for dinner. I need help with this recipe.
Let's chat for a while. It's been ages.
Why don't you come over for tea?

The second I walked through the door or hopped on the phone, I was accosted with questions. This was what I got for moving away.

"I'm sorry, Mama," I said, already feeling little beads of moisture around my brow. God, it was hot. Growing up in this heat, you developed a certain tolerance for it, but since I spent most of my time going from one air-conditioned place to another, I was a little rusty. "It was a spur-of-the-moment thing. And…" I paused, giving her a smug grin. "Like you said, I'm not a child."

"Well, I'm glad you're okay," she said before taking a sip of her sweet tea. I watched as she grabbed a cookie Molly had brought over. Barely a mother for a week, and the woman was already baking again. I swore, she was Superwoman.

That, or Martha Stewart.

Wait, didn't she go to prison for something once?

I let that thought go and took a cookie for myself.

Okay, three. I took three.

I'd run it off later.

"How is my grandbaby doing?" my mother asked, turning her attention to Molly.

The question surprised me some.

Was I being let off the hook? Had the day finally arrived when I wouldn't be bombarded with a thousand questions about my personal life?

I wasn't sure how I felt about that.

"She's good. I actually feel a little weird, being here without her. It's my first time out of the house since she was born," Molly admitted. "But Jake insisted. He said a little *me time* would be good for my mental health and that I wasn't allowed to argue with my doctor." She rolled her eyes.

"He's not technically your doctor when it comes to lady issues. That's what you have an OB-GYN for," my mom interjected, happily enjoying her cookie.

She nodded. "Try explaining that to him."

They both laughed, and I joined in, so I wouldn't seem like I wasn't paying attention, but I was seriously confused. My mom was really going to let the fact that I'd vanished for two days with a random stranger—a guy, no less—just slide?

"And the breast-feeding is still going well, too? No issues?" she asked, still enjoying her tea, like she didn't have a care in the world.

"Mmhmm, yes," Molly answered, a pleased and proud expression spreading across her face. "Very well. And we weighed Ruby yesterday at the clinic, and she's already starting to gain back what she lost after birth."

"That's wonderful. I'm so glad. Well, things are going well here. You're not to worry. Daddy and I jumped back into the swing of things with no issues. Breakfast went smoothly this morning. I made those spectacular orange scones. Oh, and there is a lovely couple from—"

"Are you kidding me?" I finally said, my eyes wide as I gripped the untouched glass of tea in my hand. There was sweat dripping down my temples from the ungodly summer temperature, making me wonder why in the world we were sitting outside.

It could have been one of the contributing factors to my outburst as I adjusted in my seat, hating the feeling of my damp shirt sticking to my back.

"What seems to be wrong, dear?" my mother asked, looking as fresh as a daisy as she leaned back in her reclining chair, drinking tea with a big, fat grin on her face.

"Oh my God," I finally said. "Did you bring me out here on purpose?"

"What?" she said, her eyebrows rising in a deliberately innocent expression.

"You did!" I rose to my feet. "You brought me out here knowing I couldn't tolerate the heat well anymore, hoping I'd, what? Sweat my secrets out to you?"

My mother, the one who'd kissed my boo-boos and sung lullabies at night when I couldn't sleep, looked up at me with that same amused, doe-eyed expression before turning to Molly. Both of them seemed like they were about to burst.

Until, finally, they did.

Laughter filled the patio.

I rolled my eyes, my hands flying up in defeat as I turned on my heels, preparing to storm off.

"Oh, come on!" Molly said. "Don't go. She was only messing with you."

Letting out a giant huff, I pivoted back around and plopped back down on the chair, still uncomfortable.

Still hot.

Still annoyed.

But, this time, I grabbed my sweet tea and downed half

of the glass in a single gulp as my sister and mother chuckled in the background.

"We had to get even with you for not responding to our text messages," my mother said. "That, and it is nice to know you actually still want to talk to me about these kinds of things."

"I don't want—"

She gave me a look.

One of those motherly don't-mess-with-me looks.

"Okay, maybe I do," I replied.

"I don't know why it's so hard to admit," she said, grabbing the pitcher of sweet tea so that she could top off my glass. She went around and did the same for Molly's and her own as well.

"Because I'm twenty-eight years old," I said. "I shouldn't need my mommy anymore."

Her face grew serious as she set down her tea and took both of our hands in her own. "My own mama died sixteen years ago, and there isn't a day that goes by when I don't need her," she said as I watched her lip tremble. "Every daughter needs a mother whether you're all grown-up"—her eyes fell to mine with a gentle smile—"or brand-new." That same smile traveled to Molly. "And I'll be here for you as long as I'm able."

She squeezed our hands and let out a breath, blinking her eyes several times, like she was willing away tears before turning her attention back on me. "Now, he must be a special one if you want to tell me about it."

I scrunched my face and looked out at the water for a moment. "It's complicated," I finally answered.

"Oh, boy," she said. "Not another one."

"Another one?" Molly scoffed. "I'm not complicated."

She folded her arms across her chest, doing her best impression of indignant.

"Oh, please!" I laughed. "Sulking around here for twelve years? And then almost marrying your best friend? That's not complicated?"

She leaned back in her chair, her eyes locked on mine until she finally gave up. Shrugging, she looked at Mom and said, "Okay, but I'm not complicated anymore."

"No, but what a hell of a time it took to get you there. I knew it was only a matter of time with your sister. You know Maria from my bridge club? Each of her two daughters? No drama. Simply met a nice man, fell in love, got married. No muss, no fuss. But my daughters? Nothing but drama!"

I didn't know if she was talking to herself or us at this point.

"So, tell me about your fellow," she finally said, her voice soothing, as I sat back in the seat, the heat no longer as bothersome as it once had been.

I clutched my sweet tea in my hands and closed my eyes as I thought of Aiden.

"He's not my fellow," I finally answered.

"But you want him to be," my mother's voice replied.

I let out a sigh, opening my eyes to the water's edge spread out before me. "We're just being casual, Mom. That's what single people do. Date. It's not a big deal."

"Now, why does that sound like a lie?"

Pressing my lips together hard, I thought back to our morning together as I tried to convince myself I could be in a relaxed relationship with no rules.

No future.

No feelings.

But every glance, every smile, and brush of his body

against mine had taken away another piece of me. Without even trying, Aiden Fisher was stealing my heart, and God help me, I was letting him.

"I think I'm falling in love," I said, his face still so fresh in my mind.

"Are you sure?" my mom asked as my head fell to my hands.

"No," I groaned, making them both laugh. Lifting my head once more, I let out a frustrated breath and answered her question once more, "Yes. But how, Mama? It's only been a few days. Love, real love," I emphasized, "can't happen overnight."

"Oh, sweetheart, there are no rules when it comes to love. Sometimes, it hits you like a lightning bolt in the middle of a summer storm. Other times, it develops slowly over time. But one does not outweigh the other. When it's real, it's real."

I nodded, feeling disheartened by my revelation. "It's real," I admitted. "More real than anything I've ever felt. And it frightens me."

"Why?"

"I'm not sure he loves me in return," I answered, suddenly remembering our conversation from earlier in the day.

"Everyone handles grief in their own way. Some hold on, grasping at whatever they can, trying to keep a sliver of hope alive."

"And everyone else?"

"They run."

"Or, if he does, there's something in the way. I don't know. I always feel like he's running in a different direction than me. Why do you think I said it was complicated? He tells me nothing, but I see the pain in his eyes from a past he won't share. He's like a treasure chest at the bottom of the ocean with no key."

"So, be the key, sweetheart."

"What? Mom, it was just a stupid metaphor," I said, feeling defeated.

"No, it was actually quite perfect. Unlock the source of his pain, and then maybe you'll find the way to heal the man you love so that he can love you in return—the way you deserve to be loved." She paused for a split second, a small smile on her lips. "Because I won't settle for any less, and neither should you."

"No, I shouldn't," I agreed.

I deserved more.

I deserved love.

The wholehearted, all-consuming kind.

The trouble was? My heart currently resided at the bottom of the ocean with Aiden.

"Be the key," my mom had said.

Sure, no problem.

"Hey, Mom? Could you maybe write out some directions on this key thing before you leave? Like a treasure map for snagging your man?"

She laughed.

Trouble was, I kind of wasn't joking.

CHAPTER ELEVEN

Aiden

Aiden,

I don't know a thing about love, but I'm fairly certain, if I were lucky enough to find it, I wouldn't let a damn thing stand in my way.

Especially this.

And, if Ben were here, I know he'd agree with me. He always did. So, listen to your brothers and wise the fuck up.

I'll be here when you come to your senses. I'd love to meet your Millie.

—James

With the stone bird my brother had carved lying on my chest, I read the note James had left on my coffee table—the one I'd managed to snag just moments before Millie's eyes descended upon it.

At least, I thought I had.

Her mood had been different since then. It'd felt almost erratic. Every touch had felt deliberate, as if she'd timed it down to the second. I'd catch her staring at me in the mirror at one of the stores she'd dragged me into, and the moment our eyes met, she'd smile and turn away. But the smile had felt forced.

She'd enjoyed herself, picking out things for both of us in the short time we had before our flight back to Ocracoke, but I could tell there were other things on her mind.

But what?

When she'd been in my arms last night, I'd thought, surely, this was what it felt like to make love. She'd cradled me, cherished me, as I buried myself in her, using her body as the ultimate remedy for my grief. I had known it was selfish when I promised her nothing, but my conversation with James combined with the anniversary of Ben's death, it had all been too much.

I'd needed her.

It was that sad realization that had me slumping in defeat.

Just like that selfish little boy who had asked his little brother to teach him how to carve his own stone figurine, I would stay here as long as I was able, soaking up as much of Millie as I could.

Because I couldn't imagine spending another day without her.

Feeling out of sorts with too many thoughts swirling around in my head, I decided a walk might be just the thing I needed. Snatching the tiny bird from his perch on my chest, I rose to my feet and placed him on the nightstand next to the bed.

Heading toward the door, I opened it and found Millie with her hand raised to a fist.

"Oh!" she gasped. "I—sorry! I didn't expect you to answer before I knocked!"

I shrugged. "We Brits are known for our punctuality."

It was a cheesy joke, but she laughed all the same.

"I was just heading out for a walk. Care to join me?" I offered.

"Actually..." she said, turning her head to gaze down the hall.

I followed her lead and found two women standing near the foyer. One was Millie's mother, whom I remembered from breakfast a few days earlier, and the other, I guessed, was her older sister, judging from how closely she resembled the other two women.

"My family invited you to dinner."

A large lump formed in the dead center of my throat. "Oh."

She pushed me back inside my suite and promptly shut the door. "I'm sorry," she said. "Please don't hate me, or think I'm one of those women who is trying to force you down the aisle. But my family is a little crazy, and...well, Southern." She said the last word like it was supposed to explain a lot. Like, *Meet Sally. She's blonde, blue-eyed, and oh yes, Southern*. And everyone would immediately nod and understand the plethora of traits associated with the word.

"Okay."

"Okay?"

"Okay, when do we leave?"

She suspiciously eyed me, so I did the same in return.

"What?" I asked.

"I don't think I've ever heard you use the word *okay*. It's weird. It's more than weird. In fact, I don't like it. Take it back."

"I can't take it back." I laughed. "I'm not allowed to say *okay*?"

She shook her head with vigor. "No. Nope. It sounds

horrible when you say it."

"It does not! Lots of Brits say it. Hell, I was watching *Jessica Jones* the other day, and the journalist character said it. Didn't sound weird then."

Her eyes glassed over a little. "Oh, yeah, him? Yeah, he's hot."

I gave her a pointed stare, causing her to blush.

"But still, no. Uh-uh. Not for you. It's like when your parents try to say something trendy. Like, just last week, my mom and I were on the phone, and she said she and my dad were going out to dinner. Then, she paused and said, 'It's gonna be lit.' It was horrible. Like *nails on a chalkboard* horrible."

I couldn't help but chuckle a little. "All right, I would be very pleased to accompany you to an enchanting evening with your family tonight. Is that better?"

Her eyes narrowed. "That will do. But I feel like you mocked me a little at the end there."

I grabbed her hand and headed for the door. "Well, you might have deserved it. Remind me to use the word *okay* at least half a dozen times tonight in conversation, okay?"

"Oh my God," she groaned.

"This is going to be fun."

Letting out a snort, she gave me an eye roll. "You say that now, but I don't think you've fully realized what you're getting yourself into."

We stopped just outside the entrance of my suite as I gave a brief glance down the hall before turning my attention back to Millie. "I've met your parents," I said. "I seem to remember your mother having a particular fondness for me."

Millie rolled her eyes as I grinned. "Yes, but now, they

know." She put emphasis on the last word.

"Know what?"

"That you and I are…" Her voice dropped down to a whisper.

"Doing it?" I said softly, making her giggle under her breath.

"Shh! Yes! And it will be like the Spanish Inquisition at dinner tonight. I tried to talk my mom out of it, but she was adamant. She wants to get to know you. I hope it's not too much."

I shook my head, placing a tiny kiss upon her nose. "I'm honored to be at your side."

She blushed, looking rather pleased as she pulled my hand down the hallway, toward the foyer.

Try as they might, her mother and sister were doing a piss-poor job of minding their own business. I smiled to myself, wondering what it must be like to have such a caring, devoted mother like Millie's.

"Mom, I'm sure you remember Aiden," Millie said.

I began to hold out my hand to the beautiful older woman but was instead pulled into a giant hug.

"So nice to see you again, Aiden."

"Mama!" I heard Millie and her sister say in unison.

"Sorry! That's just how we greet people around here," she said before letting me go.

I couldn't help but chuckle as Millie rolled her eyes and introduced me to Molly.

"This is my sister," she said. "The older, wiser version of me."

"Some would say hotter," Molly interjected.

"Some," Millie said. "But not most." She gave me a quick wink before taking my hand.

"Where are we headed?" I asked, wondering which of the three restaurants in town we'd dine at tonight.

"Oh, we're not going anywhere. Why go out when we have two of the best cooks right here?" Millie said, pointing to her mother and sister. "Plus, you can't beat the view outside on the patio at sunset."

"Sounds like a fantastic plan to me," I said. "How can I help?"

"Well, I like him already," Mrs. McIntyre said. "How are you with a knife?"

I gave Millie a waggle of the eyebrow, making her laugh. "Better with a chisel, but I can hold my own."

"Think you can handle chopping some veggies?"

I nodded, squeezing Millie's hand in mine. "I think *we* can handle that just fine."

"Great! Then, follow me."

We did as we had been told, following closely behind Millie's mom, who seemed like she was a take-charge sort of woman. I guessed running an inn and raising a family inside of it would require nothing less.

"We'll be on our own for the time being. Jake is on his way with Ruby, and she's in dire need of some mom time. Once she's fed, then I'll have Molly back in here to help me with the harder stuff."

"It's really no trouble," I said. "We can help while she rests for the evening."

Both Millie and her mom burst into laughter.

"What?"

"This is Molly's idea of resting," Millie explained. "Baking, cooking—it's like therapy or yoga for her. If she doesn't get her daily dose, she's off. And, believe me, it's not pretty."

She'd already pulled out several different kinds of veggies for an appetizer, and Millie and I jumped right in, helping her chop through all of them. I took my time, careful not to lop off any of my digits, while Millie went to town with her knife and veggies. Obviously, this wasn't her first rodeo at being her mother's assistant.

"Why so many?" I asked after a while, looking over the large piles we'd made. "Isn't it just your family and me? Or am I underestimating the size of your family?"

Millie, who'd helped herself to a carrot, made a face the moment she bit down. "Impromptu dinner for the inn. It's something my sister started a few years ago. She'll throw dinner on the grill and invite all the guests—no charge, of course. It's become a huge hit on her reviews. People love it because they say it feels like they've come home, you know?"

"Yeah," I answered, but really, I had no idea, because to me, the idea of home was still a mystery. It was the childhood dream I used to talk about with my brothers under our worn sheets while our foster parents sat in the living room and pretended we didn't exist.

"Any more veggies, Mom?" Millie asked, handing over her half-eaten carrot to me.

I grinned and took it from her as she began pilfering through the large pantry. Ten seconds later, she came back out with a marshmallow and several chocolate chips in her hands.

Now, it was me who was rolling my eyes.

"Nope, that's it. You're free to go," she announced from the counter, her arms elbow deep in oysters.

"Actually," Millie replied, "I was thinking I could teach Aiden how to make hush puppies."

That seemed to catch Mrs. McIntyre's attention as she turned to look at us. "Are you sure? You haven't made them in ages, and last time you did, they came out all—"

Millie's eyebrows rose in response. "I got it Mom, really."

"Okay," she replied, a warm smile spreading across her face as she returned back to her work.

"What was that all about?" I asked as I followed Millie into the pantry, helping her grab several items - flour, cornmeal, and salt.

"I might have burned a few things growing up. There's maybe a lack of trust associated with my baking abilities."

I grinned. "And so you thought testing them out on an inn full of guests would be a great idea?"

She turned to me, the once spacious pantry feeling quite small with us so close together. It gave me wicked ideas of what we could do in here with the door closed.

"Did you really try to impress a girl with baking?" she asked, her big blue eyes staring up at mine.

"What?"

I could see she was almost annoyed by the words coming from her mouth, but she went ahead anyway.

"The morning after we first slept together," she explained, "I asked about your expert egg-cracking, and you said you'd learned it to impress a girl."

A smug smile formed on my lips. "You're jealous?"

"What? No! Maybe. A little."

I pulled her closer, the heat from her body doing things to me that probably shouldn't be thought about in a place where flour was stored.

"It's just that there are all these things I want to do with you—like bake my grandma's famous hush puppies—but then I wonder, *Does he even like baking? I don't know. Maybe this girl dumped him, and now he actually hates all things baking-related.* The point is, I don't know anything about you, but I want to."

My heart had quickened as she rambled.

Have you even told her?

No.

Why? Don't you think she deserves to know? To have the choice?

She'll stay…and maybe it will be great for a while—really great—but eventually, I'll just become that mistake she made, and I can't be the reason she ruined her life.

A vision of us in the future, making dinner with her family suddenly came to mind. Her mother would ask me to chop the vegetables, and the room would go silent because, all at once, they'd realize the grave error in her words.

Mother, Aiden can't do those things anymore, remember?

And then the sad stares would come, and though she'd try to hide it, I'd see Millie's eyes flash with disappointment.

Because I'd failed her.

Oh God, what was I doing?

Meeting her family and having dinner like I belonged?

"I've got to go," I said, causing her eyes to widen. "Headache. I can't." I reached for my temple. "I'm sorry, Millie. Give my apologies to your parents."

I left her there, standing in the pantry, as I avoided her mother's gaze and made a beeline for my suite.

I never looked back.

The room was dark. The house had been quiet for hours, and still, I lay in bed, staring at the ceiling of the old cedar house. I thought about that first night with Millie and how she'd seemed to be a gift from heaven, sent just when I needed her most.

But I'd been in an alcohol daze, so drunk on the idea of her that I hadn't been able to think clearly.

And wasn't that the exact definition of love?

It made you crazy, impulsive, and completely irrational.

That was how I felt around Millie McIntyre.

I knew I should go. I knew I should pack up my things this very night and walk away from this tiny town and all the people in it.

It would be the right thing to do.

For everyone.

But I couldn't do it. My body was tied down to this bed, chained to this room, tethered to this woman so tightly, I didn't know how to let go.

The sound of the lock being turned jolted me upright as my eyes tried to make out the intruder making their way into my suite.

It didn't take long.

Even in the darkened room, I could spot those long, sexy legs from a mile away.

She didn't say a word as I watched her set the key on my dresser, which I could only assume she'd stolen from her parents since her overseeing days for the inn had long since passed.

Wearing only a thin slip of a nightgown, she walked over to the bed and pulled the covers back. I slid over, her eyes on mine as she found her way back to me. Her hand cradled my face as she leaned into me. Her eyes were swollen, most likely from tears she'd shed.

Over me.

I swallowed hard and tried to look away, but she wouldn't allow it.

"I'm not giving up on you, Aiden Fisher," she whispered, her lips quivering with meaning. "Not now, not ever."

"I told you I couldn't give you more," I said, feeling like the worst kind of fraud. "I warned you to guard your heart."

She smiled, moisture rimming her brilliant blue eyes. "It wasn't mine to protect any longer," she said.

The war that had been raging within me, deciding between what was the right thing to do and what my heart wanted, suddenly ended.

With a single, passionate, soul-binding kiss.

I reached for her, our lips meeting in a frenzy of words unspoken, lives now altered and a thousand crazy decisions we had yet to make.

I knew our future might be unsettled.

I knew I had to eventually tell her everything, but for now, all I wanted to do was be wrapped in her embrace for as long as I could.

Just like this.

Every time felt like the first time with Millie. Every caress of her body felt like I was exploring it anew. Removing her nightgown, I covered every inch of her beautiful tan skin with my lips, making sure to kiss away tears on her cheeks as I worked my way down.

She wore lace panties again, something I was growing quite fond of, as I took one last appreciative glance before sliding them down her long legs and dropping them on the floor.

"God, you're beautiful," I murmured.

"So are you," she answered.

I made quick work of the condom, hating that we still

had to use it, but both of us had a history we couldn't ignore, hers more recent than I liked to think about.

And I hadn't exactly been a saint either.

But none of that mattered now.

Sitting up on the bed, I pulled her into my lap. Her knees were at my sides as she straddled me, our bodies close.

So close.

"I want to kiss you, hold you, while I make love to you," I said softly, as I slowly lowered her onto my throbbing cock.

Our eye contact never wavered as she slowly melted into me. Two bodies becoming one. Two souls united.

"You feel so good, love," I groaned. "So damn good."

I didn't have to tell her what to do; she knew. Wrapping her arms around my neck, she leaned her head to the side, and her lips found mine in a surge of passion. Her hips moved, mimicking the rhythm of our kiss and frenzy and fire within.

It was magic when our bodies came together, and I knew now that I'd never be able to give her up. She was it for me. My muse, the only inspiration I'd ever need for the rest of my life.

"Oh God, I'm getting close," she cried out.

I watched as she arched her back while she rode my cock with reckless abandon, all the way through her orgasm, screaming her release for the whole damn town to hear. It was the sexiest fucking thing I'd ever seen, and as I came right behind her, I knew I wasn't going anywhere.

Not for a long time.

Not ever.

This was my home, right here in this woman's arms.

Forever.

"Twenty Questions?" Millie asked as we lay in bed, hours after making love several more times.

Neither of us could sleep, so wired from our time together that we'd decided to watch the sun rise instead.

"You know this isn't how the actual game works," I explained.

"What?" She shifted under the covers, her naked skin sliding against mine. She turned to face me, her breasts pressing against my chest as she looked up at me with hooded lashes.

"The game Twenty Questions is actually meant to be a guessing game. Someone picks something, an object or a person, and then the other person has twenty questions to guess what it is."

"Wait, have we had this conversation before?"

I grinned. "Yes."

Her face soured. "This is one of those things that happened that I don't remember, isn't it?"

I chuckled. "Yes."

"Oh God, and we played it for hours in the car. So, that whole time, you were, what? Just placating me?"

"Yes."

She nudged my bare hip, making me laugh. "Jerk."

"Well, I had questions. It was a good way to get them answered. I'm assuming that was why you started the ridiculous game in the first place. Plus, I thought it was kind of adorable."

I placed a tender kiss on her forehead as she stared up at me.

"What was it like?" she asked, resting her chin on my

chest. "Our night together."

I began to play with a strand of her blonde hair as I thought back. "It was perfect," I said. "It was the kind of night where time stood still, and we seemed to be in our own little world. We talked for hours—about everything and anything. We laughed. God, did we laugh."

"Well, we were drunk."

"We did go through a lot of your sister's alcohol stash. But still, I've had my share of drunken one-night stands."

"Didn't need to know that," she said.

"Sorry," I replied. "Just stated a fact for reference. Our night was different. And I know that because each night since has been exactly the same."

"Then, why are you running?" Her voice turned serious.

"I'm not running anymore."

"Does it have to do with that letter? And don't tell me it had to do with a client because I saw my name on it, Aiden," she insisted, her eyebrows rising in challenge.

"Is this your version of Twenty Questions again?"

"Our lives are more than twenty questions," she whispered.

I let out a heavy sigh. "I promise I'll tell you everything, just give me time. I'm not running anymore; I swear it."

I could have told her everything in that moment, but instead, I asked her to wait because, as selfish as it sounded, I needed more time.

More time like this.

"Okay," she answered.

"Oh, so it's all right for you to say it but not me?"

She nodded on my chest, a wide grin spreading across her face. "Yes, exactly."

"You know I've been living in this country for fifteen

years. That's almost as long as I was in England."

She shrugged. "And yet when I say the word *okay*, it sounds perfectly normal, but when you say it, nails on a fucking chalkboard."

"Was your family quite cross with me?" I asked, feeling like the largest ass for storming out on them.

Millie's face scrunched slightly. "My mom kind of already knew you were a tough nut to crack, so she wasn't too upset by it, although if you do it again, she might just charge after you. "

"Duly noted. I'm sorry I did. Run, I mean."

Her hand skimmed the skin on my stomach, drawing lazy circles up and down my happy trail. "I forgive you," she said. "But you'll explain?"

"Yes," I said. "Soon, I promise. Just trust me. Can you do that?"

She looked into my eyes, as if searching for something. "Yes," she finally answered. "But will you at least tell me one thing?"

"Anything."

"Who is Ben?"

My throat moved, trying to swallow the deep lump that had formed there. "My brother," I answered. "My younger brother. He died while we were in foster care together. Millie, I'm not what you read in that bio."

Her head lifted, and the motion of her hand on my skin stopped. "Aiden," she whispered. There was pain in her voice as she said my name.

Empathy.

Love.

"No," she said, reaching up to cup my face. "You're more. Will you tell me about him?" she asked.

Letting out a breath I didn't realize I'd been holding, I told the story of my brother Ben.

For the first time.

I told her how we'd met and the circumstances that brought me to him and James.

"Were your foster parents nice?"

"They were invisible," I said. "And so were we. It was an agreeable living situation—one we cherished because it meant the three of us stayed together."

"That's sad," she replied.

"No it was wonderful, because I had Ben and James. It was more than I'd ever had before, and I wouldn't trade them for the world."

"Then, why don't you want to go back? To England, I mean."

I let out a hard sigh. "When James and I scattered Ben's ashes, our foster parents handing them over to us without more than a glance, I was ready to move on. Ben's memory didn't need to live on in that shitty neighborhood with those terrible memories. I just…I thought I could honor him with more."

"So, you ran?"

I met her gaze, realizing how much of me she saw when I said so little.

"Yeah, I guess I did."

"And, now, you honor Ben through your carving?"

I nodded, going on to tell her of Ben's love for stone carving and how he'd shared that love with me.

"I have him to thank for your relentless patience then?" She smiled, turning her head up toward me.

"Ben was infallible with his never-ending patience. He would, still, to this day, say I have the patience of a gnat.

And, in comparison, he'd be correct."

"He sounds amazing."

"He was the best."

"How did he die?" she finally asked.

"He was always a sick kid," I said. "Ben was consistently smaller than the rest of us. Pale, you know? I just figured it was his coloring, but then he began to thin out even more and grow weaker. He'd shiver at night, even in the summer. When we asked him about it, he'd brush it off as a summer cold or a winter flu. It went on and on."

"He was sick all that time?"

I simply nodded.

"When he got real bad at the end, I became so angry and swore I'd go in and demand that our foster parents do something, anything, but Ben made me promise I wouldn't. He was terrified they'd separate us. But it didn't matter; James and I were about to age out anyway.

"So, one day, I finally stomped into the living room and told my foster dad off. I told him he was a sorry son of a bitch with no love in his heart. I asked him how he could sit around and watch a boy die right there, in his own house. It was the only time he ever looked at me with any sort of emotion. It was pity.

"'Ben is dying,' he said. 'He's known ever since we took him in. He just needed a place to do it.'"

"That's horrible. What awful people you lived with."

"I honestly couldn't even focus on their lack of empathy as I stood there in shock over the fact that my brother had known he was dying and didn't tell us. All that time, and he never said a word. I felt utterly betrayed."

"And what would you have done if you had known? Tiptoed around him all that time? Sat around, waiting for him to grow sicker?"

"I don't know," I answered, sitting up as she did the same. "But I could have at least done something. Maybe fought for him."

"Babe, you were teenage kids in the foster system. You can't blame him for wanting to enjoy the fact that he had a family for probably the first time in his life."

I looked down as she pulled my hand into hers, the warmth of our fingers intertwining, filling my heart with hope. "You're right. I know you're right. But, God, I wish I could have done something."

"You did do something. You gave him happiness. You filled his heart with joy every single day when you sat down with him and let him teach you how to carve, and you carry on that joy even now through your artwork. I know it for a fact."

My brow rose at her decidedly resolute statement.

Reaching over, she grabbed the stone bird that still resided on my nightstand.

"You put this bird in every piece you make. It's your signature. I remember seeing it in the memorial in Ocracoke and the piece in your bedroom that you made for the elderly couple."

A sad smile made its way across my face. "It is," I answered. "He gave that bird to me and made me promise to do amazing things with my life."

"And have you? Done amazing things?"

I looked at her, so beautiful under the rising light of the sun. Smiling, I answered, "I think I'm about to."

CHAPTER TWELVE

Millie

"W̲HAT IS HE DOING?" MOLLY ASKED, having just come in through the front door to find me standing in the parlor with a glass of iced tea in my hand, watching Aiden like a creeper.

"I don't know," I answered as she joined me, a sleeping infant in her arms. "That giant chunk of granite arrived on the morning ferry today, and, wow, you should have seen the tow truck that had to lift that sucker into the backyard."

"What? Through my garden?" My sister suddenly looked panic-stricken.

"Relax. I made sure they didn't touch a single rose."

"Oh, okay. Well then, carry on with your story."

I smiled. "Well, since the shed hasn't been used since Daddy lived here, Mama offered it up as a second workspace to Aiden—you know, to store his tools and stuff since, apparently, he can't work in the shed. Too much dust or whatever. Too small. Anyway, he's been out there ever since."

"And you've been standing here for how long?" she asked, rocking back and forth next to me.

"Since I noticed his shirt on that chair about an hour ago," I answered with a wicked grin. "Do you blame me?"

"He is…I mean…well, damn," my sister stuttered out a response seconds before we heard a throat clear behind us. Molly jumped, her hands surrounding the infant in her arms as she turned to see her very jealous-looking husband standing in the entryway. "Oh, hello, dear husband of mine. There you are!" she said, turning five shades of red. She turned to give me a death stare before scurrying off into the kitchen.

Jake rolled his eyes before his focus moved to Aiden outside. "Could he at least put on a shirt?"

My eyes followed his, and I resisted the urge to sigh at the sight of all those burly muscles glistening under the summer sun.

Damn.

"Sorry, Jake, I simply can't allow that."

His brows furrowed as his arms folded tightly across his broad chest. "So this thing between you two, it's serious?"

Taking a sip of my iced tea, I turned as he joined me at the window. I tried not to show my amusement as he put his back toward the glass to talk to me, thus avoiding the sexy, shirtless male altogether.

"It is," I said. "Or at least, it's going that way. I mean, we haven't picked out china or discussed living arrangements, but what I feel for him is definitely serious."

His gaze shifted, finding a huge interest in the wooden floor as he let out a deep sigh.

"What, Jake?"

"Nothing," he answered.

"Nothing? Since when have you been one to beat around the bush?"

"I promised Molly I wouldn't say anything," he confessed.

"Molly?" I said, my gaze traveling to the kitchen. "You guys talked about me?"

His brows lifted. "We're just worried, Mills. You've known this guy only a few days, and with the way he stormed out last night at dinner, you can't blame us for being a little concerned."

Stepping back, my fingers clutching the cold glass in my hands, I asked, "Do you all feel this way? Mom? Daddy?"

He shook his head. "Your mom believes in you—that you've made the right choice."

I let out a breath, my lip quivering as the air escaped. "But the rest of you? You don't?"

His eyes rounded. "Millie, what do you really know about this guy?"

Placing my tea on the table, no longer in the mood for it, I answered, "Enough to know he's worth the risk. I thought someone like you would understand."

"Me?"

"You came back here like a damn ghost, Jake. Twelve years, you left my sister hanging. No note, not even a phone call, and she took you back because, despite everything that had happened in those twelve years, you were worth the risk to her."

"I—"

I held out my hand, stopping him from speaking any further. "Just don't," I said. "I need some air. Just tell Aiden—if you can stand to talk to him—that I went for a walk. I'll be back later."

And then I turned and walked away, willing myself not to cry.

I made it to the threshold before the dam broke, and the tears fell.

I hadn't really thought out my dramatic exit all that well.

About five minutes into my walk, I was sweating like a dirty whore in church, wondering what I had been thinking when I decided to go for a leisurely stroll in the middle of the freaking summer in North Carolina.

How in the world did I used to run around and play in this weather?

Just as that thought rolled around in my head, two kids waved to me on bicycles, looking happy and carefree, completely unaffected by the sweltering heat or the insane humidity suffocating me from all sides.

But I refused to turn around.

If I did, it'd do nothing for my cause.

What is my cause exactly? I asked myself as I ambled down the road.

Oh yes, making my brother-in-law and the rest of my family feel bad for their actions.

Sure, they might have had my best intentions in mind, but damn it, how dare they talk about me and my love life behind my back?

At least my mother seemed to still be on my side.

My phone vibrated in my back pocket, and I instinctively reached back to grab it. After years of being attached to it for work, old habits died hard.

Speaking of old habits...

A Google alert I'd set up ages ago to monitor internet activities on the company—one I had yet to turn off since quitting, just in case my little video made the news—had just sent me something rather interesting.

Clicking on the email, I stood in the middle of the street, the sun no longer captivating my interest as it once had.

"Son of a bitch," I said out loud.

Lorenzo Russo Declares Love For Employee!

The headline was everywhere—well, everywhere that the fashion world cared about—and I couldn't click on the article fast enough, my hands a shaky mess.

If I thought I had been sweating before, it was the damn waterworks now.

Lorenzo Russo, CEO of up-and-coming fashion house Bella, went on record this morning, stating he is involved with an employee of his company and is in love.

"I didn't want this information to be discovered in the wrong way. We are very much in love and want the world to know it."

"Oh, shit," I muttered, reading further.

When interviewed, the employee, Sadie Howlett, said she didn't want to be treated any differently just because she was dating the boss.

"Wait, what the fuck?" I had to read that last part twice, my mind reeling.

Sadie?

Who the hell was Sadie?

Restroom.

We met in a restroom! Right before the meeting!

Oh my gosh, she was the newbie.

Well, that was quick.

Says the woman who is in love with another man.

Shut up, brain.

I scrolled down in the article, and sure enough, there was a picture of my former boss and lover with the woman I'd met in the restroom—Sadie Howlett.

Maybe she was the one who sent the email?

The moment my mind went there, I immediately shut it down.

Because, really, what did it matter?

Maybe it was true, maybe it wasn't. But either way, it didn't change what was happening in my life, right now.

I'd moved on.

Shaking my head, I stuffed the phone back in my pocket and went on my way.

I'd thought I'd feel more when I found out Lorenzo had moved on.

More of what? I didn't know.

Anger or sadness maybe?

But the only thing I really felt was pity, because I knew what they had wasn't love.

It was barely even lust.

Sadie was just the next distraction in a never-ending line Lorenzo kept to occupy himself. We were there to alleviate his boredom, and sure, he played the role well, making us feel special during our short little stint but we weren't.

We were what we were.

An amusement.

Nothing more, nothing less.

And, eventually, Sadie would come to this sad realization, too. I only hoped she someday found someone who showed her the true meaning of love, as I had.

Just a few days ago, revenge had been my top priority. Revenge and finding a new job. I'd wanted to prove to whoever had sent that email that it didn't faze me.

And, had I been that same girl I was then, this news would have rocked me to the core. Now, I couldn't care less.

What a difference a few days made.

Well, that, and a hunk of a man. No, not just any hunky man.

The right man.

Wiping away the copious amounts of sweat that had gathered on my brow, I let out a happy sigh. "I need ice cream."

"Are you talking to yourself?"

Nearly jumping out of my skin, I looked down to find a kid staring up at me. It took me a moment, but I recognized her as Cora's little girl.

"Hey, aren't you a little young to be out and about by yourself?" I asked, taking a look around.

She put her hands on her hips. "I'm almost seven," she answered, as if this were all the explanation I needed.

"Um, okay. Hey, where's your mom?" I asked, not really sure how to interact with kids, my only experience thus far being the few precious moments with Ruby, and she didn't exactly talk much.

"Back there," she said. "She's slow."

I looked to where she was pointing, and sure enough, there was Cora only a few houses back.

Taking another look down at Lizzie, I gave her a sideways stare. "Well, she doesn't exactly have a scooter to help her out, does she?"

She merely shrugged. "Hey, you said you were going to get ice cream. So are we. Want to go together? I can tell you how they make it on the way."

"How they make it? Don't they just freeze the ingredients?"

"Oh, you're gonna wish you hadn't asked that question," Cora said, giving me a quick wave as she finally caught up.

"Oh no," Lizzie answered. "There are dozens of ways to make ice cream. Let me explain—"

"Actually Lizzie, why don't you see how fast you can get to the end of the street? I'll time you," Cora suggested, giving me a look that said I owed her.

"Okay!" The small girl readjusted her helmet on top of her wavy dark brown hair and waited as her mom pulled out her phone.

"Ready?" Cora asked, looking down at what I assumed was some sort of stopwatch app.

Lizzie nodded.

"Set…go!"

Lizzie tore down the empty road as Cora smiled, turning to me with a satisfied look on her face.

"We have a few minutes to ourselves. I can't promise that you won't know all about ice cream rolling or the entire inner workings of an industrial ice cream maker by the time we leave the ice cream shop, but for now, we have some time to chat. How are you?"

I let out a small laugh. "Ice cream rolling?"

"Yeah, it's this super-trendy thing where they pour out the liquid cream on a—you know, never mind. How are you?"

"Fine," I answered automatically, as most of us did. But then I stopped myself and thought about it, and I ended up blurting out, "My family doesn't like the guy I'm dating. Or at least, they're not sure about him. Not entirely."

"And you're upset about this? I mean, you care what they think?"

I turned to look at her. "What? Of course I do!"

She gave a little shrug. "I'm sorry, I didn't mean any offense. It's just that you always seem so self-assured and fearless. I mean, the first time I met you, it was via FaceTime while you were walking through an airport somewhere in Italy, I think."

"Milan," I clarified.

"And you seemed like nothing bothered you, so I wasn't sure if something like this would affect you."

"Being confident at work is nothing compared to my family," I said. "And, besides, my career imploded last week, so that tenacity you remember? It's a little shaken at the moment."

"What? Oh my gosh. I'm so sorry."

I gave a quick wave of my hand. "It's fine. I had it coming. Besides, new opportunities are bound to happen, right?"

She eagerly nodded her head. "Do you have any leads?"

"Well, no," I answered. "But I haven't exactly started looking yet. I've been taking a bit of personal time."

"You mean, Aiden time?" She grinned. "I saw the way you two were staring at each other at lunch that day, and Molly has filled me in with all the details since. Sounds like it's going well?"

"Well, if Molly's filled you in, I'm not sure you've gotten all the facts right."

Her eyes were on Lizzie as she rode in circles ahead of us on her scooter. "She did express some concern, but honestly, she is mostly just glad to have you back home."

I breathed in the fresh summer air. "It is good to be back. Even if I am sweating like a pig."

"Yeah, I could definitely use some ice cream."

"Me, too. Let's pick up the pace," I said.

We did and caught up to Lizzie, who had been doing figure eights and circles for some time. Although it practically killed me in this heat, the two of us ran after her, keeping pace with her scooter the rest of the way into town. I'd been keeping in shape since arriving in town but mostly in the morning when the sun had yet to rise and the temperature was at its lowest.

This was insane.

But the light at the end of the tunnel was the ice cream.

I ordered a triple scoop, having no shame in my giant cone as I devoured that sucker before it had even the slightest chance to melt.

"What kind did you get?" Lizzie asked, enjoying her double-chocolate cone with sprinkles.

"Cookie dough, strawberry, and caramel fudge," I answered.

"That's a lot of flavors," she said as she licked her cone in perfect straight lines. She was kind of a strange kid.

I merely shrugged. "I couldn't decide. How come you went with boring chocolate?"

"Because it's the best."

"That's all?" I asked. "I was really hoping for some complicated answer with a hundred different facts."

"Sometimes, the simplest answers are the best," she said plainly.

We sat in silence, all three of us enjoying our treats in the shade. It had been a while since I was this far down on the main road in Ocracoke. Not much had changed, mind you, but I still took my time admiring my hometown. There were a few touristy shops clustered together nearby, and I found myself looking across the street to a sign in one of the windows.

"Hey, is Rita's shop closing down?" I asked Cora.

"Yeah," she answered with a touch of sadness. "At the end of the season. She's retiring to Florida."

"Man, I used to love that store. Do you mind if I pop in for a minute?"

"Not at all. We'll wait for you."

"Great, thanks."

I was already halfway across the street by the time she'd answered, my cone devoured long ago. Beachcombers was a typical store for tourists, but Rita, the store's owner, always carried a small line of clothing that I loved. It was the one place I could go on the island and pick up something to wear that didn't have Ocracoke or the Outer Banks plastered all over it. It was still considered beachwear—it had to be to make a profit here—but it was trendy and cute.

Stepping into the little shop felt like a trip back in time. Very little had changed since my high school days. The inventory had updated here and there to keep with the times, but by and large, it was like walking into a time warp, especially when Rita herself appeared from the backroom. Dressed just as eclectic as ever in a bright polka-dot top and pink pants, the plus-sized beauty hadn't aged a day.

"I heard you were back home!" she said, her voice high-pitched and full of excitement as she opened her arms, demanding a hug I was happy to give. "It's been too long, Millie McIntyre! Why haven't you come to visit me?"

"I'm so sorry, Rita," I apologized. "Time got away from me. I just heard about the shop," I said.

Her face dropped. "I know; it's a shame. But it really is time. I can't keep up anymore, and the truth of the matter is, I don't want to. I just want to be on the beach, drinking mai tais and not having a single care in the world."

I laughed. "Well, Florida is the place to do that."

"That's what I'm counting on," she said, patting her short, dark curls back in place. "But enough about me. Tell me all about you. I hear Florida has been treating you well."

I tried not to let the smile currently plastered on my face falter. "Um, yes," I said. "Very well."

"Well, I expected no less, sugar. I still remember you coming in here, grabbing pieces off the rack and making them your own. Remember that dress you bought, the same one as—"

"Suzy Mathers?"

She grinned. "Yes, wasn't it for a dance?"

"Homecoming," I clarified. "I asked her to take it back since I'd bought it first, and she refused."

"So, what did you do?" she reminded me.

"I redesigned it," I answered, remembering how many hours I'd put into that dress. By the end, it was unrecognizable and a hell of a lot better-looking than Suzy's.

"I hope you're still impressing people with those skills," she said, giving me a final pat on the back as a group of tourists came through the door.

I swallowed hard, looking up at the wall of dresses and skirts she had, and thought back to the tired, old sketchbook on my office desk—the one that held my original sketches and designs.

The one I hadn't touched in years.

Maybe it was time I dusted it off again.

I'd left my sketchbook in Florida.

Of course I had. Because, for the better part of the last

seven years, I'd been helping other people succeed while I patted myself on the back and tried to convince myself a life of travel was indeed the life I had intended for myself.

I mean, who wouldn't want to live out of a suitcase, have a closet most people would die for, and go to fabulous locations, day in and day out?

Sounds amazing, right?

It had been. For a time.

But I had been so busy, so completely immersed in what I was doing, that I didn't realize everything I'd sacrificed for that amazing sounding life.

My family, friends, an actual existence outside of work.

And my dreams.

That sketchbook had begun to collect dust on the office desk I never sat at, and soon, I'd celebrated others' success and forgotten about my own.

I'd forgotten about the girl who stayed up all night, redesigning a simple dress for homecoming into something extraordinary. I'd forgotten that sketchbook and all the wonderful ideas it had nestled inside. And I'd forgotten the woman I wanted to be.

But not anymore.

Marching back to the inn, I didn't let my misplaced sketchbook deter me. Grabbing a blank notebook I found lying around the inn, I took it to the empty parlor and got to work.

Yep, I got right to work.

With a sharp pencil in my hand and a blank notebook, I let the designs flow.

"What the hell?" I said out loud.

"Something wrong?"

I turned to see a very sweaty, very sexy Aiden standing

in the doorway. He'd just come in from the patio, and I smiled, happy that the shirt he'd left there was still absent from his body.

"I went for a walk," I said. "And I came back with all this determination to sketch out some designs, and when I sat down just now, nothing. There's nothing, Aiden. I'm a failure. All my mojo is gone."

His hands fell to my shoulders, massaging away the tension I'd developed from the frustration I'd built throughout the day. I nearly groaned as his fingers worked my tired muscles.

"You can't force creativity," he said.

"You just did." I pouted.

He chuckled behind me, deep and low. "Do you want to see what I accomplished today?"

"Yes, very much so."

I really did. I was always curious when it came to Aiden's work.

He pulled me off the couch, and I followed him to the backyard, toward my dad's old shed.

"What the heck?" I said.

There before us was the same chunk of rock that had been delivered that morning.

"Did you do anything?" I asked.

He pulled me toward him, his hands wrapping around my waist. "Yes, I did actually."

"Are you sure?" My eyebrow rose.

"Always the cruncher," he sighed.

"I should have never used that stupid M&M metaphor on you. You're going to use it on me for the rest of our lives."

He just smiled. "Now, back to your sketchbook. Give it time. Have you tried doing something relaxing? That always helps me."

"Do you have something in mind?"

Flipping me around, he gave me a wicked grin before bending over. It was the only warning I got before he abruptly tossed me over his shoulder, and the world went topsy-turvy.

"Aiden!" I screamed.

"No yelling." He laughed. "This is supposed to be relaxing!"

"I'm upside down!"

"Yes," he said. "Good for the blood flow. Now, grab the key out of my pocket. We're going to take a shower."

I did as he'd demanded, shoving my hand in his front pocket, not an easy task when I was upside down and being jostled around.

"Oh, careful." He laughed as my fingers got a little too close to the family jewels. "Actually, move your hand a little to the right, love."

Suddenly, Aiden froze in the middle of the foyer, his hand firmly on my ass, as my fingers, still in his pocket, crept toward his hardening cock.

"Uh, hello, Mrs. McIntyre."

I lifted my head and found my mom staring back at me.

"Hey, Mom," I said sheepishly.

Her eyes went briefly to Aiden's hand and my ass before focusing back on mine.

"As much as it pains me to do so, I must remind you that the inn is a place of business and—"

"We'll keep it behind closed doors, Mom," I said, swatting Aiden on the behind like a prized steed.

"Lovely to see you again," Aiden said, always the gentleman.

We left to my mother's laughter ringing out behind us.

I'd laughed all the way back to Aiden's suite.

His reaction had been a little less than amused, but after a little encouragement, I'd managed to get him back in the mood for a sexy and very relaxing shower for two.

"Remind me to thank my sister for springing for the dual showerhead. That thing is amazing," I hollered to him from the bedroom as I rummaged through a few of the things I'd brought over earlier.

I'd all but moved in, abandoning my own room in favor of Aiden's. We hadn't really discussed this new living arrangement, but he'd seemed to be pleased when he saw the large stack of my clothes appear on his dresser this morning.

I hadn't had time yet to organize any of it though, and it was proving to be a difficult process as the once tidy stacks were toppling over onto the floor while I tried to juggle the towel tied around my boobs and the too-tall tower of panties and shorts.

Silk was my ultimate downfall, and I was thankful Aiden was still in the bathroom drying off, as everything went tumbling to the floor.

Including my towel.

"Damn it," I muttered, reaching for the towel as I bent down to pick up my mess.

I smiled to myself as I caught a glimpse of Aiden's clothes strewed about nearby, remembering the way I'd ripped them off his sweaty body less than an hour earlier.

I let out a happy sigh.

Next to his shorts, a shiny black wallet had fallen out

and faced upward toward the ceiling. Not wanting anything to fall out, I grabbed it, and with all the best intentions, I meant to set it on the dresser for him to pick up when he got out of the bathroom.

I never meant to look.

But something caught my eye, and I couldn't help myself; I peeked.

There, beneath a clear plastic protector, was a driver's license.

My brows furrowed in confusion.

He'd said he didn't have a license. It was why I'd driven him around town that first full day and all the way to Mount Airy. Shaking my head, I tried to make sense of it. Maybe it was expired. Lots of people in New York had expired licenses, right?

He'd even said that, hadn't he?

And there was that *Friends* episode where Rachel's license expired, wasn't there? So, I mean, if it happened on *Friends*…

Searching for a date didn't take long, and when I found it, my heart sank. It was current.

Why had he lied to me?

"Millie, what do you really know about this guy?"

Jake's words came crashing back at that moment as I folded the wallet and set it on the dresser. Swallowing my doubt, I listened to Aiden move about the bathroom, and I closed my eyes.

I know enough, I said to myself.

And I trust him.

"Millie?"

My eyelids parted, and I found him staring at me with concern.

"Everything all right?"

Giving him a warm smile, I nodded. "Yes. Perfect."

"Good," he said, leaning into the doorframe, his dark hair still wet from our long shower together "Because I want to take you out to dinner."

"Out?"

"Yeah," he said. "What's odd about that?"

I just smiled, continuing my task of reorganizing my clothes. He watched my effort, and I couldn't help but laugh as his eyes seemed to follow every undergarment I touched.

"Going out to dinner in Ocracoke isn't quite the same as it is in New York."

"Oh? Do I need to ask permission from your father? Send you a written invitation first? Or should I arrive at your house in a horse and buggy?"

I pressed my lips together and gave him an exasperated look. "You're in a small town in the South, not 1864."

"Well then, explain the difference please. I'm afraid my Orphan Annie upbringing hasn't adequately prepared me on how to properly date a Southern Belle." For the last few words, he did his best impression of a Southern accent. It was horrible.

I rolled my eyes. "You're ridiculous."

"Have I mentioned that I worked outside all day? I'm famished, love."

"You know, that's the first time you've called me that when it hasn't directly related to sex." I grinned.

"Is not," he said.

My head bobbed up and down. "Is too."

His eyes narrowed. "Well, you are almost naked. Are you trying to get out of having a lovely meal with me?"

"What if we pack a picnic and head to the beach?"

His face sobered slightly.

"At night?" he asked.

I looked to the window and the sun that would soon be setting behind it. "Um, yes. That would be the intention. There's this great local spot I can take you. It's a little bit of a hike, but if we leave now, we can get there before it gets dark."

"And how will we get back?"

I shrugged. "There should be enough moonlight."

He quickly shook his head. "No." I could see the wheels in his head working. Thinking. Calculating. "You know, we've done things kind of backward."

"Backward?"

"Backward," he confirmed, stepping forward. I could see determination locked in his gaze. "We slept together. Then, we took a trip together, and I met your family. All that, and we haven't had a decent meal together."

"We had that lovely meal at that barbecue joint in North Carolina," I replied. "And several meals in New York."

He shook his head. "We barely touched our food at that dive in North Carolina. We were too amped up on the sexual tension building between us."

"Mmm," was all I could say.

"And I'll admit, the food we ate in New York was excellent, but I was trying to be showy and took you to some of the most well-known places I could think of, which is why I couldn't hear anything you said the entire time."

"Oh good, I thought that was just me!" I laughed.

He took my hands. "So, please, can I just take my girl out for a nice, quiet meal, where we can enjoy each other's company over a bottle of wine? And maybe, if that girl is lucky, I'll buy her an ice cream cone on the way home."

"Well"—I grinned—"since you threw ice cream in the deal."

He squeezed my hands, leaning forward to place a kiss on my lips. The rough hair along his chin scraped against my cheek; a small price to pay to have his mouth on mine.

"But I'm warning you, you and I will be the talk of the town tomorrow."

"The whole town?"

I lifted my brow as I nodded. "Welcome to Ocracoke."

He smiled, kissing me once more. "As long as everyone knows you're taken, I'm *okay* with a little talk." He put a little more emphasis on the word *okay* and threw in a wink before heading back to the bathroom.

I was full of grins, on a high of love…

Until I saw his wallet dangling on the edge of the dresser.

"Millie, what do you really know about this guy?"

Now that I'd seen that valid and very current license in his wallet, a seed of doubt had been planted and I wasn't sure how I could stop it from growing without confronting him.

Did I want to know the truth?

And would things change once I did?

That was the real question.

CHAPTER THIRTEEN

Aiden

"**A**RE YOU CERTAIN YOUR FATHER ISN'T CROSS with me?" I asked as Millie dragged me to the patio, which had been drenched in red, white, and blue streamers for today's festivities.

"For what? Bailing in the middle of dinner before you two could be properly introduced? Or shacking up with his daughter for the past two weeks and not bothering to say hello since?"

I gulped. "Either. Either will do. But we've been introduced. Remember that morning when I cooked them breakfast? That counts, right?"

"Ah, yes. But you weren't screwing me then."

I grimaced. "Could you not say screwing, so close to him?"

She rolled her eyes. "It's not like he has superpowers or anything. He can't hear us, Aiden. And, besides, he offered his shed, didn't he?"

I glanced out the window, feeling guilty for not going to him sooner, but I didn't know how to interact with fathers. Or mothers.

Or families for that matter.

"He hasn't been around," I replied defensively, feeling like the ultimate failure in front of the woman I cared for most in this world. "I would have gladly introduced myself if I'd seen him—"

Millie turned and stopped, a warm smile on her face as I tried to ignore the patio full of people who had gathered for the Fourth of July celebration the inn put on each year. "I'm messing with you. Honestly, he hasn't been around much because, unlike my mother, he isn't enjoying this little respite in their retirement. He'd much rather be watching golf or reading or basically be anywhere but here."

"And your mother is just happy to be back in that kitchen again?"

"Now, you're getting it." Her arms wrapped around my waist. "Why are you so nervous? It's a family cookout with a few extras thrown in."

My eyes darted to the window just over her shoulder.

Where I was from, family cookout consisted of my brothers and me huddled in a circle in the yard, making mud pies.

"Yes, exactly."

A comforting hand reached up to cup my face. "I'm sorry, Aiden. Forgive my insensitivity. Of course you'd be nervous. But don't worry; it's going to be great. The food supply will never end; Mom and Molly will make sure of that. Neither will the booze for that matter, thanks to Billy," she said, giving a nod in the direction of the familiar restaurant owner, who was busy tapping a keg outside. "And I'll be here to kiss you when the fireworks begin."

"You promise?"

She leaned in, her smile turning to a series of tiny kisses

against my lips. "Yes."

"Then, that's all the motivation I need. Let's go before we make your family vomit," I said, raising an eyebrow toward the patio.

She turned to see several members of her family desperately trying to avoid her gaze.

"Nosy little jerks," she muttered, making me laugh. "You know we could always spend the evening indoors."

"I don't think so," I countered. "Besides, this is my adopted homeland. I must pay my respects and wish it a happy birthday like a true American."

"With beer and copious amounts of explosives?" She laughed, grabbing my arm as we headed for the patio.

"Exactly."

The moment we walked out into the blazing heat, I took a look around and was immediately amazed by the sheer number of people.

"It looks like the whole town is here," I said to Millie.

"Damn near close," she replied, waving to several people.

"Mr. and Mrs. Lovell!" Millie exclaimed, leaving my side to greet an elderly couple. She wrapped her arms around them with a warm familiarity before turning to me. "This is Aiden," she said, pulling me into the small circle.

"Oh, we've already heard so much about you," Mr. Lovell said, a genuine smile on his worn face.

That surprised me a bit. Surely, they were just trying to keep me part of the conversation, so I didn't feel left out.

"Mr. and Mrs. Lovell have been coming to the inn since I was a kid," Millie informed me.

"Oh, before that, I'd wager," Mrs. Lovell said.

"But you don't usually come in the middle of the

summer, do you?"

Mr. Lovell, a laid-back sort of fellow dressed in khaki shorts and a Hawaiian shirt, shook his head. "No, not since the kids were young anyway. We try to avoid the rush and come in the late spring or later in the summer, but when we heard your parents were coming out of retirement?" He lifted his arms and shrugged. "Well, we couldn't pass that up."

"Plus, you get to see the newest addition to the McIntyre and Jameson clans," Millie said, motioning to her sister, who was gently rocking her newborn to sleep inside.

"Yes," Mrs. Lovell said, following Millie's lead. "She's beautiful. We just became grandparents for the ninth time last month. It never gets old."

We continued to make small talk for a few more minutes. Mr. Lovell, like most, took an interest in my work.

"It's a shame about the memorial," he said. "That sort of thing never happens in Ocracoke. Do the police have any leads?"

Millie shook her head, fiddling with her necklace as she spoke, "No. Macon Greene, one of the police officers in town, said the cameras down there were all pointed toward the ferry and not the memorial—something they're working on rectifying. But it's just awful; Aiden's sculpture was breathtaking."

The Lovells agreed.

"We were here shortly after the dedication last year. The way you captured grief." He paused. "You must have lost someone very close to you."

My chin lifted as I tried not to avert my gaze. "Haven't we all?" I said.

He patted me on the shoulder before they excused themselves to refill their drinks. "We look forward to seeing the new one on our next trip in the spring, son."

I simply nodded as I watched them walk away.

"Do you think it will be ready by then?" Millie asked.

"What? The memorial?"

Her eyes went to the back of the yard where I'd covered the granite in a large gray tarp.

"Of course," I answered, knowing it was a complete lie.

The first one had taken me nine months, and that hadn't been dedicated time. Because I'd chosen to work only with primitive tools and not saws or electric blades, everything had moved extra slow, but it was how I had been taught, both by Ben and my mentor. On the original memorial, I'd worked on it intermittently with many other projects sandwiched in between because I needed the steady income.

Now that I had the money from my gallery showing, I could afford to dedicate one hundred percent of my time to this one project, but even then, I couldn't guarantee it would be done in a year. My gut churned.

Or at all.

Not when my—

"Hey," Millie called out, interrupting my thoughts. "You have that faraway look in your eyes."

I smiled warmly, tearing my gaze away from the granite pillar in the back of the yard and back to the beautiful woman in front of me.

"I believe I was promised never-ending liquor and food today," I said, making her grin almost immediately.

"Yes, I believe you were." She tugged on my hand and dragged me to the large card tables decked out in checkered tablecloths. "Right this way," she said.

Every inch of the table was covered in food.

"Please tell me your sister didn't cook all of this."

"Not all, no," she answered. "But a lot of it. Some was brought by guests because who shows up to a cookout without bringing a side dish?"

"No one?" I answered, unsure of the right answer since I'd never attended a cookout, nor had I ever heard of the word *cookout* before this morning.

"Exactly."

We grabbed plates and began picking and choosing what went on them. I mostly just mimicked Millie because I didn't recognize half of what was being offered. Three-quarters of it was some sort of casserole, and the rest was some sort of meat.

But it all smelled delicious, which was more than I could say for the majority of the food I had been raised on, so I was happy to try just about anything.

"Hey," Millie whined as I scooped up a helping of fresh green salad and dropped it on her plate.

"You don't have a single vegetable on your plate," I protested.

She looked down. "Sure I do. See?" She was pointing to a casserole with a scattering of corn covered in cheese.

"That does not count."

"I don't like salad!"

"What will it take for a small one? Just a serving?" I asked, grabbing the tongs and snapping them shut like alligator teeth in front of her.

She simply rolled her eyes but gave in to my games. "You so owe me. The things I'm going to make you do to me tonight..." Letting out an exasperated sigh, she continued, "Fine, but know this salad is about to be covered in a considerable amount of ranch dressing."

I tried not to laugh. "It's a start."

We made our way to a grouping of tables that had been set out for today's event. Seated across from us were Dean, Cora, and Jake.

"Hey, guys!" Dean greeted us. "Happy Fourth!"

"Hey Dean, Cora!" Millie said, giving a double wave after she set down her heavy plate.

I noticed she specifically hadn't said hi to her brother-in-law, and I wondered if there was something going on there that I didn't know about. But, before I even had the chance to think it through, she was already shifting gears.

"I'm going to go get drinks. Please don't embarrass Aiden too much before I get back!"

I settled into my seat, giving a polite nod as they looked on. "I wonder if she knows that, by calling me out, I actually feel more embarrassed."

They all looked at each other and grinned.

"Oh, she knows." Jake laughed.

I nodded my head. "I should have known. Little minx. So, what were you talking about before I sat down and made things awkward?"

"Oh, you didn't make things awkward, but we were actually discussing our wedding plans," Dean said.

"Oh, lovely. When is the big day?" I asked, happy to discuss anything that didn't revolve around me.

"The day after Christmas," Dean answered confidently.

His bride though didn't look so sure.

"Why do I feel like I walked into the middle of an argument?"

Dean chuckled. "It's not an argument. Cora wants a winter wedding and with her daughter—"

"Our daughter," Cora corrected him.

"Our daughter's"—he smiled warmly—"school

schedule, Christmas time is the perfect time to do it. Everyone is already gathered together."

I nodded. "Plus the added bonus of built-in decorations."

His eyes fell to his fiancée, whose face scrunched. "You would think that, huh?"

"Not into Christmas decor?" I asked,

"Remember how I geeked out over your accent at the restaurant that one day over lunch?"

I chuckled. "How could I forget? Who do I sound like again? Was it The Doctor, Harry Potter, or someone from *Sherlock Holmes*?"

"*Sherlock Holmes*! I didn't even think of that one!" she exclaimed.

Dean wrapped an arm around his soon-to-be wife as Jake just chuckled in the background. I wondered what was taking Millie so long but immediately caught a glimpse of her at the drink table, chatting it up with Billy. She'd once told me during one of our late-night chats that you couldn't go anywhere in this town without being derailed by someone.

Apparently, that also included getting drinks at a cookout.

"I'm going to just stop right here and apologize for my fiancée. What's she's trying to say is, our wedding isn't going to be a normal one."

"So, like a comic-book wedding dress and a lightsaber cake?"

Jake's laugh grew, and from the yelp he let out, I was guessing his mate Dean had kicked him under the table.

"Just ask him how he proposed," Jake managed to say before Dean replied to my question, "I'm sure, if her dad had his way, that's how it would go. Cora's interests tend to be more book-centered, and mine lie in the ocean, being a fisherman and all. So, we're having the ceremony at the marina and the reception here. Lots of stacked vintage books and shells."

"Well, there's nothing geeky about that," I said.

"We might throw in some lightsabers in the end." Cora added.

"There we go." I laughed.

"What are we talking about?" Millie asked as she finally returned, carrying two large red cups filled to the brim with beer.

"Dean and Cora's crazy wedding," Jake answered with a wry grin.

"Yeah, when is that?" Millie asked.

"December twenty-sixth," I answered. "Or is it?"

Dean and Cora looked at each other, some sort of couple communication passing between them.

"Yeah, I think it is," Cora finally said. "Who cares if it is a crazy time of the year?"

"Exactly," Millie said, raising her glass to the happy couple. "Love is crazy."

I turned to her, realizing I'd thought those exact same words about our relationship.

"You couldn't be more right, Millie McIntyre," I said, holding up my glass to hers as our eyes met with a raw intensity. "Love is indeed a crazy adventure."

As our glasses touched, our mouths did the same, fusing together as beer sloshed down our hands. Neither of us cared because this was as close to a declaration of love as either of us had been brave enough to make.

And didn't that deserve its own toast and moment in the sun?

The sun had begun its descent into the horizon, and the anticipation for the annual Ocracoke Independence Day fireworks celebration was palpable.

"Come on," Millie said, her eyes gleaming. "Let's grab a blanket and spread it out on the grass."

I didn't have a chance to agree before she darted inside and flew back out the patio door half a second later, a large plaid blanket in hand, ready for action.

As she walked back toward me from the house, I took those moments to appreciate just how lucky I was. I'd come to this island, lost and alone, ready to give up on just about everything—my career, my future, and everything in between.

Millie, this smart, sassy woman, had breathed life back into me, and I knew I wouldn't have such a positive outlook on my prognosis if it wasn't for her.

"You're looking awfully sappy, Aiden Fisher. What's going on in that mind of yours?" she asked, tilting her head to the side as she brought her hand to her forehead to block out the setting sun.

I caught her smiling and couldn't help but do the same.

"What were you doing on this day last year?"

I wasn't sure why I'd asked, but she seemed to go with it all the same.

"Hmm." She handed me one side of the blanket while she kept the other. We raised it high in the air before neatly setting it on the grass below. "On the Fourth of July last year, I was in Paris, I think."

I raised my eyebrows as we both took a seat on the soft blanket. "That sounds horrible," I joked.

"Honestly? It was." Her eyes flickered to her parents huddled together on their own blanket nearby, sipping wine and laughing, as we all waited for the show to begin. "I was in a hotel room with a serious case of jet lag, and outside of a few people I knew from work, I didn't know anyone in the city. I remember sitting on that hotel bed, my hands running over the ridiculously high thread count sheets as I stared out at Paris. I should have been happy, you know? How many people get to live that life? But, in that moment, all I wanted to do was be in my childhood bed, roasting marshmallows like we had done when I was a kid."

"So, you much more prefer this over Paris?"

She leaned back on her elbows and gazed up at the sky, a glorious array of pinks and yellows. "Definitely. But not just for the marshmallows."

"I don't believe I've actually seen any." I grinned.

"Oh, just you wait. Have you ever even had a s'more?"

I sort of shrugged. "There was this place in SoHo that had this dessert—"

She sat up cross-legged and waved her hands. "No. Absolutely no. That doesn't even remotely count. Unless it was made in the wilderness or in your own damn backyard, it is not truly a s'more."

"So many rules."

She laughed. "Yes. And here comes another one. You can't watch fireworks without a drink in your hand."

I suspiciously eyed her. "That one sounds made up."

She shrugged. "You'll never really know, will you? But can you make mine a rosé?"

I leaned forward and planted a quick kiss on her lips. "I think you're full of rubbish."

"Pull that one out of the old English slang archives, did

you?" She laughed, palming my cheek.

"I did," I answered with a wide grin. "But that one was rather tame. Most of what my brother and I threw around wasn't exactly proper and usually revolved around sex."

She just stared.

"I grew up with a bunch of boys. Do you really have to ask?"

"That's actually kind of interesting."

I shook my head. "No, it's not."

"Sure it is," she countered. "Who knows? Maybe I might need this information sometime in my life. How do you say balls in England?"

I looked at her straight-faced and answered, "Balls."

Her head tilted to the side as she playfully hit my shoulder. "You know that's not what I meant! Come on! I want to know some slang! Teach me!"

"Nope," I answered. "I promised you I'd go refill your drink before the fireworks, and I am a man who keeps his word." I rose from my spot on our blanket. "Now, if you'll excuse me."

She looked up at me, her bottom lip protruding out, making her look ridiculous.

I rolled my eyes before heading towards the drinks station but stopped myself mid-step. Turning back around, I found her in the same position.

Same pitiful look.

"*Bollocks* is the conventional slang you'll hear often. But there is also the lesser knowns—nadgers, acorns and goolies. If you're referring to the whole package though, you might want to go with *John Thomas*."

Millie's high pitched laughter that followed behind me was infectious, and I couldn't help the smile that spread across my face as I went to retrieve our drinks. I had a feeling this wouldn't be the end of Millie's British slang education.

Not by a long shot.

Reaching into the ice chest for the pink bottle of wine Millie loved, I poured a decent amount in her wine glass before grabbing a beer for myself. Just as I was about to return to our spot on the lawn, I saw Mr. McIntyre walking toward the drink area, two glasses in hand.

Apparently fetching drinks for the women in the family was a lifelong obligation.

I had two choices—either stay or make like a tree and leave, thereby delaying my second and most important introduction with Millie's father as the new boyfriend. Only a coward would duck his head and run, and I didn't want Mr. McIntyre thinking his daughter was dating a spineless jerk.

"Mr. McIntyre," I said, placing the drinks on the table beside me to offer my hand in greeting, "I know we haven't been formally introduced…well, not since I—"

"I know who you are," he said, a pleasant smile on his face. He gave a nod to my outstretched hand but kept on toward the table with the task of refilling his drinks. "You'll find I'm not nearly as formal as most other yahoos."

Yahoos? Is that even a word?

"That's good to hear. I'm not big on it myself."

He continued to pour his wine, and I smiled to myself, seeing Millie's mother had an affinity for the same wine as her daughter.

"Really?" Mr. McIntyre said. "I always thought the English were sticklers for propriety."

"Not when you were raised in the system."

He set down his glass and eyed me. "Foster kid, huh?"

I simply nodded.

"Is it much like it is here? Foster care, I mean."

I sort of shrugged. "I guess it depends on where you end up and with whom," I said. "There are people who mean well and have their heart in it and those who don't. Unfortunately, in the city where I grew up, I think the heartless outweighed those in it for the right reasons, and I wasn't given the best upbringing, but at least I had brothers. Foster brothers. And that made it bearable."

He nodded silently to himself, thinking for a moment before replying, "Well, I don't know much about that, but I do know what it's like to grow up poor. Dirt poor. The only reason I was able to go to college was because I could throw a football. And thank God for that; otherwise, I wouldn't have met her." His eyes drifted to his wife.

"It all worked out," I found myself saying, my own gaze finding Millie.

He agreed, "It did, but there were days early on in our marriage where I would work myself to the bone, scared to death we'd run out of money—or worse, I'd fail the legacy her parents had given to us with this inn. I didn't stop working, didn't stop moving, until Molly took over a few years ago." He chuckled under his breath. "I think I've spent more hours sleeping in these precious years of retirement than I have in my whole life."

I joined him in laughter.

"I know the feeling," I said. "I just earned my biggest payout on a show in my career."

"Will it hold you?" His voice held the concern of a father.

"For a while," I answered. "For a good long while."

Our eyes met and held.

"And then? What's your next move?"

I knew where he was going, what he was asking.

Are you going to leave Millie high and dry after this job finishes?

What are your real intentions with my baby girl?

This was my opportunity to put his doubts to rest.

"I don't know," I answered honestly. "Over the last few weeks, my priorities have shifted. My career is still important, but it's no longer the primary focus in my life. Millie is. So, where I sculpt no longer matters as long as she is next to me."

His gaze narrowed, until, finally, a large hand rose up to my shoulder, pulling me into a welcoming hug. "That's all I needed to hear. But, if you could talk her into staying here, I'd buy you a house as a wedding present," he said in a low whisper, patting my back before stepping back.

My eyes widened in shock.

"Enjoy the fireworks," he said before taking his wine and heading off toward the grass. He looked over his shoulder and gave me a thumbs-up.

I followed his lead, grabbing the beer and wine off the table and walking back to Millie.

"Looks like you and my dad were having a meaningful talk over there," she said as I took a seat and handed over her rosé.

"I'm pretty sure he offered to buy me a house."

"What?"

"Nothing," I said.

"Oh! The fireworks are starting!" She cuddled up to me, both of us ignoring the ridiculously humid temperatures as the first firework lit up the sky.

"What were you doing on this day last year?" she asked.

I thought back, trying to remember my Independence Day a year ago.

"You're smiling," she said.

"That's because I just realized what I was doing at this moment one year ago."

"If you say banging another chick, I will literally end you right here."

I chuckled as the memory floated back in my mind. I could still feel the sweat dripping down my face as the sounds of fireworks had lit off in New York while I worked in my studio. "I was putting the finishing touches on the memorial."

"Our memorial?" she asked, looking up at me, her face aglow from the lights above.

I nodded. "I chiseled the last part of the bird at the base just as the fireworks ended that night."

"Wow," she said, her gaze turning upward. "I know this is horrible, but I'm really glad some asshat destroyed that thing."

A smile stretched all the way across my face as my chin rested on top of her head. "Yeah, me too."

Me, freaking, too.

The sun had barely risen over the water when I rose the next morning, its golden rays sending glittery flecks of sunlight across the top of the water for miles. Millie still slept soundly next to me, a tribute to how thoroughly she'd enjoyed herself the day before. Usually, she was the one poking me in the ribs, calling me lazybones and telling me to wake up and grab a morning run with her.

I savored this rare treat, watching her chest rise and fall and the peaceful way her mouth parted just ever so slightly as she dreamed. I silently chuckled to myself, wondering if her dreams were of giant dancing s'mores. God, that woman loved her junk food.

I was going to have to learn how to hide some spinach in her food. That, or figure out how to make her love some sort of vegetable.

Careful not to make a sound, I shifted out of the bed and made quick work of throwing on a pair of jeans and a T-shirt.

No need to scare any of the other guests by running around half-naked through the inn.

Not that any of them were up.

Grabbing my phone, I stepped out into the hallway and headed for the patio. The house was quiet, but the old floors creaked under my bare feet. Making my way across the parlor, I opened the door that led out to the large patio and stepped out, the heat blasting me in the face almost instantly.

"Damn," I muttered. "Starting early today."

Taking a seat in a chair nearby, I stretched my legs out in front of me and took a moment to appreciate the view. Beyond the patio, bright green grass spread out in front of me before giving way to sand.

And then there was nothing but water as far as the eye could see.

Millie called it a bay, but from where I was sitting, it might as well have been the whole damn ocean because the view seemed endless.

I could have sat here all morning, staring at that view, but I'd come out here with a purpose. Pulling out my phone,

I dialed a number and waited.

"Do you know what fucking time it is?"

I grinned. "Why yes, I do. Good morning."

"Jesus, why are you so bloody chipper?"

"It's the day after a holiday. Don't people usually get those off?" I asked, leaning back in the chair.

"What? No, not the Fourth. Those of us who aren't temperamental artists actually have to go in and work today."

"Oh," I said. Why didn't I know that? "Well then, consider me your alarm clock."

James groaned. "My alarm clock was set to go off in an hour."

Pulling the phone away from me, I checked the time once more. "Really? An hour from now? Isn't that kind of late? What kind of doctor are you?"

"A tired one."

I let out a laugh.

"Seriously, Aiden, what do you want?"

I blew air out through my teeth. "Help," I answered. "I'm ready to ask for help." I looked out at the view before me, squinting more than I had a few weeks before, and I knew I needed it.

A solid few seconds went by. "Are you serious?"

"I am."

"What changed your mind?" he asked. I could hear him rustling. Obviously, he had decided to get out of bed after all.

"You know what."

"So, you told her?"

I swallowed hard, the blue water of the bay winking back at me. "No," I replied.

"What? Why?"

"I…" I couldn't find my words. No, that wasn't true. I knew exactly what I wanted to say. I was just ashamed to say it. "I just want to be me a little while longer," I confessed.

I could hear him sigh on the other end. "You'll always be you, Aiden."

"No," I argued. "Once I tell her, I'll be different. I'll never be this Aiden again. I'll be a different version of myself. And, for now, I want to be uncomplicated Aiden—the guy I hope she is falling in love with."

"All right," he relented.

"So, you'll help me?"

"Of course I'll help you! I've been trying to help you from the very beginning! It's you who's been avoiding—"

"I get it," I said, making him chuckle. "So, what do we do now?"

"Why don't you come home and—"

I adamantly shook my head. "No."

"But, Aiden, I need to be able to examine you. To retest and see how much worse it's gotten and then come up with a plan."

"Then, come here."

"To North Carolina?" He sounded incredulous.

"Yes. Why not?"

"Well, for starters—"

"Can we figure it out? That's all I need to know."

He breathed out a sigh of frustration. I could hear his wheels turning from here. "I guess I could figure something out. It might take me a few weeks though. Your case isn't exactly textbook. If you were a fifty-year-old patient coming into my office, I'd know exactly what to do, but you're not. You're thirty-three, and this is—"

"Rare. I get it."

"I'm sorry," he sighed. "Yes, I can do it. I'll research everything. I've already put some feelers out, trying to get in contact with a couple of colleagues who've had similar patients. But can I ask why? Why are you so intent on not coming home?"

I paused for a moment, my gaze focused on the lawn and the sparkling water beyond. "Because this is my home now, James. With her."

"And when your brother shows up to help you out with this mystery medical problem you haven't told her about?"

"Let me handle that," I said. "Just worry about your end."

"Okay," he said.

This time, it was me who chuckled, hearing my brother say the word that drove Millie crazy.

"What?"

"It doesn't sound odd when you say it," I said before hanging up on my clueless brother.

I rose from the chair and slid my phone back in my pocket. With one last glance at the bay, I headed back toward my suite.

To Millie.

James had said it might take him a few weeks, which meant my time as this Aiden was limited.

It always had been, but now, it felt real.

I'd always known I'd eventually have to tell her, but knowing and doing were two very different things.

And the closer I got to the reality of it, the more scared I became.

CHAPTER FOURTEEN

Millie

"IS THIS YOUR DAILY ROUTINE NOW?" MY SISTER'S voice filled the parlor as her quick steps came up behind me.

"Nice to see you, too," I replied, leaning back in the plush sofa chair I'd repositioned to face the large glass windows that overlooked the backyard and bay. "What about you? Is this *your* daily routine? Showing up after breakfast to inspect Mom's handling of things?"

I glanced up to see her standing next to me, Ruby snuggling up to her chest in one of those infant carrier devices that always baffled me.

Molly's mouth hung open until she finally turned. "I do not—that's not why I'm here."

I made a sound of disbelief that closely resembled something I'd heard Ruby make the other day when spitting up milk.

"Well, at least I don't sit here all day, swooning over my boyfriend."

"I'm not swooning," I answered.

"Oh, so you're not sitting here staring at him while he…"

She glanced out toward the shed. "Hey, where'd he go?"

I put my pencil down, a little put off that my sister hadn't noticed any of the work I had spread out in front of me. "Didn't you hear?"

"Hear what? Oh my gosh, he didn't leave, did he? If he did, I swear to God, I will track him down and—"

Crossing my arms in front of my chest, I turned. "He didn't leave."

"Oh," she simply said. "Well, that's good because I don't think I'm in my best fighting condition yet after giving birth." Pink tinted her cheeks, showing her embarrassment.

"It's good to know you've grown confident in Aiden's and my relationship though."

"I have!" she argued as I pivoted away, readying to gather up my stuff. "Millie, I'm sorry. I just—maybe it's a knee-jerk reaction."

"Why? Because I'm not worth hanging around for?"

"No," she answered. Her hand touched my arm, pulling me back toward her. "Because I wasn't."

I let out a deep sigh.

Now, it was me who felt like a jerk.

Jake and Molly had been high school sweethearts until one day, after the devastating death of his mother, Jake walked away.

From his family, his hometown, and most importantly, Molly.

"I thought you were over all that."

Her eyes rounded with warmth. "I am," she said. "Well, ninety-nine-point-nine percent of me is, but there will always be the tiniest sliver of doubt."

Doubt.

The word resonated with me so much. Ever since I'd

gazed down at that valid driver's license, a tiny piece of mistrust had been lodged in my heart.

"How do you ignore it?" I asked.

"That's just it; you can't. By ignoring it, you allow that doubt to grow and fester inside you."

"So, you face it head-on," I said. "Why am I not surprised? Is there anything you're bad at?"

She smiled, ignoring my question. "Jake and I talk about it sometimes, yes. It helps reassure me that he's not going to up and leave again."

"If he did, I'd be the one running after him to kick some ass."

Her smile widened. "I wouldn't expect any less. Now, what is this news I didn't hear?"

"Oh." My gaze turned to the shed. "Daddy and Aiden hit it off so well after their talk at the party the other day that, apparently, he's become kind of an apprentice to Aiden."

"You're kidding."

"I really wish I were," I said.

"Our father, the one who has basically made napping in hammocks a full-time profession?" She laughed.

"Don't forget golfing. That man loves his time in Myrtle Beach."

"Right," she agreed. "How could I forget? So, where are they?"

"Well, that's the other part of the news. Daddy felt bad that Aiden had been working so long out in the sun."

"Meaning Daddy didn't want to work out in the sun himself." Molly laughed.

"That's probably more accurate. Anyway, he went out and bought an air-conditioning unit for the shed—one of those window units—and put it in himself, so they'd have somewhere to rest because, up until now, Aiden would just sit out in the shade, refusing to come inside because of all the dust. So, now, the shed is like their little man cave."

"Well, I'll be damned."

"That was pretty much my reaction as well," I said, leaning back in the seat.

"Does it bother you that your boyfriend and Dad are so chummy?"

I thought about it for a moment, picturing Aiden as a little boy with no family to speak of for so long. "No," I finally answered. "Aiden doesn't have a father; he never did. He's more than welcome to share mine. That is, if it's okay with you."

Looking up at her, I saw a warm smile spread across her face.

"Perfectly okay," she replied. "Now, what is all this?" she asked, pointing to the sketches I'd been working on all morning.

It was about time she noticed.

"Oh, just some ideas I've been playing with," I said, waving my hand in front of me like I didn't care that she'd taken a whole ten minutes to ask.

In reality, I was dying to show them off.

She reached for one of my favorites, a long maxi-style dress with cutout detailing on the sides and a stunning back. "This is gorgeous," she said. "Very beachy. Is that what you were going for?"

My eyes drifted to the view in front of me. "I guess I was just inspired by my surroundings."

"It reminds me of that dress—do you remember the one I'm talking about?"

"My homecoming dress?"

She nodded. "I still have it. It was hanging in the closet in our room for the longest time, and I found it when I went to clean it out before Cora and Lizzie used the rooms last year. It's hanging in my closet now, if you ever want to try it on again."

I rolled my eyes. "Oh, please, like it'd even fit."

She gave me a hard stare. "Don't even, little sister. Your figure hasn't budged an inch since high school. Don't ask me how, considering the crap you eat, but I'm quite certain that dress would look just as good on you now as it did back then."

"Hmm, I would like to take it down to Rita's shop and show it to her before she closes up, for old time's sake. When I was down there a few weeks ago, she mentioned it. It would be kind of fun to even give it to her as a going-away present."

"She would love that. You were always her favorite, growing up."

"I know," I said, looking down at my sketches. "She tried to get me to work in the store on several occasions, but I was terrified of getting tied down. I didn't want anything standing in the way of my exit strategy."

Molly simply rolled her eyes, but then something changed. Like a lightbulb flipping on inside her head. "What if you bought the store?"

My brows furrowed and I wondered if, instead of a lightbulb turning on, it had actually exploded instead.

"Say what now?"

She turned, pulled up a chair, and sat down next to me. I guess this was going to be a deep conversation.

"Hear me out, okay? You're unemployed, right?"

"Yep, thanks for pointing that out again. By the way,

why hasn't Mom or Dad said anything about the fact that I've been home for weeks without any plans to go back to Florida?"

My sister's face turned red.

"You told them, didn't you?"

"Maybe. But don't be—"

"Honestly, I don't even care. I mean, what was I going to do? Keep lying? One can only have so much vacation saved up. But please tell me you at least kept the part about my boss to yourself?"

"Yes. Oh God, yes. Mom and Dad do not need to know about you boinking your boss. Dad would have a heart attack for sure."

I made a sour face. "Could you please refrain from using the word *boink* around my niece? Or anyone. Gross."

She laughed. "Anyway, back to the store. I heard from someone in town that she still doesn't have a buyer, which means the store will be empty after she leaves in September. It's a perfect situation."

"For what?" I asked, feeling butterflies beginning to flutter in my stomach. I didn't like where my sister was headed with this.

"For you to take over, silly! Or totally start anew. Sell your own designs!"

"Do you have any idea how long it takes to create an entire line of clothing, let alone get it into production?"

"No," she said. "I really don't have a clue, but I'm sure you do. I'm sure you have all the skills, Millie."

She looked at me, really looked at me, with those bright blue eyes that matched my own.

"This is crazy," I said. "I don't even know if I want to move back to Ocracoke." My gaze drifted to the shed.

To Aiden.

There were too many unanswered questions to begin with. His life was in New York.

But, for the meantime, he was here.

Would he stay after the memorial was completed?

There was that doubt again.

I guessed it was time to face it head-on.

Turning to my sister, I said, "Let's go get that dress."

Her eyes brightened. "Does that mean…"

I shrugged, but I couldn't hide the small bit of glee that escaped as I rose from the chair.

My own store.

My own line of clothing.

Yeah, it was a pipe dream, but it was mine.

And damn if it wasn't about time I started having those again.

By the time we made it to the store, I was leaking sweat out of every pore on my body. I'd never purchased anything like this before in my life.

Unless you counted my apartment.

Oh crap, my apartment.

I'd probably have to sell that now that I was moving.

Moving…

Was I actually moving?

So. Much. Sweat.

Even the idea had my heart galloping to an unknown destination in my chest.

"Are you nervous?" Molly asked as we walked up to Beachcombers.

"Yes," I managed to say.

"Excited?"

"Yes."

"Do you hate me for suggesting the idea?"

We both stopped at the entrance as I tried to steady my breath.

"A little," I answered. "But, more than that, I'm disappointed with myself for not thinking of it. I've spent too long working on other people's dreams and ambitions; I've kind of forgotten what it's like to have my own. I kept rising through the ranks at my company, believing that was enough, but really, I was just moving further and further away from what I wanted. I mean, this is why I wanted to go into design in the first place." A memory flickered back to the forefront of my mind. "I think I told Aiden that."

"You think? Is that part of the whole drunken night coming back at you?"

"Yeah." I smiled, happy I'd shared it with him. Apparently, I was more honest with him drunk than I was with myself sober.

"Well, let's see if we can get you one giant step closer to those dreams of yours, shall we?"

With my gorgeous hand-sewn masterpiece of a homecoming dress in my arms, the one that had started it all, we stepped into Rita's shop.

"Yes. Let's."

"Two McIntyre girls at once!" Rita exclaimed the moment she saw us enter. "Well, isn't it my lucky day? And is that a little angel sleeping on your chest, Miss Molly?"

"It is," she said, looking down at Ruby, who had been fed just before we left Molly's house after picking up the dress.

I swore, that infant slept more than she was awake.

But I guessed it was hard work, growing that fast.

I remained relatively quiet while Rita fussed over Ruby, and the two moms talked babies for a few minutes.

"It's amazing how quickly they grow," she said. "Soon, little Ruby will be starting kindergarten, and then, before you know it, she'll be off to college. Heck, I remember the two of you coming in here, shopping for clothes, like it was yesterday."

This was it.

My moment.

"Actually, that's why we came in," I said, stepping forward, the dress still at my side as my heart raced in my chest.

"Oh? You need something? I'm afraid I don't have a lot in stock. I've put mostly everything on clearance, trying to sell off what I have before I close in a month."

A month? That was really soon.

I gulped down the dread.

"No, well, actually, I might take a look around, but that's not why we came in. I wanted to show you this," I said, holding out the dress. "And to make you a proposition."

Okay, I said to myself, letting out one last breath, *here goes nothing.*

―∞―

"Why isn't this town bigger?" I asked as my sister drove us back to the inn.

"Um, well, it's an island. It can only be but so big. And why are you asking?"

I didn't think I'd blinked since we left the store, the whole of Ocracoke passing me in a blur. "Because I need more time to process this. I just bought a store, Molly."

"Well, not quite. You have a contract, but there is still the matter of money. You'll need to apply for a loan—"

"I have the money," I said.

"You what?" She nearly drove off the road.

I nodded, my eyes still wide and scary-looking. "I have the money. I've been working my ass off since college. With the exception of my apartment, which I'm going to sell, I've hardly spent any of the money I've made over the years, and I've made a lot of it."

"But your clothes… and the shoes?"

I shrugged. "Most of it I got as swag from shows or as just a perk of my job."

"That's a nice perk."

"Yeah, it was. But not as nice as owning my own store," I finally said, a sly smile creeping up my cheeks.

"So, it's starting to process?" she asked.

"Yeah, I think so."

"Good, because we're home."

I looked up at the inn and let out a happy sigh. "I bought a store today, Molly."

My hands were clinging to the preliminary paperwork Rita and I had signed, which the realtor had brought over after I shared my plans with Rita. I looked down at them to make sure they were still there.

Still real.

"You once told me everyone needed a little bit of nomadic time in their lives, where they could wander and explore and truly find themselves. It's that advice that pushed me to finally step off this island and discover who I was without Jake. And it's that advice that ultimately gave me the courage to find the path that led back to him. Are you sure your nomadic days are behind you?"

Looking up at our childhood home, remembering all the crazy moments we'd shared within, I smiled. "Who said you always had to be a nomad to find yourself? Mom and Dad raised us in this unconventional inn, surrounded by strangers, and yet we had a perfectly normal upbringing. Maybe I, the one who couldn't wait to leave, am supposed to come home to find myself."

"It sure would be poetic, wouldn't it?"

"Yeah"—I laughed—"it would. Plus, this island could use some style."

She grinned. "It really could, and I know I, for one, would really appreciate not having to get on a ferry every time I wanted something cute to wear on a date. Do you think you could do something about that?"

I gave her a once-over. "You've always been a work in progress, haven't you?"

Her eyes widened just before we both stepped out of the car. "I thought my sense of fashion had greatly improved over the last few years!"

"We'll keep working on it. I'm here now; don't worry."

I was pretty sure I heard her mutter something under her breath as she said good-bye and hopped back in the car. Since I'd called her out on her coming over to see how Mom was handling the inn, she knew her plans had been ruined.

I had known maternity leave was going to be hard on my sister, but this was downright ridiculous. Taking a quick look around the street and parking area, I noticed neither of my parents' cars was around, which meant Aiden was alone.

Finally.

I wanted to go straight to the backyard and tell him all

about my day, but I felt like a mess, and I was in desperate need of a shower after the stressful afternoon I'd had. So, rather than heading for the patio, I went toward our suite, loving the fact that it was now ours.

I hadn't been in the other room in weeks.

Unlocking the door, I set down the papers on the dresser and breathed out a content sigh. Seeing all of our things commingling together in this room filled my heart with joy. It was messy and small, but I didn't care.

I could spend the rest of my life crammed with this man in the tiny, little suite.

And it'd be the happiest life I could imagine.

Of course, I just spent my life savings on a storefront in a town dependent on tourists, so who knows? I might need to live here the rest of my life, surviving off the kindness of my family.

But it could always be worse.

I could be forced to move in with Molly and Jake... or my parents.

A very real shudder went down my spine.

God, I hoped this dream of mine worked out.

Trying to keep a positive outlook on things, I stripped off my clothes and jumped in the shower, eager to go see Aiden. It had been a few days since I was outside and really took an up-close look at the progress he'd made on the memorial project.

Now that he'd been working on it for several weeks, I was starting to see the progress of it, but it was slow work. I now understood where the need for patience came from. I'd given him a hard time about M&M's and such, but the work he created was beautiful.

After my shower, it didn't take much longer to get

ready. I threw on a cute dress and a bit of makeup, and with one last look at the contract I'd left on the dresser, I stepped out of our messy suite to go share the news with my man.

And I hoped he'd share in my dreams because there was no one else in the world I wanted to have by my side in this crazy, new adventure but him.

CHAPTER FIFTEEN

Aiden

ARCHING MY BACK, I STRETCHED MY SORE muscles, feeling the hours of work I'd put my body through today. Glancing up at the granite boulder I was slowly molding into the vision I'd created in my head, I felt a sense of satisfaction, knowing it was heading in the right direction.

Ben would have loved to get his hands on something like this. He would have loved to expand his talent, to let it grow into what I was afforded.

It had always been a dream of mine to start our own business. Two brothers creating art together. We'd have moved out to the country and gotten our own studio. We'd have lived off the meager earnings we made off our work. It wouldn't have been much, but it would have been a good life.

Two brothers.

Two stone doves.

I remembered telling him all of that out there in our backyard as we'd chipped away at the stone, day by day.

I realized now that he'd known all along it would never happen.

He'd just wanted to appear normal to James and me, for as long as he was able.

The thought sobered me.

I guessed I was no different, hiding the truth from Millie. But, unlike Ben, I planned on telling her.

I only needed a little longer.

A little more time like this.

"It still looks like a giant rock."

I turned to see Millie walking from the house, a big smile on her face. Her blonde hair blew in the breeze, and I noticed she'd changed her clothes since I saw her this morning, opting for a tropical print dress that dipped low in the front and nearly dragged on the ground, her bare feet peeking out with each step she took.

Damn, I was a lucky man.

"That's because you're not looking close enough," I said, pulling her towards me. "You smell good. What is that? Vanilla? Jasmine?" I tucked her into my arms, wrapping them around her as she leaned into me, both of us glancing up at the giant stone pillar.

"Yes," she simply stated. "I picked it up at a store in town today."

The way she'd said it told me there was a story behind her words, but instead of sharing it, she stepped forward, her hands caressing the granite as she began checking my progress. I watched in silence, feeling an extreme sense of pride. Seeing her lay her hands on that stone, it did things to me.

"You never told me how you became Aiden Fisher, master stone sculptor." Her head turned back toward me, a slight smile on her lips.

"It's not a very good story," I answered, stepping forward

to join her. I pressed my hand on top of hers, spreading our fingers wide over the dusty stone. "I knew what I wanted to do, but I wasn't exactly equipped with the cash to go to art school. So, I found a sculptor—an old-school type of chap who—"

"I can't believe you just used the words *old-school* and *chap* in the same sentence."

I grinned. "Do you want to hear this story or not?"

"Go on."

"Like I was saying, Dalton—that was his name—wasn't a flashy sculptor. He didn't use saws or anything modern. He was just a basic chisel-and-hammer type of guy, and he wasn't interested in taking on an apprentice."

"Is that why you don't use saws?"

I gave her a pointed look.

"Right, sorry. Your story. Continue."

"But I was young and hungry. Quite literally. And I knew, if I didn't have a job or at least a career path by the time James tracked me down, he'd drag me back to England so fast, my head would spin."

"Wait, you left without telling your brother?"

I sighed. "Yes, I was angry. It was foolish and selfish, but he forgave me. Besides, he got a good deal out of it."

"Oh?"

"Well, he stayed, didn't he?" I said, watching as she guided our hands along the stone, careful to avoid the chalk lines I'd drawn.

"Right. He's a doctor, isn't he?"

I had mentioned that as some point or another, I think. Just not a doctor of what.

So many lies, I was losing track.

"Yes," I said, clearing my throat. "Anyway, I was very

persistent with Dalton, to the point of being annoying. No, *annoying* isn't the right word. *Desperate* might be more accurate. Finally, he caved."

"He must be very proud of you."

My hand froze briefly as I remembered the gruff, old man. "I wouldn't know," I replied. "He died shortly after I went off on my own."

"Aiden." The way she said my name, it held weight and compassion. Turning, she lifted her eyes toward mine. "I'm so sorry."

"We weren't that close, to be honest. He made it very clear from the beginning that I was his student and nothing more. I don't think he was in the business of letting many people in, which was tragic, considering the number of hearts he touched with his artwork. It's scattered all over the city. I'm sure even you would recognize some of it."

"Really?"

I nodded.

"What about you? Is there anything in the city of yours that I could see?"

I pinned her between both hands, her back resting against the warm stone. "Not yet, but maybe someday."

I could see my answer bothered her. The idea of someday.

We hadn't spoken about it—whether I'd go back when I was done with this job. I wasn't even certain if she was staying. But one thing that had changed was that we'd stopped talking about leaving, and we'd started just living in the now.

And that was all I wanted right now.

With a very limited time until James came down with whatever cockamamy scheme he'd come up with to help me battle or prolong the war that had begun inside me, thanks to a couple of really crappy inherited genes from my birth parents, I just wanted to freeze time.

To remember how beautiful Millie looked under the setting sun, leaning against the stone, with her golden hair framing her face as she gazed up at me with such love and trust.

"Come on," I said, taking her hand.

"Where are we going? Are you taking me to the man cave?"

I laughed as we trotted toward the shed. "The man cave? Is that what you call it?"

"Well, yeah. I mean, you and my dad hang out in here. It's pretty small and not very well lit, so it's kind of the perfect name."

I pulled her inside.

"Oh, wow, it's really bight!"

I took a look around while she did the same. "I made a few modifications."

Specifically the lighting.

"I guess," she said. "It's like being in direct contact with the sun. Why so many lights?"

I cleared my throat. "I just like to be able to see when I work."

"I thought you worked outside," she countered, taking a look around. Her hands touched everything. The chisels, every single hammer, even the larger chunks of granite I'd chipped away and stored in a pile.

"Not always," I said. "Remember how I said I sometimes work with clay?"

"I do." Her eyes immediate began to scan the shed. "Oh my gosh," she exclaimed when she finally found what she was looking for. "It looks just like the original."

"Well, not exactly like it," I said, walking to the spot where she was standing. I smiled as she gazed at the small clay replica of the memorial I'd created for the town—the one that had been destroyed. "It's quite a bit smaller."

She gave me a sideways look, sticking out her tongue. "Funny."

I allowed her time to examine it a while longer. She leaned forward, taking in all the details even though there was very little. The beauty of this memorial was its simplicity.

"Will you teach me?" she asked.

"How to work with clay? I'm fairly certain anyone can do that. It's pretty straightforward."

"No." She slapped my shoulder in a playful manner. "And I'm quite sure you just insulted every clay sculptor in the world with that comment."

I simply shrugged.

"Will you teach me to carve?"

My chest tightened. Just when I thought I couldn't love this woman more.

"Yes," I answered, my voice strained with emotion.

It was the reason I'd brought her in here, but I'd thought I'd have to talk her into it.

The fact that she'd beaten me to it...

It made my heart swell.

"It requires a great deal of patience. Are you sure you can handle it?"

"Well, you had an excellent teacher. I'm sure I do as well," she said.

My thoughts went to my brother for the briefest moment and our matching stone birds.

"I think, unfortunately for you, mine was better."

"Let me be the judge of that."

Her attention was already shifting to the long wall where I'd laid out my chisels.

"Why don't you grab a chunk of granite, and I can teach you how to make your very own stone animal?" I suggested.

"Why can't you teach me on the memorial?" she asked, her gaze drifting to the door.

Mine followed where the sun was already setting behind the house, the sound of crickets filling the air.

"Uh, well…"

"You don't trust me?" Her face carried a smile, but beyond that, I could see a deep worry setting in.

Shit. It wasn't that I didn't trust her. I could guide her stroke and make sure every tap of the hammer was accurate.

I'd be there every step of the way.

My eyes shifted to the door once again and then to the small window next to it. It was nearly black outside. Finally, I looked back at Millie, her smile wavering.

"You're right," I said. "A stone animal is for amateurs. Let's go see how you fare with the big granite rock."

She beamed with happiness. "Now you're talking!"

"Why don't you head on out? I'm going to see what I can grab for lighting, and I'll meet you out there."

She hopped over to me, placing a kiss on my cheek. "Good idea. We wouldn't want to be blind out there."

"No"—I swallowed hard—"definitely not."

I'd done the best I could with adding extra lighting around the stone pillar, but the majority of the lighting inside the shed required electricity—something that was sorely lacking outside of it.

"Do you maybe want to do this tomorrow?" I asked, walking up toward her after setting up a few strategically placed flashlights. It was woefully unimpressive.

"In the heat?" She adamantly shook her head. "I've seen how much you sweat and believe me, I'm already hot enough out here as it is. Besides," she said, looking around with a certain gleam in her eye, "this is romantic, which is kind of perfect because, after our lesson, I have something pretty exciting to tell you."

My interest piqued, something she'd obviously counted on. "Then why not just tell me now?"

"Because someone promised me a carving lesson," she countered.

My hand reached out, pushing back a tendril of light-blonde hair from her face. I would never be able to say no to her.

I'd forever be trying to give her the world for the rest of my life.

"Okay," I said, making her lip twitch. "I mean, righto, miss."

She rolled her eyes as I bent down and grabbed a chisel and hammer before handing it to her.

"Is this all we need? Don't I need that mask thingy you usually wear?" she asked.

"No," I answered. "That mask thingy is called a respirator and protects my lungs from the dust, but for what little we're doing, I don't think it's necessary." I paused, remembering her first comment. "And what else do you think we need?" I asked.

Turning toward the granite, her gaze traveling the length of it, she shrugged. "I don't know. I guess I just thought it would require more things. Doesn't look very hard."

My brow lifted. "You think more tools equates the level of difficulty?"

"I don't know. It just seems so simplistic."

A tiny smirk played upon her lips. She was goading me. Time to give her the first lesson.

"Grab your chisel," I instructed. "And place it here." I pointed with my finger to a location I'd been working on earlier in the day.

"Oh, I like it when you're bossy." She batted her eyes, the smirk on her face widening.

"I know," I replied, giving her a wicked grin in return.

She did as I'd told her, placing the chisel against the stone. "Here?" she asked.

I nodded, leaning in real close to double-check one last time. I adjusted it slightly to make sure the angle was correct, so the impact of the hammer would take off just the right amount of granite in the right direction.

"Now, grab your hammer."

She did, holding it high in the air, like she was ready to ward off an intruder.

"Closer," I said, my voice deep as I guided her, wrapping my own hand around the tool and closing the gap. "Not too far, but not too close. You need to make sure the impact is with purpose but not out of control. Ready?"

"Oh crap, I'm nervous."

"I'm going to step back now."

Her eyes widened. "What? Why?"

"It's going to take more than a tap to get through that granite, love."

"Right. Okay." She looked terrified.

Honestly, I was a little terrified myself. But I trusted her.

And, even if she messed it up a little, I was early enough into the piece that I could always fix it.

Hopefully.

My heart picked up a bit of speed as her arm pulled back a little, probably more than necessary and—*oh God, were her eyes closed?*

The familiar sound of metal hitting stone sounded through the air.

"Did I do it?" she asked, her eyes still closed.

I stepped back toward the granite and grinned. "Well, you made a dent."

"What?" she groaned, her eyes jerking back open to see the tiny mark she'd made. "But I hit it so hard!"

"There's that crunchy attitude again. You have absolutely no patience. Do you think I learned how to do this in a day?"

"Well, why don't you show me how it's done, master sculptor?" Her voice purred.

"Haven't you seen me hit a hammer dozens of times now from your perch by the window there?"

She gave a coy smile, her fingers running down the length of my shoulder. "Yes, but it's so much better up close. But lose the shirt first."

Her words made me feel cocky and delirious. I'd show off for her any day. My mind had already jumped ahead several steps, plotting out how I'd pound out a couple of strokes of the hammer as she watched, and then I'd toss the tools on the grass and throw her over my shoulder, so we could pound it out in a completely diferent way indoors.

Reaching up over my head, I pulled the T-shirt over my head, dirty and stained from my work throughout the day.

Knowing she was watching my every move only propelled me forward.

God, this woman made me feel wild.

Desperate.

Complete.

"I will never get sick of looking at all that," she said, the moment my shirt hit the ground.

"Yeah?"

A satisfied smile spread across her face as she took me in, her gaze traveling along the hard lines of my body, earned from years of hard work. "Yeah," she agreed.

She handed over my hammer and chisel, looking eager and wicked all at the same time. I willingly took them and stepped up to the same spot in the granite she'd attempted, smiling when I felt the small dent she'd made. It really did take quite a large amount of force to break through granite. I should have started her off with something softer, like soapstone or alabaster.

Lining up my chisel, I held back my hammer and then let it fly. The crack was loud and caused Millie to jump.

"Okay, I didn't hit it quite that hard." She laughed. "Wow, you're strong."

I gave her a quick grin. "Well, I didn't get these arms from going to the gym."

"No, definitely not. Do it again."

"I feel like I'm your cheap entertainment for the evening. Do you need to go make popcorn? Maybe pour a glass of wine before I begin again?" I asked, leaning against the stone as she took her fill of me.

"Mmm, just a few more. And then we'll go in, promise."

That image of me throwing her over my shoulder came to mind once more. "Deal."

With sex on the brain, I lined up my chisel once more and pulled back my hammer, making sure to double-check as I went. Another crack.

Millie was just as pleased as the first time.

So, I did another one and another. With every swing of my hammer, my thoughts grew more focused on her and less on what I was doing.

Once again, I lined up my chisel and swung.

But this time, I missed.

"Fuck!"

Searing pain went through my entire hand. I'd missed the chisel entirely, my hand crushed in the process. Dropping both tools to the ground, I tried not to panic.

"Oh my God, Aiden!" Millie rushed to my side as I grunted in pain, pulling my hand to my chest. Her eyes widened as she took in the full extent of my injury.

"I'm calling Jake." Her gaze tried to avoid my hand, which could only mean one thing.

It was bad.

Really bad.

I'd taken a swing or two at my fingers before but nothing like this.

Nothing with such force. Such power.

I'd been sure of my lines.

A random thought drifted through my brain.

The coffee cup.

The one I'd broken those first couple of days after meeting Millie. I'd been so sure I'd set it on the countertop.

I swallowed hard as I watched Millie run toward the house to retrieve her phone, the silhouette of her body so fuzzy around the edges.

I'd been trying to ignore it over the last few weeks, how

much worse it'd become.

But the truth was as plain as the test results on that sheet of paper I still carried around with me. I was so frightened Millie would find it and discover the truth before I was ready to share it.

I was going blind.

Quicker than I'd imagined.

And, soon, the world would be nothing but an empty, black void, and there wasn't a goddamn thing I could do about it.

Except for wait as my world came crashing down around me.

"We can take the ferry," I argued, my head alternating from a very worried Millie to a somewhat equally worried Jake.

"No," Millie replied, ushering me out toward the car.

Jake had been here in minutes after she made the call, confirming what we'd both already known. I needed to go to the hospital as soon as possible.

"We're flying. I've already called Jimmy, and he's agreed to take us."

"It's just a broken hand."

"It's more than a broken hand, Aiden," Jake chimed in, both of us looking down at the alarming rate my hand was swelling. "I think some of those bones are shattered. I can set a bone, but if it's shattered, that requires surgery."

Great.

I could see the fear in her eyes as she helped me into the car, assisting me with my seat belt since my injured left hand made it difficult.

"Thanks," I said a second before she pulled away.

Her eyes glistened, and her voice wavered. "I'm so sorry, Aiden."

"Why are you sorry?" I asked, my good hand resting atop hers.

"Because I'm the one who pushed you, who asked you to keep going. It's my fault."

I let out a breath through my teeth. "Believe me," I said with conviction, "this is not your fault. Do you understand?"

She nodded, but I knew she didn't agree. A single tear fell from her cheek as she pulled away and shut the passenger door.

I'd done that.

I'd caused that pain.

Because I'd been selfish and kept my secret.

Because I'd lied.

Because you'd stayed.

We didn't say much as the three of us drove to the airport, Jake tagging along since I was now officially his patient, and according to Millie, he was pretty damn dedicated, so he'd be with us for the foreseeable future.

Just another item to add to my list of things that made me feel guilty—taking a new father from his family for an entire night. Thankfully, Jimmy was already waiting for us when we arrived at the small airport, his tiny plane parked in the middle of the parking lot, like I remembered it from the day I'd arrived here a month earlier.

I hadn't expected to leave so soon.

I hadn't expected to leave at all.

"Damn, that looks pretty bad," he said the moment I stepped out of the car.

"Feels fucking brilliant," I said, looking over at him with

a rather dry expression.

He chuckled under his breath. "Well, at least he still has his humor. Let's get this poor guy to the hospital, shall we? Which hospital, Doc? Outer Banks or Virginia Beach?"

We stepped onto the private plane, and I saw Millie give a pleading look to Jake before he answered, "Outer Banks Hospital should be fine. No need to take him farther away."

Millie mouthed the words, *Thank you*, to her brother-in-law before he gave a quick nod as I settled into my seat, resting my head against the back as I tried to breathe through the pain.

"How are you doing?" she asked, her fingers warm and comforting against my forearm.

"Good," I lied.

Honestly, I wanted to throw up, but I'd rather die than tell her that and cause her more pain.

There were a lot of things I'd rather do than cause her more pain.

And wasn't that something to think about?

My brain spiraled, going down a rabbit hole of self-doubt and loathing, as we traveled the short distance up the coast. By the time we made it to the hospital and I was checked into a room, I was sick with fear over my future with Millie.

I was on autopilot as I sat in the room with the nurse, answering questions on medical history, while Millie went to go make calls to her worried family members.

"Is there anything else?" she asked, pulling me out of my funk.

I saw her turn away from the small tablet she had on the counter, and her eyes met me head-on. I swallowed hard, my gaze shifting between her and Jake, who'd been quiet this whole time, waiting to speak to the doctor who was assigned to me.

"I, uh…" My throat went dry. "I have macular degeneration in both eyes."

Jake's eyes widened, flickering toward the nurse and back to me.

The nurse just kept typing before she spoke again. "Early onset?"

"No," I replied, thankful for the small bit of research I had done after storming out of my brother's office. Often, with many eye diseases, there would be an early onset in childhood, like a warning sign that signaled of the dangerous journey ahead. "No vision problems as a kid."

"You're only thirty-three." Jake blurted out. " Age related macular degeneration doesn't usually start until mid-forties, if not later."

I nodded. "Pretty shitty luck, huh?"

The nurse had already begun typing.

"Can you give us a minute?" Jake asked.

"Sure," she replied. "I can finish typing this at the nurses' station. The doctor should be around shortly."

"Great." Jake waited for her to leave, before he turned his attention back toward me.

"How long have you known? Does Millie know?"

I sat up in the uncomfortable ER bed, doing my best to hold my arm against my chest. "My vision started to change a few years ago. I just chalked it up to getting older," I said. "That, or Karma."

"Karma?"

"My brother is a ophthalmologist," I explained. "A bloody good one, too. He would constantly badger me to come into his practice and get my eyes checked—preventative eye health and all that—but I always told him I was fine and ignored him. Finally, when it got bad enough—"

"How bad?" he asked, his arms folded across his chest. I wasn't sure if he was asking as a friend or a doctor.

"Blurry spots in my vision," I explained, "Sometimes, what I'd see as wavy lines were actually straight. Stuff like that. I went in to see James, asking if I might need a pair of readers—you know, those silly little things you pick up in a drugstore?"

He nodded, looking slightly put out. "I know what readers are. Half of my patients wear them."

"Right, of course. Well, apparently, what he saw he didn't like. He ran me through a bunch of tests, none of which turned out good. He said my parents must have had it too—which probably contributed to why I got it so early on—the bastards."

"And my other question?" he pressed.

"No, she doesn't know."

"Know what?" Millie's voice caused me to jump.

Both of us turned to see her stepping into the small room as I felt a bit of panic come on.

Not like this.

Not yet.

"That Aiden wants you to call his brother," Jake intervened.

I let out a sigh of relief. Not quite the lie I would have chosen, but it was good enough.

"Oh!" Her spirits seemed to perk up.

Jake gave me a look that said I owed him and also one that said he wanted to kill me simultaneously.

I got it. Really, I did.

"Well, why didn't you just say so? Of course I can call

him. Hand over your cell," she suggested.

"Actually," I said, "if you could just dial, I think I'd like to tell him. Maybe you could get me some ice chips."

"Absolutely." She seemed to like being useful, a common symptom of guilt.

Not that she had anything to feel guilty about, but I knew it helped soothe the ache in her chest.

Taking my phone from my shorts pocket, she found my brother's phone number and tapped the screen, the phone ringing almost immediately.

With a kiss on my cheek, she went off to find me ice chips while I broke the news to my brother.

The news that things were far worse than I'd let on, and I doubted any device or harebrained idea of his was going to stop what we both knew was coming.

No matter how hard I tried to fight it.

That left me to decide, was I going to go at it alone, like I'd originally planned, or take everyone I loved into the darkness with me, ruining all our lives, one terrible accident at a time?

CHAPTER SIXTEEN

Millie

IF EVER THERE WAS A TIME WHEN I NEEDED TO LEARN the art of patience, it was over the next few weeks after Aiden's accident.

In the days that followed, there was extensive surgery to repair the damage he'd done to his hand, and then the news that it would take months for him to regain full mobility. Thankfully, he didn't have to stay in the hospital long, he only needed to return every so often for physical therapy once the initial healing began.

So, our separation wasn't long.

I tried to see that as a good thing.

I made every effort I could to make sure he was comfortable when he returned to the inn, but after several quiet days, I could see a distance growing between us.

At first, I blamed the meds. Even I knew pain medications could alter a person's state of mind, and add that to the devastating news he'd received in the hospital, it was no wonder he might be a little depressed.

But even I knew I was lying to myself.

More than once, I heard heated arguments coming

from the suite when Jake came to visit, and then there were the hushed phone calls with his brother.

Something wasn't right.

One afternoon, I found Aiden out of bed, staring at the papers I'd signed with Rita. I'd pulled them out after she called, wondering if we still had a deal. It had been some time since we spoke.

And, at this point, I wasn't sure.

"What is this?" he asked, holding his injured hand to his bare chest.

I tried not to stare, tried not to feel guilty.

But the ache still burned in my chest at the memory of that night.

Does he blame me? I wondered, for taking away his livelihood, his career?

His life.

"Nothing," I answered. "Just a silly idea I had. I think it's almost time for your meds. Why don't you head into the kitchen, and I'll make you some lunch?"

He shook his head, his brows furrowed as he stared down at the contract. "I don't want to take them anymore. They make me fuzzy."

"But you'll be in pain, Aiden—"

"I'll manage. It's been long enough since the accident." He paused, still staring at the contract. "You bought a storefront? In town?"

"No," I said. "Well, not officially. No money has been exchanged."

"And you have it? The money?" he asked, suddenly very chatty. This was honestly the longest conversation we'd had since that hammer collided with his hand.

"Yes. It's going to take every cent I have, but yes. I've

been saving for a long time. I didn't know what for, but I think it might be a good investment. For the future."

His eyes hadn't left the small stack of papers, like the gears in his head were on overtime. "You know how risky it is, to start a business like this? Especially here?"

I felt the air in my lungs dissipate. Of all the reactions I'd expected him to have, this was not one of them.

Shock mixed with a bit of surprise and excitement? Sure. But this?

"Um, yes. I did grow up here," I reminded him. "I've seen quite a few shops and businesses come and go in my lifetime."

"Then, why would you do this? Why risk your life savings on something with no guarantee?"

My brows knit as anger rose in my throat. "I wasn't aware anything worth the risk in life came with a guarantee."

He let out a silent breath of air, and finally, his eyes met mine. "Why are you doing this?"

"Why? Because it's my dream. Because I've spent far too long helping others chase theirs. I figured it was high time I focused on one of my own for a change. And someone once told me nothing should stand in the way of getting what I wanted."

"But why here? Why not back home in Florida?"

My heart ached as deep emotion swelled in my chest. "Because this is my home."

His jaw clenched, his emotions getting the best of him. "Don't do this because of me," he warned, turning away, his shoulders slumped forward as he paced the room.

Where have you gone, Aiden?
You promised me you wouldn't run.

"See, that's the thing," I said, pivoting toward the door.

"I thought I was doing it for us. I guess I was misinformed."

And then I walked away.

Because the heart could only handle so much abuse, and lately, mine had been through the wringer.

After our turbulent conversation over the storefront, things between Aiden and me didn't improve.

The vast walls he'd erected around himself only seemed to grow, the walls becoming so tall and thick, I wondered if I'd ever see the real Aiden again.

But then, late at night, when the inn was quiet and he reached out for me, I'd find the tiniest crack in the protective fortress around his heart. His hardened gaze would soften as he held me, his touch would steady as his fingers grazed my skin, and for a moment, I'd believe he'd come back to me, but as fleeting as it had come, it would end just the same, and he would be gone again.

"Maybe he's just still feeling the effects of the accident. He did some serious damage to his hand, and I'm sure it's caused quite a lot of depression, considering what he does for a living," Molly said one day after a particularly rough day of playing nursemaid.

"Molly, it's been three weeks. I'm trying to be sympathetic here, but I'm not sure how much longer I can handle the silent treatment."

"You're not thinking of leaving, are you?" she asked as we sat outside on the patio, something we'd come to enjoy during her maternity leave.

She couldn't seem to stay away from the inn, coming around at least twice a day with Ruby in tow, ignoring

Mom's insistence that she should enjoy her time away, so I'd done what any good sister would do.

Instead of sending her away, I distracted her.

With iced tea and gossip.

Lately, the gossip all seemed to revolve around me, but it was nice to have her around to talk about it.

Even if she was a little too perceptive.

"Oh my gosh, you are thinking about leaving. What about the shop, Millie? What about not wanting to put your dreams on hold any longer?"

I looked out onto the water, a cool glass of iced tea in my hand, as I thought about the day I'd spoken to Rita. I'd never felt so scared and excited in my life.

"Don't do this because of me."

"I don't know," I said, Aiden's voice still so clear in my head. "I thought I was building a new life here, Molly, and now—"

She leaned forward, her hand on my knee as her eyes met mine. "That man loves you," she said with conviction. "I know I was leery of him in the beginning, but I've seen the way he looks at you, little sister."

"Clearly, you haven't been paying attention lately," I scoffed, my head turning from hers to hide my pain.

"Don't give up on him Millie, and don't give up on your dreams. Fight for your happiness. Remember what mom said about being the key."

"That was just a stupid metaphor, Molly," I said. I had believed, up until a few weeks ago, that I'd unlocked the temperamental lock that was Aiden's heart.

But now? Now, I was unsure about everything.

"It doesn't make it any less true," she reminded me.

I held on to these words as we said our good-byes, and

I sent her back to her own house to do whatever it was that you did on maternity leave—wash baby bottles, stay up all night, and send four thousand pictures a day of your newborn to every person you knew.

That sort of thing.

I didn't know how long I sat out on that patio by myself.

Spending time with my sister had given me a glimmer of hope. Maybe I was acting a bit rash. I wasn't the best at practicing the art of patience after all, and my inclination to act impulsively was always at the forefront of my mind.

Aiden had asked me to trust him, and I needed to follow through with that, even if I got a little banged up in the process. Everyone had their plights, and relationships were sometimes about supporting each other through those rough times.

Even if it hurt.

Walking back to our suite, I made a mental note to contact Rita and let her know I was going forward with the contract. This was my home. I was here for better or for—

"What is all this?" Pushing open the door to our suite, I found suitcases.

Packed suitcases.

Our once messy room had been straightened.

No, not straightened. *Emptied*.

All of Aiden's things had been removed, packed into the suitcases that now stood in a straight little line next to the bed.

"I've decided to head back home," he answered, refusing to meet my gaze.

Funny, I thought you were already there.

I swallowed hard, my heart squeezing tight in my chest.

"For a visit?" I asked.

He finally turned, his expression grim.

No, definitely not for a visit.

"The project has been delayed for several months, love."

"Don't call me that," I spat. "Not anymore. Not when you're—" I couldn't finish.

He sighed, a heavy sigh that filled the room momentarily as he took a seat on the edge of the bed. His head hung low, as if this were a burden for him.

As if I were a burden he needed to be rid of.

"The only reason I stayed was because I loved the inspiration the area gave. That, and—"

"And what?"

"Well, I knew it'd be easier to keep you here, in your hometown, rather than talking you into joining me in New York for a spell. And I liked having you around."

"You liked having me around?"

"It is quite dull around here, and I knew I wouldn't make it without someone to keep me occupied."

Every word cut my heart a bit deeper.

"You're lying," I said, my arms wrapped protectively around my chest like armor. "You said that night together, our first night, was perfect. You said—"

"I said a lot of things, Millie. I told you, I'm in the business of emotions, and I play off of others well. Didn't I tell you to guard your heart around me?"

"But you love me," I demanded. "We were going to make a life here together!"

"When did I ever tell you that? Did I ever say those words?"

I thought back, tried to remember a time when I'd heard him say those three little words. I'd felt them hundreds of times, in the way he'd held me, the deep devotion in his gaze... but had he ever spoken them?

"What we had, Millie was a long-term distraction. I needed someone to keep me entertained on this dreadful island, and you needed someone to help you get over how disappointing your life had become. It was mutual and it was lovely, but now, I need to get back to my life."

"You don't mean that," I said, unable to stop the tears from flooding my eyes. "You're just running. You said you wouldn't run, Aiden."

His throat worked up and down, and he met my gaze. "I'm sorry. The only love I have room for in my life is my career, and you nearly ruined that a few weeks ago when you distracted me. So, if you don't mind, I'm going back to New York where I can get proper medical care that doesn't require a three-hour journey, and then I'm going to put my life back together."

"What about the memorial?" I asked, my mind reeling as my heart fell to pieces on the floor.

"It can be shipped back to my studio in New York. It will be a welcome change to be back in my temperature-controlled warehouse with all the equipment back in place."

I'd thought he liked working here.

I'd thought he liked working here with me.

I'd thought a lot of things, none of which were true.

A distraction—that was what I was.

Just another damn distraction.

Was that all I was ever going to be?

I blinked several times, the shock wearing off as I tried to figure out what to say to the man who'd just broken my heart.

Because, unlike with Lorenzo, this time, it was definitely broken.

No, not broken. Utterly destroyed.

Thanks to Aiden, I now knew the difference.

"I was actually thinking of leaving, too," I said, making his head turn back toward mine.

"Oh?"

Trying to keep my voice steady, I nodded. "Yeah, after what you said about the storefront, I started to get cold feet. I mean, I would have to be crazy to start a business on this island. It's empty half of the year and filled with tourists intent on spending their money on junk. Who would want to buy my designs?"

For one brief moment, his face softened, but just like the nights when he'd held me and I'd seen his walls crack for a split second, it was gone again.

"You're absolutely right. Stupid risk. You're much better off."

I wiped away the dried up tears from my face as I watched him walk out the door.

"Don't give up on him, Millie. And don't give up on your dreams. Fight for your happiness."

I heard his suitcases roll down the old hardwood floor. There was a pause, ever so brief, and I wondered if he'd changed his mind.

Maybe this was all a dream.

But then the front door opened, and he was gone.

I'm sorry, Molly, I thought. *I can't fight anymore.*

I've lost the war.

The key went into the lock with surprising ease.

I didn't know why I thought it wouldn't.

I guessed I'd thought walking back into this empty, upscale apartment after my life had fallen apart would be harder.

Again.

But, at this point, I just felt numb.

Molly and the rest of my family and friends had begged me to stay after Aiden's abrupt departure. Well, actually, they'd first begged me to go track him down and cut off certain parts of his anatomy.

It was a sweet offer, but after a few days of sulking around the inn, I'd needed the space.

Being in Ocracoke right now would have been suffocating. Everything had reminded me of him, and I'd already shed far too many tears over that man.

God knows he'd probably forgotten all about me the second he stepped foot onto the mainland. Hell, he'd probably already found himself a new distraction now that he was back home with his perfect warehouse art studio and top-of-the-line medical care.

Dropping all my stuff on the floor in the middle of the living room, I went for the kitchen. Knowing I probably had nothing to eat, I went for the wine.

Now, wasn't this a serious case of déjà vu?

Bottle of wine, lonely party for one.

Yep, I'd done this before.

Only this time, it hurt so much worse.

Just as I was about to make it a full circle event and take my pity party into my closet like I'd done before, a quiet knock sounded on my door.

It was probably the nice old lady who lived next door. She was one of the only people I knew in the building, having spent the majority of the time I lived here traveling, but

I always managed to carve out a bit of time for her and usually brought a little something back for her from my travels.

Unfortunately, this time around, all I'd managed to bring was heartache, and I doubted she'd want any of that.

With the bottle of unopened rosé still in my hand, I the door and pulled it back open, expecting to see Mrs. Metzler standing on the other side.

Instead, I was met with an impressive dark-haired man wearing a designer suit I could call by name, based on the pin-striped pattern and the buttery dark gray fabric.

"Millie?" he said as I was admiring his attire.

"Yes?"

"You are a hard woman to track down. Do you mind if I pop in? I've been all over, the place trying to find you."

His accent was distinctly English, something I was trying to avoid these days.

"Do you mind telling me who you are first?" I eyed him suspiciously. A good fashion sense could only get you so far in my book.

"My name is James Griffin. I'm—"

"Aiden's brother," I said, finishing his sentence. "What are you doing here? Is he okay?"

His hands flew up in a calming manner. "He's fine, I can assure you. Well, as fine as he can be."

My brows furrowed. "What is that supposed to mean?"

His gaze went to the living room and then to me.

"Oh, right. Come in, please. I'm sorry."

I stepped to the side as he made his way in, and I allowed myself a moment to take him all in.

He was taller than Aiden's six-foot-two-inch frame and had a bit less bulk. But he was handsome in a very sophisticated, *Fifty Shades of Grey* sort of way.

"You said you've been trying to find me?" I asked as he took a seat on one of the two sofas in my living room. I held up the bottle of rosé I still held in my hand, offering him some.

He shook his head before answering my question, "I flew to Virginia Beach and then Ocracoke, but my very chatty pilot, after finding out who I was coming to visit, said you weren't on the island any longer—that he'd flown you to the airport just hours earlier."

"That would be Jimmy. We go way back."

He nodded as I helped myself to a glass of wine, listening as I popped the cork.

"He actually flew me down here."

I stopped mid-glass. "To Florida? Jimmy? He flew you all the way down to Florida?" My mouth gaped open. "But that man doesn't even like to fly to the other side of the state. He does tours for tourists and airport runs, and occasional trips to the hospital in a pinch. But that's it. He likes to stay close to the island."

"That's what he said—until I told him why I needed to get to you."

My heart beat a little faster in my chest as I took my glass of wine to the living room and sat down. "And why is that?"

"I'm about to violate HIPPA privacy rules for what I'm going to tell you—not to mention, if it ever got out, I could lose my medical license—but he's my brother Millie, and for a good portion of my childhood, I didn't have any sort of family. He and Ben were it for me."

"I don't understand," I said, my head spinning the second he started mentioning HIPAA.

"I know you don't. My stubborn brother has made sure

of that. And, right now, he's miserable because of it."

"You said he was okay. Has something happened with his hand?" I asked. *Oh God, did he reinjure it?* Maybe it had been too soon to travel.

"His hand is fine," he reassured me as his gaze leveled with mine.

In that moment, I knew something was about to change. It was like all the air had been sucked out of the room.

"Aiden is going blind."

"What?" I felt my body react to the news quicker than my mind. Tears welled in my eyes as a sob tore through me. "Are you sure?"

He took my hand in his, and it felt warm and comforting. He didn't answer right away, giving me a second to breathe. "Yes, I'm sure. I'm the doctor who diagnosed him."

"He never told me what kind of doctor you were," I said.

He smiled. "No, he probably would have kept that to himself, too. I'm an ophthalmologist. A pretty damn good one too, if you ask me."

"Is there a cure? Can you fix it?"

He shook his head. "What he has is degenerative. I can help with prescriptive eye wear to help him see at night, or even some medications have been found to help slow it, but his is happening so fast and at such a young age. It's really like—"

"Working blind?"

"Unfortunately, yes," he answered.

I let out a staggered breath, remembering all the times he'd seemed nervous about going out at night... the picnic at the beach, my damn carving lesson.

No wonder that shed had been lit up like a Christmas tree. He probably could hardly see anything the night he hit his hand.

I shook my head, so many things suddenly shifting in place.

"So, why fly all this way to tell me? It doesn't change anything," I said.

"Don't you see, Millie? This changes everything."

"He doesn't love me," I said. "He went back to New York."

He let out a shallow laugh. "Yeah, and he's been doing his best to drink himself to death since he returned."

My eyes widened.

"Look"—he sighed—"I know what my brother might have told you to push you away, but do you think I would risk my career to come down here if I didn't know for a fact that he loved you?"

I still wasn't convinced. I wanted to be, but Aiden's horrible words were on replay in my head.

I was a distraction.

Nothing but a distraction.

"He told you about Ben?" Even though he'd formed it as a question, it was somewhat rhetorical, as if he already knew the answer.

Still, I nodded in reply.

"Outside of the anniversary of his death, Aiden doesn't talk about Ben—to anyone. Not even me. But he told you." His gaze was steady, his eyes full of meaning. "He didn't leave you because he doesn't love you—"

My hand suddenly went to my lips.

How many times had he pushed me away, only to pull me back again? And then, just when things had been good, when our happily ever after had seemed plausible, a dose of reality had set in. In a moment of carelessness, he had gotten injured, and he'd pushed me away again.

"He left because he does." The words fell from my lips.

Silence feel between us as I clutched my untouched wine, trying to make sense of everything I'd just learned.

"What a complete and utter idiot," I said under my breath.

"Yes, well, he never was the brightest of the three of us. The most reactive? Sure. The most passionate? Definitely. Stubborn? Without a fucking doubt."

I stood up, not hearing a word he was saying and slammed my wine down on the coffee table. "I'm going to go give that man a piece of my mind."

"What? Now?" he asked, rising from the couch as well.

"Yes, now."

"Of course. Because why wouldn't I want to hop on another plane today? Sounds like a great time."

I blinked, realizing for a moment that he was probably exhausted. "I'm sorry," I apologized. "I'm usually a much better hostess than this. Or a least, I think I am. It's been a while since I've actually entertained. Do you want to crash here for the night? You don't have to come back with me."

"Are you sure?" he asked.

"Of course. Just drop off the key with Mrs. Metzler next door when you leave, and don't eat anything in the fridge. Seriously, not a thing. I don't know how long some of that stuff has been in there. There are menus in the drawer next to the silverware. You can have practically anything delivered."

"You are a goddess among men, Miss McIntyre."

"We shall see," I said, turning toward my luggage that was still waiting for me in the middle of the floor. I guessed that worked out well.

"Give him hell for me," James said as I turned around, my hand already on the handle of my luggage.

"Oh, I will," I promised.

He stepped forward, his hand reaching into his pants pocket. "And, when you do, give him this." He pulled out a small stone bird, much like the one I'd seen before, except this one was rougher.

Unfinished.

"Aiden has one just like this," I said. "He said it was Ben's."

"It is. And this one is Aiden's. He never finished it."

I took it from his hand, my fingers running over the jagged lines. I could see the intent, the path he'd laid out, but the journey had never been completed.

"It's not going to be easy to convince him. Once my brother has his mind made up, it's hard to deter him."

"And you think an unfinished bird is going to help?"

He smiled. "I'm sure you'll find a way. You've worked a miracle already in my brother's heart. Now, we just need to remind him of it."

I looked down at the stone bird and squeezed it as my eyes closed in a silent prayer to the heavens.

Okay, little bird, let's get to work.

CHAPTER SEVENTEEN

Aiden

"YOU LOOK LIKE YOU COULD USE A DRINK."

That's the understatement of the year, I thought as I walked into the familiar gallery in Manhattan, the one I'd thought would make all my dreams come true. That was when I'd thought all my dreams revolved around stone and a chisel.

The last few months had shown me I had so much more to live for.

And so much more to lose.

"That'd be great. Thanks, Harry," I said, happy to see my old friend.

Harry had been the director here for several years and was the first person to take a chance on me.

I owed him much.

"I'm sorry for dodging your calls and emails," I said. "I've been…away."

He made a dismissive motion with his hand as he poured us each a glass of whiskey from the private stash he kept in his office. Harry liked to think he was a character from *Mad Men*. Crystal decanters lined sleek wood shelves, which only accentuated the plush leather sofas.

It all went very well with the priceless modern art that adorned the walls, and, of course, the man himself, who had discovered some of the biggest names in a decade.

Including myself.

"You forget," he said, offering me a seat before he took one himself, "I work with artists on a daily basis. I learned a long time ago not to take it personally when one of you vanishes for a while. Just last month, I had a painter who needed to go off the grid. He hid out in a dark cave for two weeks, resetting his senses or whatever. Came back and painted me a fortune's worth of canvases. So, I get it. I mean, I don't really, but I understand who I'm working with."

"Harry, I'm quitting."

The news nearly had him spitting out his top-shelf whiskey all over the designer sofa he'd probably paid a hefty sum for.

"Come again?" he said, setting down the glass on the ornate coffee table in front of him.

"My heart's not in it anymore. I can't keep carving if I don't feel my work."

He leaned back, his finger finding his chin as he assessed me. "This wouldn't have anything to do with that hand you're trying to hide from me?"

I pulled the sleeve of my hoodie down a bit lower to cover my cast.

"Oh, come on, Aiden. It's August, for Christ's sake. Who wears a damn hoodie in the summer? Plus, you're babying the thing like a wounded animal. I'm not an idiot."

"It was an accident," I said.

With his eyes still on my hand, he let out a huff of air. "Look, so you banged up your hand. A hazard of the job, right? Take some time off. Go travel, and get inspired. Meet someone. Hell, meet several someones, and then come back and see how you feel."

I didn't need to meet anyone.

I'd already met the one.

And I'd let her go.

Every moment since had felt like a fucking struggle to breathe. Like a tiny thread had come loose in my heart when I walked away from her, and every step I took tugged harder and harder, tearing open that seam until my chest was ripped wide open, and everything was hanging open to the elements.

I'd lied to her.

Her eyes, the utter betrayal in those blue irises when I'd used her own insecurities over her affair with her former boss and said she was nothing more than a distraction?

I'd never forgive myself for that.

I'd made a mockery of our love, and for that, I didn't deserve anything from this world.

"No," I finally answered, "I can't."

He watched me stand, and I began to walk out the door before he called out to me. "Listen, Aiden, I say this as a friend and not a man trying to make another buck or two off of you. Don't give up on your talent. I've seen a lot of carvers come by my door, but you, you're the real deal."

I let out a sad sort of laugh. "You should have met my brother," I said. "He was the real talent. I just had the drive and a great deal of patience, which I happened to learn from him as well."

"Sometimes, that's what matters most of all," he said before pausing. "Good luck, Aiden, wherever the road takes you."

Luck? Luck and I had never been fast friends.

No, wherever I was headed…I just hoped they had a decent supply of whiskey.

"James, where the hell are you? This is the third message I've left for you today. Your office said you took a personal day. Since when do you need personal time? I thought workaholics didn't do shit like that."

I knew I was rambling as I walked into my apartment building, giving a short nod to the doorman, but it was odd for my brother to just up and leave his office. He ran that place like a well-oiled machine, and the last time I remembered him taking a day off was…well, never.

"For a man who wanted to start treating me right away, you're sure tough to find. Not that any of it is going to help. Well, except maybe this fine bottle of whiskey I just bought. You know where to find me. Or don't. I don't really fucking care anymore."

I was going to go bury myself under a rock and practice the art of drinking myself to death. I pressed the button to the elevator, and it sprang open right away.

"Oh," I said, remembering one more thing before I ended the call. "Stop sneaking into my apartment when I'm not there. I don't need your food. I'm not a bloody charity case. I can take care of myself."

I hit End on my phone and let out a sigh.

I should have never given him that key. It was like having a mother hen on my back twenty-four/seven, and now that I was crippled and half-blind, I knew I'd never be rid of him.

I knew he meant well.

I knew he cared, but right now, I was disgusted with everyone, but mostly myself, and the only companionship I could stand was the bottle currently taking up occupancy in my hand.

Stepping off the elevator on my floor, I walked the short distance to my apartment and slipped my key in the lock. It was midday, and I was met with rays of sunbeams shining through my windows, lighting up my otherwise dreary apartment.

Placing my beloved bottle on the kitchen counter, it took me a moment to notice the stone bird lying there beside it.

But it wasn't the stone bird I was used to seeing.

It was the one I'd hidden away so very long ago.

The one I'd given up on when Ben died. My fingers fell to the raw, unfinished edges, a lump in my throat as I picked it up.

I caught movement in the corner of my eye, and as I looked up, I felt my heart beat for the first time in days.

"Millie," I breathed out.

She stood in the center of my living room, looking more radiant than I'd remembered.

Was it possible that she'd grown even more beautiful in our short time apart?

I stepped forward, wanting to run to her, to pull her into my arms and never let go. But I stopped myself.

Nothing had changed.

I was still going blind, still tumbling into darkness.

And I wouldn't drag her down with me.

"What are you doing here?" I asked, my emotions betraying me. I cleared my throat and stood straighter, but it was hard not to see that she was destroying me with her mere presence.

"I flew home today," she said. "Or rather, I flew back to Florida. I can't really call it home any longer because it never felt like it. But I went anyway because I couldn't stand to be in my actual home because of you."

"I'm sorry—"

She held up a single finger, cutting me off. "No, I'm speaking now. You had your chance. It's my turn."

I went to put my hands in my pockets, until I realized the giant cast I still had prevented me from doing so, causing me to just stand there awkwardly instead. "Very well."

I could see she was struggling with her words, her emotions on edge. "I went back to Florida to get some much-needed air. I needed time to figure out how to move on from you."

I swallowed down a lump of guilt into my gut.

"But not five minutes into my well-deserved pity party, I found myself face-to-face with your brother. And that stone bird."

"What?" I glanced down at the bird and then back to her, my eyes wide with shock.

I could tell by the look of betrayal written all over her face just what my brother had gone to her to do. He had gone to do what I couldn't.

Tell her the truth.

And I'd never felt so ashamed in my life.

"It wasn't his place to tell you," I said softly.

Her lip quivered as she tried to keep her composure. "No, it was yours."

This time, I did move. I trekked forward, intent on closing the gap between us, but she held up her hand, and I stopped.

"Please don't," she whispered. "Otherwise, I won't be able to get this out, and you deserve better. We deserve better."

"I don't understand."

She looked down at her feet, fumbling with her hands, a show of insecurity as she found her words. "You once asked if I trusted you. Do you remember?"

I nodded. "Yes."

"You asked me to trust you, and so I did. I did so because I loved you, because I believed you would someday trust me in return with whatever it was you were holding so tightly to your chest."

"I do trust you," I whispered.

"No," she said, "you don't. That's the thing about trust, Aiden. Trusting someone means allowing that person to make their own decisions because, in the end, you trust they'll do the right thing. You never even gave me the option."

"You would have stayed," I said. "You would have wasted your life with me, a blind ass—"

"Don't you dare finish that sentence." Her voice quivered with emotion.

"I'm not worth it," I whispered, feeling more like the orphaned foster kid than I had in years.

She folded her arms across her chest. "See, this is where we disagree." Her eyes flickered toward the stone bird on the counter. "Tell me about it."

"What? My bird? Why?"

She shrugged, but it was a halfhearted motion to distract me from the effort it took to keep her tears at bay. "Seems your brother thinks it will help somehow. I'm guessing there's a story behind it. So, humor me."

I glanced over at it, letting out a frustrated breath. "I never finished it. There isn't much else to say."

"But why? You carry around your brother's bird like a talisman, but you bury your own like a dirty little secret? I don't understand."

I looked down at the deplorable bird, remembering the fights I'd had with Ben over it.

"It's no good, Ben! I'm not like you," I hollered. "I can't do this!"

"Yes," he answered calmly, "you can. You just need to keep practicing."

"This is bollocks!" I shouted. "I'm never going to be as good as you."

"Because I was horrible!" I roared. "Is that what you and James want me to admit? Ben was amazing, and I could barely make a goddamn bird. I worked on that bloody thing forever and barely got the general shape before my brother died."

Her eyes rounded, but she stayed put, keeping her position in the center of the living room. "Then, why keep at it? Why not just give up?"

I looked over at the horrible-looking stone figurine once more, my shoulders slumping. "Because it was the only way I could keep him alive."

"And, in doing so, you found your own passion. Your own voice."

"I promised him I'd do great things," I said, my eyes falling to the floor.

The sound of her sandals against the wood floor caught my attention as she slowly walked forward. I caught the smell of her vanilla-jasmine perfume as she took my hand in hers.

It had only been days since we touched, but it felt like years.

"Don't be the boy who gives up too soon," she said as our fingers twined together.

"I can't ask you to do this," I said. "My life, it's not going to be easy. The accident with the hammer, it's just the beginning. I'm going to be a burden, a—"

"I don't recall offering just yet." She smiled, her eyes still wet from unshed tears. "You hurt me, Aiden Fisher. More than anyone ever has. Knowing you did so out of love, well, it helps a little, but I still don't know if I can trust you."

"You—"

Her finger fell to my lips.

"I'm talking, remember?"

I nodded.

"We need time to heal and maybe a little time to grow."

Her words stung.

"I'm taking that storefront, and I'm going to make it my own, on my own. I've realized I can't put my dreams on hold any longer, and nothing is going to stand in my way anymore. Ocracoke is my home, and I'm not going anywhere."

She was fierce in her conviction, and I'd never been more proud of her. I'd felt like an absolute fraud, telling her to walk away from the biggest opportunity of her life, fearing it would tie her to a life with me.

I was glad she was taking it even if I might not be part of the picture.

"And what about me?" I asked hopefully.

"You work on this stone bird," she said. "Relearn your craft. Take up a new one. Hell, I don't care, but figure out how this new Aiden fits into the world, because I will not allow the love of my life to wither and die under the weight of his disability."

"You want me to learn how to carve blind?"

She reached into the pocket of her dress, something I didn't even know she had, and pulled out familiar-looking candy. Dropping a few peanut M&M's on the counter next to my stone bird, she said, "I saw a singer on TV who was deaf. She used the vibrations to differentiate each note. Anything is possible, Aiden, with a little prayer and patience. At least, that is what my father used to say and I believe you know already know a thing or two about patience."

"I'm the love of your life?" I breathed out.

She smiled, pressing her lips to mine. Reaching for her, I palmed her cheek, wanting the kiss to last forever, but she pulled back far too quickly.

"I guess that's up to you," she said. "You know where to find me."

And then, before I could argue, she was gone, leaving me alone in my apartment with a handful of M&M's, an ugly stone bird, and a life to rebuild.

I guessed I'd better get started.

CHAPTER EIGHTEEN

Millie

"**M**OLLY, REMIND ME WHY I THOUGHT IT WAS a good idea to open this place in March?" I shouted from the stockroom.

"Because," my sister shouted back, "it's a good time for a soft opening. Remember, spring break?"

I took a deep breath. "Right, spring break."

God, what was I thinking?

Open a store, I'd thought.

What a great idea, I'd thought.

It would be easy.

It wasn't.

I'd drained every dime I had and then some, selling my apartment in Florida and half of my closet to stock the store with pretty things that people would hopefully want to buy, and for what? A small influx of spring breakers?

The island wouldn't be jam-packed with people for another three months.

I could be sitting on this inventory for three months.

Thank God Molly was still allowing me to stay at the inn, free of charge. No one had complained about the weird family member lurking about who stole bagels and scones in the morning and drank all the coffee.

So, at least my living situation was good—in the event that I went bankrupt.

"You look panicked. Are you panicking?" Molly asked after finding me stuffed in the corner of the stockroom, rocking back and forth.

"What? Who? Me?"

"Yeah, you're definitely panicking. I'm going to go get you ice cream from across the street."

"No. I'm fine," I said before adding, "Get me cookie dough. And chocolate. With sprinkles. Oh, and maybe some strawberry?"

She rolled her eyes before slipping out of the stockroom.

I should probably do the same.

There were still a few more things I needed to do before our official opening tomorrow.

Like throw up a couple more times.

Looking around the stockroom, I tried to smile. I was pretty pleased with everything I'd gone with as far as inventory was concerned. As much as I wanted the place to be filled with my own stuff, that simply wasn't possible so early in the game. I needed income and I needed it quickly, so establishing a steady stream of cash was priority number one. Once I had that done, I'd slowly start introducing my own designs.

Or at least, that was the plan.

For now, I had an eclectic mix of boho and beachy styles that would appeal to young and old alike. It wasn't your typical touristy shop, but it wasn't so high end that it would scare off the typical traveler.

God, I hoped this worked.

I'd never wanted anything so bad in my life. Well, that wasn't exactly true. But not everything worked out the way you wanted it to.

It had been seven months. Seven months of waiting and wondering.

Seven months of hoping to hear something. A friendly text, a call—something.

I didn't know how long to wait before I faced reality and moved on, but I didn't want to move on. Ever.

So, for now, this store was my everything.

And I was pretty okay with that. Mostly.

Now, if I could just keep this place afloat.

Just as I was trying to decide how many more dresses to pull into the front, the front door chimed.

"Did they have sprinkles?" I hollered, waiting for my sister to reply. When she didn't, I stood up from my spot on the floor. "Hello?"

No answer.

Okay, great. Either I was being robbed or someone was loitering in my store, and I would have to shoo them out.

Because nothing said warmth and hospitality like kicking people out of your brand-new store.

"Um, we're not open," I said, the confidence in my voice astounding even me. "So, if you could just come back tomorrow…"

No door chime, which meant the loiterer was still here. I guessed I'd have to leave the stockroom now and confront the person.

Great.

I was pretty sure I had a stain on my shirt from the taco I had eaten at lunch and dust all over me from hauling and unpacking boxes. Maybe I'd scare them away from my appearance alone.

Stepping out from the stockroom, I took a brief look around but stopped immediately when something caught my eye on the checkout counter.

A single stone bird.

My breath hitched as I looked up and found my loiterer.

Standing on the other side of the counter was Aiden, holding the matching bird. His matching bird.

Only now, the raw edges had been smoothed. The beak was pronounced, and tiny, intricate details had appeared all over its beautifully shaped body.

It was finished.

My heart nearly exploded as I took him in. His hand was mended, no longer in a cast, and his eyes... they held me captive.

"You're here," I said. "I didn't think—"

"You didn't think I'd come back," he finished.

"It's been seven months."

"You never were a patient one." He smiled, stepping forward to place the figurine down next to its mate. "You asked for the impossible, love. I had to make sure I could deliver."

I watched as he joined the two birds together, the two halves fitting together as a whole. Their necks slopped toward one another, like they were embracing. The craftsmanship was seamless, and I felt my eyes well with tears, knowing how much work it must have taken for him to do it.

"It's beautiful."

"No, you are," he said as he stepped forward.

It was then that I noticed the walking stick, and my heart bled for him.

"Aiden."

"It's not as bad as it seems. My brother has put me on

a medication that is slowing it some, and I have these ridiculous glasses that help in darker situations. But I'm adjusting—"

"But the bird," I said. "It's flawless."

He smiled. "A requirement for me to come home, I was told."

My eyes widened. "You're staying?"

"Well, it was a hell of a jaunt to get here. I wasn't planning on leaving—"

He grunted as I leaped over the counter and into his arms. He was here—in my shop, in my arms—and I was never letting him go.

My legs wrapped around him as he pushed me up onto the counter, his fingers finding my face as our eyes met. I could see his struggle to focus now, and I knew I'd find a way to make sure every single second of sight he had left was cherished.

Starting now.

"I love you, Aiden Fisher. Will you be the love of my life and live with me on this crazy, beautiful island?"

"Yes, but only if I can rent some space out in this lovely shop of yours."

"What?" The look of surprise on my face wasn't hard to miss.

He pointed to his bird. "You didn't think that little guy was all I did, did you?"

My mouth opened, but I came up dry.

"You wanted me to rediscover myself, to figure out who I was with this disability. I couldn't do that by carving just one little bird. So, once I finished, I kept going. And I did it all while blindfolded."

"You what?"

"I knew I would one day be unable to rely on my eyes, so I took them out of the equation. It wasn't easy at first, but slowly and with patience," he said, giving me a hard look, which made me laugh, "I figured it out. Some of my stuff is a bit rougher than it used to be. I took more time and care with the bird because I wanted to impress you and earn my spot back in your bed. And your heart."

I felt him squeeze my ass, causing shivers to go down my spine.

"But I think I can do it, and I owe it all to you."

"No," I said. "You owe it to yourself."

He kissed my forehead. "Thank you for believing in my dreams. I love you, Millie."

"Thank you for first believing in mine. Now, how about we go create one together?"

"I like the way you think." He smiled, that single dimple I'd missed so much making an appearance in his cheek. "But, first, does that stockroom door have a lock? It's been a long seven months."

My eyebrow rose as he looked at me with lustful intent. "No, but the front door does."

"Wasn't that your sister I saw across the street at the ice cream shop?"

"Yeah." I laughed. "But she'll understand. Now, go lock that door. And hurry."

"Okay." A wicked grin spread across his face.

With his return, he'd brought the other half of my heart with him, and I finally felt whole again. I knew what challenges lay ahead for us, but together, I knew we could face anything.

As long as we had each other.

EPILOGUE

Millie

One Year Later

"Did you look at those bridal magazines I bought for you?" Molly asked as we took our seats.

I shook my head, making a sour face. "No, not even a little."

"Millie! How am I supposed to be your matron of honor if you won't even help me plan the wedding?"

I looked up at the stage, the sparkling blue water setting the perfect backdrop, as Aiden and several other members of the town congregated before the ceremony.

My sister nudged me. "I mean, you won't even share with me the proposal story! The least you could do is let me do my job."

I turned, slightly annoyed. "Okay, first of all, sometimes things are too personal to share—"

"He proposed during sex, didn't he?"

I pressed my lips together, trying not to smile as the memory of Aiden's head buried between my legs came back to mind.

Oh, boy, did he.

"Like I said, some things are too personal to share. And, secondly, I never made you matron of anything!"

She made a whiny sound, something I was sure she'd picked up from her toddler. "Oh, come on, I want to plan a big wedding. Everyone wants a big wedding!"

I huffed. "No, not true. Because I don't."

"Will you just take a look—"

"Molly, I did. And you know what I saw. A bunch of stuff I don't need. A giant, over-the-top dress my husband wouldn't even be able to see. An elaborate cake that would be demolished ten seconds after we cut it—that my husband also wouldn't be able to see."

"Millie, I'm—"

I smiled, taking her hand. "I'm not saying this to make you feel sorry, Molly. I'm just trying to make you understand. All I want to do is marry that man up there. And it could be in a courthouse—"

"No, that's not acceptable."

"Or," I continued, "in a backyard. I honestly don't care. I just want to be his wife."

She smiled. "Well then, set a date."

I smiled to myself. "You'll be the first to know. Now, shut up. I think they're starting."

"There are a lot more people here than last time," she whispered as we both took a look around.

I hadn't been to the first memorial dedication in Ocracoke, but it was clear to even me that the area around the ferry terminal was loaded. Highway 12 was packed with cars, parked on either side as far back as I could see.

And the media had come out.

I was glad I wasn't the one up there speaking.

I sent a silent prayer up to the heavens as Dean took the podium, and although he and Jake were two of the actual survivors of the ferryboat accident—the reason for the memorial—I thought the majority of the crowd this time around had come for someone else entirely.

The blind stone carver.

Aiden had tried to keep a low profile, not wanting to make a spectacle of himself. A simple life—that was what he'd wanted.

He wasn't joking when he'd asked to rent a space in my shop for his work.

We'd negotiated on the price, and he paid me well for it. But not in cash.

At first, the sales had been few and far between. His stuff wasn't cheap. But then word had gotten around, thanks to a few local bloggers, that Ocracoke had itself a blind sculptor, and sales had kind of skyrocketed after that.

So much so that I'd had to kick him out of my store and force him to get a real place of his own. Now, he took commissions like a proper artist again.

And he was about to deliver his biggest one to date…to the town of Ocracoke.

"As much as I'd like to believe you're all here for me," Dean began, causing muffled laughter among the crowd, "I know that's not entirely true. The town of Ocracoke grew a bit larger a year and a half ago when Aiden Fisher came to stay with us. I can honestly say I was puzzled when he agreed to come to our sleepy town and carve a replacement for the beautiful memorial we'd lost to a thoughtless vandal. But what I've realized over the years is that this town has a way of being a beacon for those who are weary, lost, or even a little broken."

Aiden's gaze met mine and even though I knew he couldn't see me—his sight so poor now that he could only make out blurry images from such a distance—I gave him a warm smile.

"This memorial is about survival, perseverance, and honoring the ones we lost so tragically. I couldn't imagine a more perfect individual to capture these ideas into our memorial, and I am honored to introduce him to you today. So, without further ado, Mr. Aiden Fisher."

The crowd erupted in cheers, and I joined them. Jake and James, who flanked Aiden on each side, stood up and helped guide him to the podium. When I'd offered, he'd shaken his head, saying he wanted me to be in the crowd.

"Knowing you're out there will calm me, love," he'd said.

So, I'd agreed, and allowed someone else to be at his side.

I took a moment to drink him in as he took his place up in front of the crowd. He might have lost his sight, but it hadn't diminished the power or the raw sexual magnetism he had.

And, with all the carving he was doing, he was still every bit as ripped.

If not more so.

I couldn't help but smirk a little.

Standing before them, I watched as he turned his head toward the memorial.

"How does it look?" he asked, making everyone chuckle a little under their breath. "I'm sorry it took me so long to get it back to you. I know this town has gone on a while without it, and I thank you for your patience as I figured out how to do the impossible."

His gaze turned back to me, and he smiled. "You see, I'm engaged to a wonderful woman who reminded me a while ago that nothing is impossible with a little patience and prayer. Well, she can attest to my mastery skills in the practice of patience, but prayer, that was a little harder. But I took her advice anyway, and you know what I found?"

He paused for dramatic effect.

"You," he said simply. "I found a town eager to take me in. I found a soon-to-be father-in-law willing to step out of retirement and become my assistant."

I leaned over and found a big, happy smile across my father's face.

Their bromance or father-son thing they had going on really was adorable.

Possibly bordering on disgusting.

He really had become the father Aiden never had, but always wanted.

"And I found a family and love. Love that will last through all the trial and tribulations life has to offer. You, Ocracoke, are the answer to the prayers I hadn't even realized I was sending up to the heavens. So patience and prayer," he said once again, his voice growing heavy with emotion, "you'll find it at the base of the memorial next to my signature."

My eyes followed everyone else's. He'd changed the familiar bird carving a bit. It was no longer one bird but two, as he'd realized he had his own path to live, outside of honoring his brother. From now on, he'd be remembering Ben and forging his own path at the same time.

"I hope that, whenever you find yourself up against the

impossible, you'll come here and remember the blind carver who made a beautiful life with just a little patience and prayer. Thank you."

I stood the second he finished his last word, so filled with pride that my eyes were leaking. I rushed the stage along with the rest of my family. I knew he'd be flooded with media asking for interviews, but I needed to get my hands on him first.

Jake and James were doing a pretty good job of giving him a wide berth from the crowd. Too much commotion caused him to panic when he was in an unfamiliar area, but the second they saw me, they let me through.

And he caught me the moment my body collided with his.

"It was perfect," I whispered in his ear.

"Yeah?" His hands tightened around my waist.

"I love you," I said, pulling back so that he could see me.

Up close, he could still make out features, like the color of my hair and the gentle slope of my nose.

He smiled gently. "Wanna make that official?"

"Shh!"

"Do they have a clue?" he asked, his voice lowered, as I turned us away from our prying family members.

"No, and let's keep it that way. Meet me back at the inn? After your adoring fans?"

"Fans?"

"There are media trucks all over the place."

"Great." He sounded less than thrilled.

"Two words," I said. "I do."

"Temptress. All right. But only because—"

"Shh! I'll see you in a few hours."

I quickly kissed him and then disappeared before he could say another word. After all, we'd worked hard to pull this one off.

Wouldn't want to risk ruining it at the last minute.

Aiden

"I've never loved you so much in my entire life," I said as my brother helped me out of the car.

We'd just arrived back at the inn after he singlehandedly handled a dozen news crews like a bloody pro.

"Save the poetry for your fiancée. By the way, are you ever going to share how you popped the question? Knowing you, it was probably something well thought out and bloody boring."

I grinned. "No, it wasn't and not a chance."

He suspiciously eyed me. "Bollocks. Did you ask her to marry you while you were shagging?"

I rolled my eyes. "No one says *shagging* in America, James. Who are you, Austin Powers? You've been here for fifteen bloody years. Acclimate!"

We walked to the front of the inn, my home for nearly a year, until I finally talked—to the extreme pleasure of Molly—my blushing bride-to-be into buying a house of our own. It had taken a lot of persuading, her nerves on high alert with the business still just starting out, but I'd assured her I had enough to keep us going for a while.

And now that I finally had her all to myself, I was never letting go.

"Acclimate. You acclimate, you damn jerk!" my brother

muttered as he helped me to the front door.

"See"—I laughed—"there you go. Perfect. Now, perk up. There is a lovely party inside in my honor. Try to enjoy yourself."

And, before we entered, I stopped him.

"What?" he asked. "Is there something wrong?"

"No," I said, suddenly feeling awkward.

With Millie, I could bare my feelings without a second thought. Doing so with my brother though was…

Difficult.

"Thank you," I quickly blurted out before taking a deep breath. "For never giving up on me. I know I'm stubborn and a flight risk, but you never gave up on me, and I just—"

"You're my baby brother," he said.

"Perhaps you could leave off the baby part when introducing me to people?" I grinned.

"Not a chance."

He pulled me in for a big hug before we entered the inn, the old house full of energy and warmth. I didn't know how but I could feel her the second before Millie's arms wrapped around my middle.

"I thought you'd never get here."

She placed a quick kiss on my cheek, and my hands found her as I smiled. She was wearing the dress I'd picked out. The one with the soft silk fabric that felt like butter to the touch. Up close, I could see the subtle blue color, which made her tan skin look radiant.

I would cherish these memories forever.

Especially the one that was about to follow.

"You ready?" she asked.

"I was born ready for this," I said.

She took my hand and ushered me to the center of the

parlor. Everyone quieted, probably expecting a speech or a toast.

And they were going to get a hell of a one.

Just not the one they expected.

"Hi everyone!" Millie began. "Thank you all for gathering here tonight to celebrate my wonderful fiancé, Aiden."

They all clapped.

I kind of felt ridiculous.

"But, actually, we had a different plan for the evening, if you don't mind."

It was already dark, the benefit of early March, and if everything went according to plan, Millie was going to let go of my hand, walk over to the switch on the wall, and flip it, illuminating the patio—bingo.

The entire crowd of family gasped.

Thankfully, it was a happy gasp as they took in the altar of flowers and lights that Millie's mom and dad had put together earlier that day.

We'd needed someone's help, and I couldn't exactly marry their daughter without asking permission, which they'd given.

In spades.

"You're getting married?" Molly squealed. "Right now?"

I felt Millie's hand return to mine.

"Yes," we both answered, her grin so infectious that I couldn't help but kiss her.

I may be blind, but even I could see the love radiating between us.

"Well, what are we waiting for?" someone shouted, most likely my brother. "Let's get these two married!"

I turned to the woman I loved, knowing, in just

minutes, I'd take her to be my wife.

This was exactly where I was supposed to be.

Taking that flight down to Ocracoke was the best damn decision of my life, and it didn't matter what obstacles life threw at us from here on out. We'd face them together.

With a little patience, prayer, and a whole lot of love.

PLAYLIST

The Blower's Daughter—Damien Rice

With or Without You—April Meservy, Aaron Edson

Little Do You Know—Alex & Sierra

Can't Help Falling In Love—Ingrid Michaelson

Hold Me—The Sweeplings

Crazy In Love (Remix)—Beyonce

Walking On A Dream—Gardiner Sisters

Lies In The Dark—Tove Lo

Unsteady—X Ambassadors

The One I Love—Mirror Fury

Lights Down Low—MAX

Love At First Sight—The Brobecks

The Fire—Kina Grannis

ACKNOWLEDGEMENTS

Number fifteen! What? Okay, let's see if I can make this quick, without babbling. Shoot, I think I already am. First and foremost, I must thank my amazing husband Chris and our daughters. Without their constant support, I wouldn't be half the author, or person I am today.

Behind the scenes, I have an amazing supportive team and I'm going to try and not forget anyone.

Jill Sava—thank you for being my right hand. Literally.

Ami Waters—Thank you for being with me from the very beginning. For realsies.

Nina Grinstead—Thank you and everyone at Social Butterfly for getting my new releases out in the book world.

Sarah Hansen—Thank you for making yet another beautiful book cover. You are beyond talented.

Jovana Shirley—Thank you for editing each and every one

of my books, and making sure my hero doesn't do weird things like sit down twice in the same sentence.

Stacey Blake—You are a formatting genius. Thank you.

To my beta readers, Katy Nielsen and Carla VanZandt, thank you for being my guinea pigs and muddling through my completely unedited manuscripts. You are amazing.

And a double thank you to Katy Nielsen for lending her proofing skills to this book.

Berg's Book Reviewers—Thank you guys for all you do! I truly appreciate the time you give to my books!

Berg's Bibliophiles—I love you guys!

Bloggers—Thank you for reading and reviewing. What you do for the book world is so important.

READERS—Thank you for reading my words and making each and every one of my dreams a reality. Here's to number sixteen…

ABOUT THE AUTHOR

J.L. Berg is the *USA Today* bestselling author of the Ready series, the Walls series, the Lost & Found series and more. She is a California native living in the beautiful state of historic Virginia. Married to her high school sweetheart, they have two beautiful girls and two pups. When she's not writing, you will find her cuddled up, watching a movie with her family, obsessing over fandoms or devouring anything chocolate! J.L. Berg is represented by Jill Marsal of Marsal Lyon Literary Agency, LLC.

Website: www.jlberg.com

Newsletter: bit.ly/JLBergNewsletter

Facebook: www.facebook.com/authorjlberg

Twitter: @authorjlberg

Goodreads: www.goodreads.com/authorjlberg

OTHER BOOKS
BY J.L. BERG

The Ready Series
When You're Ready
Ready to Wed
Never Been Ready
Ready for You
Ready or Not

The Walls Duet
Within These Walls
Beyond These Walls

Behind Closed Doors

The Cavenaugh Brothers (includes Within These Walls, Beyond These Walls, and Behind Closed Doors)

Lost & Found
Forgetting August
Remembering Everly

Standalones
The Tattered Gloves
Fraud

By The Bay
The Choices I've Made
The Scars I Bare
The Lies I've Told
The Mistakes I've Made

Made in the USA
Middletown, DE
29 September 2020